W9-AZS-458

Finding Frances

Janice M. Van Dyck

Winston-Higgins Press, LLC
2840 West Bay Drive #222
Largo, Florida 33770

This book is a work of fiction. Names, characters, places, and incidents are either products of the author's imagination or are used fictitiously. Any resemblence to actual events or locales or persons, living or dead, is entirely coincidental.

For information regarding special discounts for bulk purchases, contact the publisher at the above address or info@winstonhigginspress.com

Manufactured in the Canada.

Cataloging-in-Publication
Van Dyck, Janice M.
Finding Frances / by Janice M. Van Dyck.
p. cm.
LCCN 2010920169
Paperback: ISBN: 978-0-9826140-0-6
Hardcover: ISBN: 978-0-9826140-2-0
E-Book: ISBN: 978-0-9826140-1-3

1. Death–Fiction. 2. Families–Fiction.
3. Terminal care–Fiction. 4. Advance directives (Medical care)–Fiction. 5. Bereavement–Fiction.
6. Psychological fiction, American. I. Title.

PS3622.A5855F56 2010 813'.6
QBI10-600012

This book is dedicated to nurses everywhere,
our "Guardian Angels"

Finding Frances

1

FRANCES Baldwin was ready to die, but not like this. She'd always imagined dying in bed with proper notice so they would find her in the morning, arranged artfully on the pillows, bedclothes smoothed, and her eyebrows penciled in just right. *She died in her sleep*, they would say. *So peaceful. It was a blessing she didn't suffer too much.*

A dignified death. Yes, that was the way she'd envisioned it. Not this terror that grasped her throat in the middle of the night, draining her mercilessly, bleeding her of oxygen heartbeat by heartbeat, leaving invisible pools of Frances all over the floor and the bed. The events of the past few hours were not part of the plan, and Frances was fast losing the ability to think clearly or to do anything about it.

Earlier she'd thought, *my heart is going crazy, it's running like a million little feet across a tin roof. Maybe this is how it starts. Maybe I am going to die now.* The thought excited her and made her breath come up shorter than ever. *I knew it. I knew it was coming. I've felt it for months now.* She glanced heavenward, smiled, and made the sign of the cross on her head and shoulders. *It's as good a time as any. I'm ready, Lord.*

She stumbled over to the long bureau, the one she and Bill had bought over fifty years ago when they'd first married. *Try to be quiet*, she told herself as her hand knocked the perfume bottle. She waited for a moment and listened, but there was no sound from the room next door. *Good.* He was still asleep. He would never approve of what she was doing. He'd have the ambulance here before she could say, "Go back to bed," and she didn't want to leave anything to chance. Not when she'd gotten this far.

She picked up her natural-bristle brush from the doily and fixed her hair. After smoothing the lines beneath her eyes with a dab of makeup, she got into bed and waited for the end to come.

It's okay. No one will be surprised, she assured herself. Everyone knew she had the emphysema from smoking for so long. Smoking was a passion for Frances, so she'd accepted the diagnosis without regret; after all, everyone had to go sometime. She hadn't even stopped smoking. She believed in letting nature take its course.

She'd accepted the gradual decline as easily as she did all the other indicators of her advancing age: when her thick brown hair faded to an unruly frizz, she'd tied it back in beautiful barrettes; when her joints stubbornly declined her demands, she'd stopped her ballroom dancing; and when her jowls softened she'd exercised them for a week before forgetting about them altogether. Like her poor digestion and sleeplessness, the heaviness and the fluid in her chest now seemed normal.

Frances lay still, waiting, trying to concentrate on something—the pattern on the sheets, the needlepoint flowerpot her daughter made the summer she had mono, the blue braided rug. Anything to keep her focused. Her eyes fell on the collection of family photos on the side table. William and Diane on their honeymoon. Sugar and the boys. Randy, so handsome in his suit. *No, don't look at them*, she thought as she drank in their smiles and felt them begin to wash away the bittersweet taste of her determination. *I can't think about how much I love them. It's so hard to leave them all as it is*. Frannie's heart now filled with a different kind of ache, this one impossible to bear. She wheezed in a long breath.

For as long as she could remember, Frances had been trying to separate from them all, gradually, so her leaving wouldn't be a shock. But now that Frances could see exactly what her death was going to look like, even she was mourning the loss. She hadn't expected that.

She'd tried to ready them for this night, this night when a little part of them would die and the rest of their lives would begin to grow into the little places she'd tried so hard to carve out as her own. Tears formed in the corners of her eyes as she imagined the significance of her life evaporate, but they disappeared quickly as she moved her concentration away from the photographs and back to the small pink bouquets on the wallpaper.

I hear you, God. I'm coming. She prayed the Our Father, then waited. She wasn't quite sure what was supposed to happen next. The actual dying had taken Frances quite by surprise, like the interruption of an important news bulletin in the regular programming that had become her life.

She again imagined being found in the morning, looked around, and again tried to tidy her bed. It was a bigger effort to arrange the pillows artfully now that her breathing had become more labored and noisy. She could feel her heart beating in every capillary in her body, pounding through her skin. There wasn't enough air, barely enough air, even though her heart was working harder and harder to get the oxygen she needed. Her chest began to hurt more than it ever had before; minutes went by as Frances waited for her heart to stop beating. Or explode. Or something.

It can't go on much longer like this, she told herself as she waited for the next breath to be impossible to take. She waited. And waited. Waited for God.

An hour passed.

And her heart kept beating. Faster. Wildly, uncontrolled. It beat on and on and on. Still Frances waited, certain that it was her time. But what if it wasn't?

When she felt the crushing weight on her ribcage, she began to panic. The pain increased until she could barely move from the mattress, as if a car had struck her and was now stopped on top of her chest, the doors opening and closing, the trunk space filling with suitcases and boxes, children bouncing up and down on the rear seats. Another hour went by.

This is worse than death, she told herself as the fear and panic began to overtake her determination. As the time went by, Frances began to believe that she was not going to die after all, but rather that she was condemned to live for years taking half-breaths and never having enough oxygen, unable to speak as the pain eclipsed her completely, alone and afraid her heart would beat ten million times more just beneath the skin until the only sound she could hear was the throb in her ears and throat. What could be worse?

I have to do something, she finally decided, *I can't stay here like this. I have to make it stop.*

Frances rolled off her bed and stumbled into the kitchen for the breathing medicine. The inhaler had sat unopened on the shelf since she'd brought it home from the pharmacy almost a year ago, nearly forgotten next to the other medications the doctors had given her but that she'd never taken. She tried desperately to inhale the aerosol spray, but she couldn't coordinate her movements. Fumbling in pain and fear, her whole body shuddered as the device fell from her hands. She leaned over to pick it up, but lowered herself clumsily to the floor instead; she had no energy to stand. Her arms were so heavy now, and she couldn't move her legs at all.

"Bill, wake up, I need you."

Her voice was weak. She knew Bill wouldn't hear her. So she began to rattle things around in the kitchen, hoping to make enough noise to rouse him. She pulled the mixing bowls down from the shelf beside her, unable to take a breath deep enough to call him again.

Bill heard the noise and he called to her. "Frannie?"

"Call 911," she replied hoarsely. Then she put her head down.

Frances Baldwin didn't want to die like this, crumpled up in her old pink nightgown with the inhaler in her hand and her husband hovering over her as she looked up from the tiled floor. She closed her eyes and lost consciousness.

2

WILLIAM Baldwin watched his wife bustle in and out of the room. Each time she appeared around the corner, she searched his face for some reaction, some signal. But he gave her none. Finally, he grabbed her arm, motioning that he was ready to hang up the telephone, and Diane relaxed into his grasp and stared up into his eyes.

The flash of anger in his glare startled them both. He didn't even know how he felt yet, and he sure didn't want his wife figuring it out before he did. He let go of her arm and looked away, remembering to breathe only when he felt a rush behind his eyes that made him dizzy. Diane began to occupy herself with newly important chores that involved taking only a few steps between the kitchen counters.

He nodded and spun his hand around as if it might make his sister hurry through her words. "Okay, Sugar. Let me know what happens. Give Mom a hug and let Dad know he can call me if he has any questions. I'm only as far away as the telephone." He pushed his long, blond hair back from his eyes as his heart began to slow down. He no longer listened to Sugar's voice. Instead, he heard the movie of his life replayed in his ears.

"Okay." He finally smiled, thinking of the softness of his sister's face and the rough day she must have had. "I will. Love you, too."

He walked from the sink to the built-in desk to replace the telephone receiver in the cradle, although he really only had to push the button on the cordless. Diane waited as he pulled his lips into a number of distorted positions. Then he leaned over to catch his breath as though he'd just finished running a sprint.

"Your mother's in the hospital." Her voice had no emotion and it was a statement, not a question. However, she clearly intended it as an opening for him to elaborate. But he couldn't, not yet.

"Yes." William was still squeezing his facial features, first his lips, then his eyes and forehead, until they wrinkled tightly then fell into forced relaxation. It helped, but it couldn't make the vision of his mother on the kitchen floor disappear.

"And it's her heart? Is she going to be okay?" Diane was impatient. She always wanted immediate answers. Why couldn't she just wait?

"Congestive heart failure with continued atrial fibrillation. Respiration shallow, BP elevated. My guess is they've got her on warfarin, oxygen and some sedatives."

"You sound like an ER doc. I guess old habits die hard." She laughed, although it wasn't the right time and it sounded slightly callous. But that was Diane's way, at least that was Diane's way when she spoke to him. It had evolved that way over the last year or so, and he was becoming used to it. He didn't seem to have any warmth to offer her these days, either.

"Remember? I quit med school and went into hi-tech so I wouldn't have to deal with death. I'm not good at it. I never have been." He walked to the cabinet and took a glass from the shelf. "And I don't really plan on starting now."

He went to the stainless steel refrigerator and filled the glass with filtered water, then drank most of it down in three long swallows.

In the same monotone she used before, Diane responded, "She's your mother, Will. Apparently, you have to."

Her voice was getting on his nerves. He didn't answer for a moment. His legs finally couldn't hold him anymore, and he pulled out one of the wheeled chairs just in time to collapse into it. He put his elbows on the table and wiped his face with his hands, smearing his nose and eyes into his cheeks.

"Give me a break. My mother almost died, Diane. Sugar said she almost died, but she woke my dad at the last minute. Apparently, it had been going on for hours. A few minutes later and it would have been too late. They wouldn't have been able to save her." He choked on the last few words, his mother's reprieve stuck between the muscles in his throat.

"And she didn't wake Bill?" Diane's voice rose a note or two, and she blinked in disbelief. "She had to have known something was wrong. The pain would have been terrible as her heart kept pounding to get her oxygen. And she wouldn't have been able to breathe once her oxygen was depleted." She had slipped into her doctor mode: her face froze, her eyebrows stopped moving, and she stood straighter as she paced slowly. William had seen it coming. Now, on top of everything else, he had Doctor Diane Metcalf to answer to.

"Why didn't she wake him?" She sat down at the table. On the opposite side.

"You already know the answer, Diane." William's voice was flat, the words barely making it out. "She's been ready to die for years."

He'd given up trying to rearrange his face and had begun

smoothing out the wrinkles in his pants, pressing hard into his thighs with long, kneading strokes, still trying to control his breathing.

"Yes, so you've said. Then why did she wake Bill? She could have just died last night if that's what she really wanted."

The truth was cold, and it began freezing William's gut when he first heard his sister's voice on the telephone. But now that the adrenaline had kicked in, his face was flushing and he was finally loosening up.

"Gee, I don't know, Diane. Let's see. Think back to what we know about the hypothalamus. Anatomy 101. Maybe she didn't die because respiration and heartbeat are both controlled in the base of the brain, the same spot where primitive emotions are formed. Maybe it all just got mixed up. If she couldn't breathe, she must have panicked." He was exaggerating his explanation, as though he were talking to an elementary-school student. "Survival instinct, you know? Maybe her body's basic instruction to live just overrode her rational thoughts."

He couldn't help but take her simple agitation as aggression and felt his tone of voice was justified.

"Wanting to die isn't rational," Diane corrected. She wasn't giving an inch. "Not when medical treatment is available." She sat back in her chair, and William felt his wife slip even further away with the motion.

He spoke louder, as if she'd gone across the room.

"Why do you always have to be so rational?"

Her tendency to accept the straight answer had impressed William when they were in med school together, but now it was one more thing that separated them. William was always thinking in the grey zone and had found there were no straight answers in marriage—or in life in general. Diane still appeared calm and focused, in great contrast to his own turmoil.

"You're the one who's always looking for a broader explanation, Will. I was just trying to put it in context. Wanting to die is not normal. Admit it, even if she is your mother."

"Wanting to die and being ready to die are different things, Di." He pounded his fist on the table and stood up. He stood at the window as the color drained from his face. "And I'm not ready for either one, okay?"

"Ahh," Diane crossed her arms over her chest and nodded as if she'd just met an answer she already knew. "So it's all about you. I see."

If William hadn't known she was a dermatologist, he would have assumed by her manner that she was a psychiatrist. He spun and snorted.

"Of course it's about me!" His voice came from deep within, blowing like the Santa Ana winds on a brushfire. "It's all about me! My mother is going to die, maybe sometime soon. I'm the one who has to keep on living without her. She'll be dead, she won't even miss me. But for me, everything will change."

"You managed to live without her after med school." Diane's tone was softer now, her anger consumed by William's. "You barely spoke to her for ten years."

It was true, but it didn't make things easier. "My mother never understood the reasons I couldn't become a doctor, and it crushed her when I changed careers. We had a stand-off that lasted most of my adult life."

He curled and straightened his fingers, as though exercising them. Then he shook his head and found his wife's eyes for the first time since he'd hung up the phone. "I don't know, Diane, the last three years have been great. It feels like this is the first time I've ever been acceptable to her. Forgive me, but I like it. I like having a mother who loves me. Is it all that bad?"

His bluster was gone, but the storm inside William was just getting started. He could feel his emotions, thoughts and beliefs all spinning in his gut, like a shaken can of soda. It was just like him to spew out his anger all over the ceiling, walls and floor, leaving only half of himself inside.

"Listen, I'm sorry I yelled, it's just that—." He didn't finish. What more could he say?

Diane nodded to acknowledge his admission, as she'd done all the times they'd reached an impasse before. William flopped back into his chair and rolled it closer to her.

She patted his arm and pushed his hair behind his ear.

"I know, baby, but you knew your mother had COPD. You knew she was going to die. It can't be all that surprising."

Despite the tension they'd learned to live with day to day, she was doing what she always did for William, listening to him explore the situation from all points of view until the edges wore away, until the situation grew softer in his hand and could be held closer or put away in a cabinet with all the other memories. The only time the technique hadn't worked was when they talked about the future of their marriage. That was a spiny urchin with poison spikes, no place to hold on to, no place to set it down without puncturing the inflatable California lifestyle they'd chosen. William was sorry about that, too, and the vacuum of it sucked his breath away. Perhaps his marriage was just one more dying thing this drop-out doctor was going to have to learn to deal with.

"You're right. I knew she was sick." He turned his palms

upward then let his hands drop to his sides with the weight of his desperation. "But I guess I just figured it would take longer to happen. I thought she had more time left."

Tears started to form as he added, "I thought I had more time."

"Are you going to fly out there?" Diane's words were now barely audible. It ended up sounding like a suggestion. Maybe she would be glad to be rid of him.

"No. I've got to keep my distance. It's the only way I'll make it through this." He didn't know much right now, but he did know he couldn't go back into the family structure and play the role of oldest son. The room grew quiet, and William thought they'd said everything that could be said at the moment.

"Distancing is not a technique that has worked very well for you," Diane added. "Historically, I mean."

She cleared her throat and stood, leaving the thought on the table. It was almost a whisper, and it roared in his ears long after she left the room.

3

BILL Baldwin sat in the artificial twilight at Lower Valley Hospital alongside his sleeping wife. He tried not to notice the smell of death and desperation and cafeteria trays, tried not to listen to the hushed crying of the waiting family next door, tried to ignore the endless rolling of stories down the hallway. So far, nothing was helping him recover from the chaos that had started when Frannie pulled the metal bowls onto the floor last night.

He tried to pinpoint the moment he'd begun to lose control. Finally, he traced his misfortune back to a single day, to a moment back in June when Frances had announced that she had poison ivy, to the very sigh that had escaped her lips and carried her away from him.

What had begun as a normal summer working in the garden had turned into the worst couple of months Bill could remember.

He could still see her standing in the mid-day sun, wearing a hat to cover her fair skin, a scarf around her neck. Her hands were bare. They were both sweating and winded in the heat. Bill pulled his baseball cap down over his forehead. His white, button-down cotton shirt was stuck to his back, and his pants were flecked with grass and seeds. Wearing his grey leather gardening gloves, he pulled together an armful of twigs, branches and weeds. In his mid-seventies, he didn't stand as tall as he had when he was younger. That day he was slightly bent and moving slowly.

He'd already cut the overgrown shoots off the bushes that bordered the east side of his manicured yard. That was hard work, and he laid the power tool and trimmings beside him. Beyond the bushes, the neighbor's chain link fence bared its metal teeth at him. Bill shuddered and scowled back. He hated the feeling of being enclosed, hated the idea that he was shut out, hated the idea that his territory had become so defined. So he'd done the only thing he could do—he'd reduced the whole thing to a landscaping problem.

The flowering shrubs he'd planted a few years back were coming along nicely, just a few seasons short of camouflaging his resentment entirely. If his domain was going to be cramped in like this, it would be on his terms. Bill stepped back slowly to survey things, arms folded and a slight smile on his lips. His property was like a well-groomed woman on his arm, her flowering dogwoods, hostas and hydrangeas the envy of the neighborhood.

Bill always thought his wife looked like a movie star. She acted like one, too, always a step ahead of him. A small-boned and graceful woman, Frannie's hair was mostly grey now. For better or for worse, over the years everything there was to know about her had been documented on her face. Strangers often reacted to the struggle she wore there. They sometimes believed she was an unhappy woman, but she wasn't, at least Bill never thought of her that way. She described herself as a realist, although he never really saw that in her, either.

She always told him that many things could be true at the

same time, and her face reflected just that kind of contradiction. Alongside the lines of laughter and joy at her mouth and eyes, chapters of labor and hardship were written on her brow. The weight of determination and perseverance camouflaged her best feature—that spontaneous smile, a flash of light and laughter that could fill a room and lift the hearts of everyone in it. Bill lived for that smile, although after a half-century of marriage he still hadn't figured out how to bring it about. Frances wasn't smiling that day in the garden.

"We should have started early this morning, Bill. I wanted to start at eight but you can't seem to do anything before ten. This sun is too much for us old people." Her voice was irritated but not angry, a tone he had grown accustomed to during their fifty-six years together.

His reply was meant as a "Yeah," but sounded more like a grunt as he maneuvered his pile toward the trash can.

"And if you had put the compost pile over in the corner this winter, I wouldn't have to be climbing behind it to clear out these bushes." Her voice, matter-of-fact, was still accusing but not upset. He knew that tone well. This may have been the one-millionth conversation in which she complained that he'd done something to make her life harder, and yet neither of them had regrets. He did not regret his transgressions; she did not regret having to point them out.

Frances moved her thin body between a tall, overgrown Rose of Sharon bush and a pile of wood chips and grass. Coughing and sneezing from allergies and emphysema, she bent over to pull weeds and used the rake in her left hand to steady herself. Bill watched her rake the loose threads into a pile and pick them up with her hands. When they were in the trash can she pulled off her scarf, wiped her face and neck with it and tied it back on, smoothing the edges and her hair back into place. She still looked good for a woman her age.

He turned and grunted again as he finished clearing his pile of twigs and stood up. Almost done. He turned his attention to the vegetable garden and smiled.

It already looked good. This was going to be the best crop yet. He tried to calculate when he'd be able to pick a few tomatoes to ripen on the window sill. Maybe July. His mouth watered at the thought of a hundred red tomatoes, softball-sized green peppers, and baskets of zucchini and carrots. He was hungry for some of Frannie's zucchini bread. And stewed tomatoes. Fresh vegetables were one of the summer rituals they shared. He grew them; she prepared them in salads and sauces and all kinds of dishes. For many years, they both enjoyed the flavor of the sunshine and the earth they owned together.

"How many years have we been growing the vegetables, Fran?" He was full of pride as he picked a little beetle off one of the large, green tomato leaves and crushed it between his fingers. The early fruit was well-developed, sculpted unevenly from the growth following heavy rains.

Frances sighed heavily, not from the work, not from the memory. Just a heavy sigh that seemed to have the weight of her whole body and a hundred more behind it. "'Bout all of them, Bill, wouldn't you say?" The reply was stilted as if the idea stuck in her throat, as if the few words were too much effort.

Bill almost hadn't noticed her mood change, but it was there, creeping into his reverie. He tried to shake it off.

"Let's see, Fran. We started planting when the kids were small. Remember Randy was still a baby. Only about three. His job was to water with the hose when we were done. I'd dig out the holes with the post-hole digger. You n' Sugar would put in the seedlings." He chuckled. "God, she was cute."

Sugar, whose real name was Cynthia, had earned her nickname before anyone had a chance to call her Cindy. She was the firstborn, his little girl, a sweet kid who charmed them all from the very beginning. Sugar. No one had ever thought of calling her anything else.

He squinted and removed his hat. He'd been transported almost forty years at the memory, back before there were fences and power tools, back to the time when hard work wasn't so hard.

"I guess it was William who worked behind me to put in the fertilizer," he continued. "We all worked together, every year, one night at sundown. Then we'd squirt the kids all off with the hose and put them in bed. Remember that, Fran?"

Frances looked up from her task. She couldn't help but smile at the thought of those three little bodies, soaked through their tee shirts, laughing, playing in the outdoor evening shower they'd contrived.

The telling of the story closed the space between Fran and Bill, as if filling the gap of the years. Bill realized now that it was he who moved toward his wife; she had no inclination to do anything other than just stand in the garden on that summer day. He wanted to be closer to the time when the kids were smaller and life was still new, but Frannie just stood in place, another heavy sigh still in her chest, yet to be exhaled.

It was barely an hour later, as they finished up outside, that Frances noticed the rash on her arms. "Poison ivy," she said to no one in particular. Then the sigh she'd been choking on finally came. Bill had known she'd had one left.

The blisters couldn't have taken Frances by surprise; she'd had poison ivy before. When she felt the creeping tingle at her neck, she removed the scarf and felt the welts with her fingers. She said, "My face."

He could already see it reddening, she could probably feel the tightening. She turned toward the house and began to cry, resigned.

This took him by surprise. Sorrow didn't seem the right emotion. After all, it was only poison ivy. Her life had been full of challenges and pain, and this was nothing compared to what she'd already survived.

"Bill?"

The sound of his wife's voice pulled him back to the present. Frances was stirring in her hospital bed, her breaths coming in long sighs, his name carried gently in the arms of her whisper. She opened her eyes and blinked them quickly as she looked around.

"Bill?"

"I'm here, Fran. You rest now. You're in the hospital. Everything is going to be fine."

"I thought you were an angel. You're all white."

She motioned to the IV beside her, but forgot the question. Then she closed her eyes, but she didn't relax. Ideas floated on top of her turbulent reality like oil, shape-shifting and colorful, both interesting and alarming, moving in all directions. Bill made no further explanation, and she stilled.

The prognosis was good, and with any luck he'd be able to take his wife home in a few days. They'd kept Frances lightly sedated since they'd brought her in last night, trying to keep her from panicking again. They put her on oxygen to make her breathing easier. Although things were better, neither remedy had set her heart beating on a proper pace. It was still thumping randomly as if it had forgotten the tune it was supposed to play.

But he was sure she'd be better soon. The poison ivy had been much slower to heal.

Frances didn't believe in taking medicine, and he suspected that was part of her agitation now. She had lived her life so far with only a few antibiotics and an aspirin or two.

When she had her poison ivy, she tried calamine lotion for her rash, but it stung and burned off the first layer of her sensitive skin. Bill remembered finding her crying in the bathroom, her face and neck bright red with open, oozing sores.

"Leave me alone," she said.

"I can't, Frannie, c'mon. It will get better. Trust me." He tried to take her arm and lead her into the hallway.

She shook him off. "No it won't."

It took a few weeks, but he was right. The rash finally improved on its own. But Frannie felt worse. While the rash was confined to her neck, the deterioration of her spirit continued. She just wanted to be alone. She hadn't allowed visitors for months.

One afternoon he grew frustrated and took matters into his own hands.

"Frannie, Sugar called and is coming over with the kids. We thought it might cheer you up. They're on their way." Bill acted as if they'd never discussed the matter before. The best way, he'd found, to get around her resistance to a thing.

Her anger was quick. She moved toward him in one giant step, then passed him by as if she'd changed her mind about throwing herself against him and pounding on his chest. Although she hadn't touched him, he could feel her fists of rage, now strangely impotent.

"What have you done, Bill?"

He was confused, or at least he appeared to be. He'd known his wife would object, but she just couldn't sit in the house another week without seeing anyone. It wasn't natural.

"It's only poison ivy, Fran. And you're getting over it." He tried to soften his voice, to move closer to her.

She moved away again, as if he had physically threatened her, but he knew it was her own emotions she didn't trust.

"You." Her voice quivered. "You, Bill, never know the right thing, do you? You never have a clue about me. Whatever I ask you for, you never give. You give me just the opposite. I said I didn't want the kids to see me like this. I told you that. But what did you do, Bill?"

He didn't understand why she hadn't left the house all summer and wouldn't let her daughter and grandsons visit. She seemed okay when she spoke to her friends and family on the telephone. She laughed in desperation about her plight and looked for their support. Why wouldn't she let those closest to her offer it?

He walked toward the front door to see if Sugar had arrived. He knew better than to stay close to Frannie when she was like this.

She was still pacing the kitchen, muttering to herself,

stopping and starting a string of chores that had already been done. Finally, she reached for a cigarette and lit it, exhaling her anger with each puff of smoke.

"And that Sugar. I could kill her. I told her not to bring the boys. She never cares about what I want, it's always about what she wants."

Frances banged around the house, making noise instead of screaming the way she used to do. She hated to be without power, hated not to be in charge of herself. Hated that Bill was no longer paying attention to what she wanted. When she heard Sugar's car pull up outside, Frances folded her apron and put it on the counter.

"Tell them I'm asleep. I'm not going to see them, Bill. I told you that."

She closed the door to her bedroom and sat very still. Bill knew she was listening to him and Sugar and the boys visit together. Frances was farther away from them than she'd ever been.

He did the best he could to cover for her, although he could tell Sugar was offended and confused that her mother had avoided her all summer. She kept looking down the hall in the direction of her mother's room, unconvinced that the door would remain closed, trying to will it open with the sheer force of her concern.

In the quiet words between them while the boys watched television, Bill and his daughter discussed their resentment that Frances was putting herself first. They didn't like that her vanity, or whatever it was, got in the way of the family.

And now here we all are, Bill thought at his wife's bedside. *Brought together at the hospital. Gathered around Frannie, supporting her the way we wanted to all summer. It's funny how things turn out.*

Despite the circumstances, he was more sure than ever that he'd been right all along. Satisfied, he kissed his wife on the cheek and went home for the night.

Frances opened her eyes and silently watched her husband leave. The medication was wearing off, so she was beginning to think clearly. And she didn't like what was going on here, no, not one bit. This was not part of the plan. When she heard the elevator doors close, Frances pressed the button for the nurse.

"When can I go home?"

The overweight woman with cornrowed hair was barely through the door frame when her hip brushed it on one side. She frowned and rubbed the spot where she'd made contact.

"Mrs. Baldwin, we're doing everything we can to get you out of here. But I told you earlier that you can't go home until your heart is beating normally." She fiddled with the IV monitor and moved Bill's chair back against the wall.

Frances felt the flutter like wings under her ribs. It didn't hurt. It just felt like her heart might fly away without notice, leaving her to die from a hole in her chest. Somehow that was much closer to the ending she'd imagined last night. She could accept that.

"Well, maybe it's never going to beat right again. Maybe we all just have to get used to it." Frances scratched at her nose, and the finger clipped by an oxygen sensor nearly poked her in the eye. "I can't stand all of this," she said.

She pulled the monitor off, and it fell between the bars of the guard rail onto the floor, the long cord weighting it down.

Frances rather liked the effect. It was as if she'd stomped her foot, which obviously she was unable to do at present. It was hard to make an impression on people from a hospital bed, so one had to use the tools one had.

The nurse retrieved the monitor, rolled her eyes and bit down on her frustration.

"Mrs. Baldwin, please." She reached for Frannie's hand and clipped the monitor back on her middle finger. "Your procedure is scheduled for the morning. Get some rest. Do you need something to help you sleep?"

"Sure. That's all I need. More drugs." She flung her arm down beside her and pushed the button to change the slant of her head. "No. I do not need anything to help me sleep."

Frances was wide awake now, her body resuscitated by the adrenaline that sprung from the indignity of it all. The bird was beginning to fly.

The nurse looked at the heart monitor and pulled her lips together tightly.

"You have to calm down, Mrs. Baldwin." She picked up the telephone and called the nurses' station, speaking slowly and quietly into the receiver.

"That's easy for you to say," Frances mumbled to herself. "What's the procedure anyway? Maybe I don't want the procedure."

"Your husband and your daughter know all about it." The nurse had resumed her soothing voice. She hung up the telephone then tucked Frances' blankets in again, swaddling her tightly like a fussy baby.

"We're talking about me. About my body," she wheezed. "Why didn't anyone ask me if I wanted the procedure?" Frances felt her breath shortening again, but this time it was anger that had its hands around her throat.

A second nurse came in and injected a clear liquid into the IV line.

"You were sedated, Mrs. Baldwin. We couldn't ask you. Look at it this way. The procedure is going to set your heart beating right, and you can't leave the hospital until your heart is fixed. So the procedure will be a good thing. Right?"

"I guess so," Frances agreed even though the nurse had missed her point. What was her point? She felt suddenly like every muscle in her body had given up at the same time. Even her eyelids. Her body relaxed, unwilling to do her mind's bidding.

The nurse's voice moved toward the door. "Okay then. Try to settle down and be patient. These things take time."

4

DR. Safiya Al-Biruni, the resident cardiologist, entered Frannie's room with a smile.

"I've got good news, Frances," she said. "The conversion procedure worked and your heart is now back to normal. You're well enough to go home today!" The doctor was a fortyish woman with long, thick hair tied back tightly in a ponytail. She had a slight accent and smiled as she signed off on Frannie's hospital chart.

"Well, that's great, Doctor, but what did Dr. Linden say?" Bill stood and walked toward her. He was already there to manage things even though it was technically too early for visitors. Frances had been in the cardiac unit four days, and she'd never given up trying to go home. Bill had the same goal, but he thought the best way to accomplish it was to make sure she followed the doctors' orders. Frances wasn't in a position to bargain.

"Dr. Linden?" Dr. Al-Biruni was puzzled as she began paging through the chart.

"The pulmonary guy. The lung doctor." Bill sighed but remained calm.

Frances restrained her impatience with a lasso that resembled a noose. She hated doctors, but Bill felt they were owed a certain amount of respect no matter how difficult they made things.

"Oh. Well, I don't know," the doctor answered nervously. "Does Frances have a lung problem?" The pages were still turning.

What Frances wouldn't give for someone who knew how to talk to doctors, because obviously they didn't talk to each other.

They waited together all morning, watching television, until the doctors conferred and signed all the papers for Frannie's release.

It was a hot August day. Bill pulled the car into the driveway of their one-story, red brick house and fumbled with his keys. He smiled from ear to ear even though his skin was soaked from both the inside out and the outside in from the humidity. Over six feet tall, he was a handsome man; his full head of hair was still mostly dark. To look at, he could easily pass for ten years younger, but he was an old man in the ways that counted. The heat and stress were making him unsteady. He carried two flower arrangements from his sons and Frances' small suitcase, puffing loudly as he held the door open.

Sugar was still dressed for work, her sculpted blond locks curly in the weather.

"I haven't seen your hair like that since you were a teenager," Frances said. "It looks pretty. You don't look so haggard."

Sugar sighed and helped her mother out of the car.

Now that she was out of the hospital, Frances was ready to get back to her life. And that meant sending Sugar home to her family. She'd been at the hospital every day, and even though the situation had been difficult, Sugar laughed a lot and kept the conversation going. The time had gone fairly quickly. It turned out that Frannie had missed her daughter terribly, and they had done a lot of catching up. But after nearly a week of juggling her job, kids and parents, Sugar had to be as ready for normalcy as Frances.

"Are you okay, Mom? Happy to be home?"

They maneuvered toward the front door, and Frances dropped her daughter's arm once she reached the porch.

"Yes, I am Sugar. Even if it is with another handful of prescriptions."

"I'll get those filled for you and bring them over later."

Frances sighed, relenting. She'd promised to become a good COPD patient, not because she wanted to live, but because she'd wanted to go home and get out of the medical system. She'd had to promise. It was the only leverage she'd had.

When she walked through the door, despite her best efforts, Frances felt the gloom descend. She stood in the very spot where she'd fallen on the kitchen floor and was nearly knocked out by the lingering weight of her fear, the vacuum of her despair, and the unbidden disappointment that she'd missed her chance. Bill caught her changing expression and tried to shift its momentum in another direction.

"You sit down, Frannie, it's been a big day for you. Do you want some coffee?" He plugged in the coffee maker and fumbled for a filter.

She always had a cup of coffee in the afternoon, and they'd only served her decaf in the hospital. She was ready for the real thing. She inhaled, coughed, and gathered what remained of her resolve.

"I'm not sitting down, Bill. I've been lying in bed for days.

And don't you start acting like I'm some kind of invalid. I'll make the coffee."

As they waited for the pot to brew, Sugar kissed her mother goodbye on her right cheek, where her mother preferred it. This was their ritual for greeting and saying goodbye. Frances allowed no other physical contact between herself and her children; she made the rules for how they would love her.

As Sugar rushed off to meet her kids at the school bus, she said over her shoulder, "I'll bring the boys over later, Momma. They've missed you so much. And don't go to any fuss. They love you just the way you are."

She was gone before Frances could respond. Frances realized she missed the boys, too.

She unconsciously fluffed her hair and straightened her clothes. It was true. She was still a little vain at seventy-four. She had hated the poison ivy because she didn't want to look bad and she didn't want her grandsons to be embarrassed by her. They were at that age—ten and thirteen. Having always felt unattractive, and having learned over the years not to call attention to herself, Frannie allowed herself this level of narcissism.

But there was more to it than vanity.

Only she knew the bigger truth. By the time the poison ivy began, she had already begun withdrawing from her life. Like the heart failure, the rash had threatened to bring her back to the physical world, away from the introspective and intuitive place to which she had begun to gravitate. She resented the distraction from what had become, in the last year, her real purpose in life—to prepare for a dignified death.

Although the doctor's x-rays had found no visual changes from her cigarette smoking—that is to say there was no cancer growing—Frances' lungs had begun to harden. When she'd received the diagnosis last fall, she'd been surprised. She'd thought smoking only caused lung cancer. But they said she had COPD and gave her an appointment card for a specialist and a glossy brochure. The brochure cover had photos of older people playing with their grandchildren next to the words *Chronic Obstructive Pulmonary Disease*. Inside were more photos and the words *chronic bronchitis* and *emphysema*.

Frances hadn't understood COPD at first, thinking it was just an inconvenience she would recover from. But hidden in the brochure was the truth that like cancer, it, too, would eventually kill her. And perhaps with less pain and fuss. That would be just fine.

For some time now, she'd noticed it was getting harder to fight through the fluid in her lungs for each breath. She tried not to call attention to it by moving too quickly or for too long, or by talking too much. In truth, the poison ivy gave her an excuse for isolation. She'd found little need to talk at all during these last months.

A year or so ago, Frances had gone to the bedroom at the end of the hallway when she'd needed to cough and clear her airways. She hadn't wanted anyone to hear. It irritated her throat and esophagus, and overworked the muscles in her chest and back. It left her tired. But over time the breathing eventually became more difficult and noisy, and she found herself coughing more and more in every room of the house.

That was the reason, not the poison ivy, she'd stopped attending social events, having guests, and seeing her grandchildren during the summer. But she had let them think it was because of the rash on her face.

There was plenty of time to deal with the truth.

Frances drank her coffee at her usual place at the table, looking out the window. The kids were passing by on their way home from school. A day like every other day: the chatter of soft little voices like the songs of birds floating in her window. The girls skipping and flirting, the boys tagging and teasing.

She loved to hear their laughter freed after a long day of repression. It made her smile, her own laughter trapped just behind her lips. How many times had she sat in this very spot, watching them, drinking a cup of coffee and smoking a cigarette?

A cigarette. The mere thought made her crave a cigarette with her coffee, made her crave it badly. After a few moments, she needed a cigarette like she'd never needed one before. Every cell in her body focused on a single goal: nicotine. Making a silent pact to have only one, Frances stood up and went to the cabinet where she kept her carton.

It was gone. And so was her lighter. Of course, Bill had taken them away. She knew they were no longer in the house, instinctively, like a bird knows north. Frannie reminded herself that a promise was a promise, dumped the rest of her coffee down the drain, and tried to figure out what to do next. It had been four days since she'd had a cigarette. She resolved to make it five.

"What shall I make for dinner tonight, Bill? Do you feel like chicken? I'll bet you've been eating fast food while I've been in the hospital. Your cholesterol's probably off the charts."

She got up from her chair, wiped the Formica counter clean with the dishrag, and not knowing what else to do at the moment, resumed her life right where she'd left off.

"You know, Bill, the physical therapist said if I have COPD I should live in a dust-free environment," Frances said the next morning.

She hadn't mentioned to her daughter that she, one day out of the hospital, was planning a housecleaning. Sugar would have hired a cleaning woman, threatened her, or at the very least tried to talk some sense into her. But Frances didn't want sense. And she surely didn't want to be told what to do. Sugar was bound to argue that it wasn't a good idea for her to go stirring up dust, climbing the stepladder and hauling heavy linens and curtains from one end of the house to the other.

For when Frances Baldwin housecleaned, no spider, cobweb or dust bunny was safe. Twice a year she moved the furniture out, she got down on her hands and knees to scrub. She wiped baseboards and moldings, she took everything out of closets and changed the curtains. Frances always said it was the best exercise she could think of.

"How many seventy-four year olds can still do all this?" she would ask Bill proudly.

As if she had no physical impediment, Frances directed, "Let's roll up the rug in my bedroom, and I'll sleep with my bed on the wood floor. I can keep that clean a lot easier."

After Bill had complied, she added, "Can you reach up to that curtain rod? I can't get it, even with the ladder."

"Welcome back." Bill gave her a brief hug.

Frances began the day optimistically. Maybe they had fixed her up at the hospital, after all. It had been months since she'd been as upbeat and full of energy, and nothing seemed to make Bill happier. He watched as Frances alternately wiped down the walls of her bedroom, tended a big pot of spaghetti sauce simmering on the burner, and put a big pork roast in the oven. The washing machine and dryer were both running.

"It's good to have you back. At last."

Bill smiled as he carried all the big things for her, and she was careful to heave the furniture gently, so as not to irritate his knee. She liked when her husband pitched in. It made her feel for a moment that she was not as alone in her life as it seemed.

Bill helped her make the bed and pack away the summer linens in the closet. The chilly nights they'd been having meant fall was coming, and Frannie made up her bed with a light blanket and a rust-colored striped bedspread. She went into Bill's room and blanketed his bed in the same manner. She didn't want him to be cold.

From time to time she stopped for a cup of coffee or to catch her breath. She still had a lot to do. She didn't have the strength she remembered, but it was much easier to do housework than it was to be in the hospital. So she pushed herself harder than she might normally have done. She didn't stop for lunch. No cigarette. She busied her hands.

She went back to her cooking and packaged up the extra food for future night's dinners. Bill looked on, his stomach growling, while Frances went through her routines. He put his nose in the air and picked the smells out one by one, naming them as he imagined his dinner in detail.

"I feel like I'm at a smorgasbord," he laughed. She gave him a meatball to taste. He cut it in half on a small plate and savored each bit.

"My favorite." He laughed and licked the fork. His eyes twinkled.

Frances remembered how much she liked cooking for people, how her meals satisfied them in a way her company never seemed to do. She made a mental note to have Sugar and the boys over for spaghetti the following night.

By four-thirty she was beginning to slow down. Her body was tightening up from all the bending and carrying, and the coffee no longer seemed strong enough to keep her fueled. In a way, it was a relief to have so much to do. It distracted her from paying attention to every swoosh, hammer, gurgle and push going on inside her body. At times she struggled to keep her body going in the waves; it felt like the tide was rapidly going out. But she still had dinner and the dishes to take care of.

The oven timer buzzed. The roast was done. Frances made a thick pork gravy from the pan drippings then made up Bill's plate full of meat and mashed potatoes and his favorite Brussels sprouts, adding a big, buttered slice of bread. The two carried their dinner plates into the family room to eat, as they usually did, in their designated chairs watching *Jeopardy*.

As the theme song began to play through the ten-year-old, nineteen-inch television set, Bill smiled.

"I really think everything is going to be okay," he said and bit into his soft bread. He tipped his glass of milk as he swallowed and added, "Good to have you back, Fran."

The last thing Bill expected on Thursday morning was bad news, yet there she was, doubled over in pain, as he watched his favorite morning game show.

Frannie had done what they all wanted in the hospital—she'd taken all of the tests and treatments and medicines—she'd done all that and quit smoking, too, so she might live the few more years everyone expected. But despite all that, despite acting like she was back to her old self yesterday, despite almost wanting to be the mother and wife they all wanted her to be, deep in her heart Frances knew the effort was useless.

Her life was, she was positive now, coming to an end. There was a profound pain, deep in her gut that had never been there before. She remembered her father dying of colon cancer: the pain, the blood, the anguish. This must be what he'd felt.

She didn't want to panic this time. She wasn't going to wait for hours and hours for them to take the pain away, and she wasn't going to take an ambulance. Too much fuss. No, she would do this her own way.

"Bill, I need to go to the hospital."

She spoke calmly and simply, looking around her home for the last time, breathing in deeply the memory of her cohabitation, of the life she had known. She was ready. She took her handbag and a small suitcase packed with her makeup, hairbrush, face cream, and the new nightgown from the shelf in the closet that she had reserved for such an event. She hated those tie-back gowns at the hospital. Heading to the car before Bill had even gotten up from his recliner, she stumbled on the porch and grabbed at the furniture for support. She righted herself and her thoughts with the utmost determination.

Now it was Bill who couldn't breathe as he waited a moment to either lose consciousness or to regain it from what must be a bad dream. When neither occurred, he dialed the telephone and his throat seemed to close around the words he used to tell Sugar what was happening.

"Stay strong, Dad. I'll meet you at the hospital."

"I'm not sure I can. I know too much now."

Disoriented, he took his keys off the front hall table as he looked out to see Frannie already sitting in the front passenger seat of the car.

5

ACROSS the country, just outside Los Angeles in a 1970s-era rancher set back amid the tall trees, all William could think was, *This is it. It's really going to happen. Now.*

"We all thought it was behind us, at least for the time being," Sugar explained in a small voice on the telephone. "But now there's this pain in her stomach."

William asked a few questions about how his mother's symptoms had presented and what tests had been ordered. Based on his training, William thought it likely that a blood clot had formed during her heart failure and had lodged in her abdomen. When the heart beats normally, it keeps blood pushing through at a normal pace. But when the normal rhythm is interrupted the way his mother's had been, some of the blood can remain in the heart. If the patient is unlucky, clots can form in the stagnant blood. *Of all the places a clot could have traveled*, William thought as the weight of the idea sunk down his legs. Having it lodge in her abdomen was bad because it meant the blood flow to her digestive system would be blocked off. He kept this information from his sister because he knew it was a serious complication and suspected that it might be fatal.

"Should I come out there?" He knew the answer but hoped she might say no anyway.

"Yes, I would if I were you." She said it as if it were solely his decision. "I don't know if this is the end or not, William", she said more cautiously, "but this is the time we will be dealing with all of the issues."

William wasn't quite sure he knew what *the issues* were, but it sounded ominous enough that he didn't ask.

"You know how Mom feels about medicine and doctors and hospitals. She'll die before she lets herself become an invalid."

Sugar's voice was beginning to plead, and William felt his choices narrowing.

"And she won't live connected to machines."

William knew that was how his mother felt, yet she'd still expected him to be a doctor and save other people long after they stopped wanting to live. This was where his conflict originated.

He could see both sides of the argument clearly: medical intervention saves lives, but there is a point when medical intervention stops being a life-saving measure and starts interfering with a natural death.

Many people didn't even know that refusing medical care at the end stage was an option, and their doctors rarely told them. In his experience, most people seemed more comfortable making a decision that, despite the odds, might result in continuing some form of life—no mater how compromised—when the alternative was a certain death.

There was only one thing he could say.

"I'll be there tomorrow."

He'd known all along he would. But that didn't mean he wanted to. Sugar was obviously relieved.

"And would you mind calling Randy?" Sugar asked quietly and politely. She couldn't call their youngest brother herself because they hadn't talked in four years.

"Sure. Someone should give him the choice of being here, too."

William hung up and sat quietly in a chair by the window, processing his thoughts. He looked out for twenty minutes before he managed to take action. Two thousand miles away from the inevitability of his mother's death, he was coming to terms with the idea of going home.

He knew what his mother said about dying, but he also knew her to be religious woman. *If she believes God has the upper hand, then what issues and choices could there be for us to deal with?*

"I'm going to Philadelphia." William made the announcement in a clear voice to get his wife's attention from across the room. "Would you mind getting me the red-eye flight out tonight?"

He couldn't help but think his wife was relieved as he explained the situation. He was satisfied with that because he didn't want to repeat their earlier confrontation about his mother's motives. Yet Diane was so cooperative and supportive that William again suspected she'd be glad to get rid of him. He was afraid she'd get used to his absence.

"Is there anything else I can do?"

He considered her question. As far as he could tell, her offer was sincere.

"No. Thank you. I just have to get there."

"Maybe the time away will be good." She added, "For us, I mean."

William knew exactly what she meant and wished that instead of dealing with his mother's issues, he could deal with his own now. His issues were a wall that had kept him constrained for most of the time Diane had known him. Their marriage had been stretched into an unnatural position for a while now. His emotions bound each word of love she needed to hear him speak. During one of their recent conversations about the children he seemed unable to commit to having, he'd asked her, "Why don't you give up on me?"

She hadn't answered.

He asked her the same question now. His eyes filled with his love for her, and he tried to will it from spilling over.

"Because there are too many things I still love about you."

The words floated from Diane's desk at the window, over the couch, and out to the doorway where he stood. He shifted to block their escape.

"You're nuts," he nearly whispered. The tears fell. "I adore you."

"I know. Now go get ready."

He tried to convince himself as he headed up the stairs that time away from each other would help them find some perspective. He wondered how day-to-day living had become so stiff and routine, how their ever-growing list of issues forced such structure on the ease they had once enjoyed.

They met in medical school in the days when women represented a small minority and beautiful women represented a separate field of study. William was one of a number of sex-starved intellectuals tagging along behind the beautiful, tall, auburn-crested woman whose easy smile and confident manner could have taken her to Hollywood as easily as her brains had taken her to the top of the class at the UCSF School of Medicine. She was every man's fantasy. Beauty to distract them, a great body to stoke their imaginations, a clever mind to challenge them. Coming up against her sharp wit substituted for foreplay.

For her part, Diane said she'd abhorred the attention but had fallen in love with him despite her best efforts, mainly because of his non-scientific approach to the science of medicine, and, she once admitted on a night of too much tequila, his boyish appearance and cute tush.

In school, she spent hours trying to understand his opinions on healing and the role of medicine in American and Western societies. He always had additional insight to the technical information they studied, challenging it with philosophy and religious principles. Even as a young man he'd tried to make sense of death and dying, and now at forty he was no closer to making peace with it. The older he got, it seemed, the fuzzier his thinking became.

Diane didn't really understand the complexity of William's arguments and had been exhausted with the thoughts she did have on the textbooks she memorized. The details of physiology and chemistry were unimportant to William, and their interest in medicine eventually diverged. While they were both good students with promising futures, it hadn't surprised Diane when he announced that he wouldn't finish the last months of medical school. Likewise, it hadn't surprised him when Diane graduated summa cum laude and pursued a career in dermatology.

He had been happy to put the topics for which he could never find an answer to the back of his mind and make a living in computer network design. In this field, he always knew how the pieces fit together, and he could control the inputs and outputs. And no one ever cried over a network design, he often said.

He gathered his thoughts and a small bag for his journey, expecting to stay only a day or two. As a second thought he packed up his notebook, the journal that he kept from time to time when things really bothered him. He threw it in his carry-on along with the paperback thriller from his nightstand.

William called Randy, and then his father, while he waited for his flight. With determination, he turned his mind from the recurring thought, *My mother is going to die now,* which he'd been repeating over and over unconsciously since he and Diane drove to the departure terminal at LAX, and explained to his father that he would be taking the late flight to Philadelphia.

"Is there anything I can say to stop you from coming?" his father asked.

William was confused. "What do you mean, stop me from coming?" *My mother is going to die now.*

"She won't see you. She doesn't want anyone to see her like this. She would want me to tell you to stay home. I'm sure of it. Since she got the poison ivy, she hasn't wanted anyone to see her."

"You're kidding."

"No, I'm not," his father insisted. "She hasn't had visitors all summer long. Since the poison ivy."

William wondered what his father could be thinking. It seemed impossible that Bill didn't grasp the fact that they weren't talking about a skin rash. The situation was grave and uncertain. His mother might die, maybe even before he could make the flight across the country. But he couldn't have that conversation with his father right now; he hoped that it would wait until he arrived.

"Then don't even tell her I'm on the way. I'll sit down the hall in the visitor's lounge if she doesn't want to see me. If my presence doesn't mean anything to her then I'm coming for me, Dad. Not for her." When he said this, William knew for the first time that it was true. "You can't deny me that."

"I wish you'd stay home."

"I know."

My mother is going to die now.

And I need to be with her.

6

William's Journal

AUGUST 24, 2005. In many cultures, like the Hmong, the dying person is ushered to death by loved ones and by prayers to ensure a peaceful transition to the next place. They believe a person's thoughts at the moment of death will define what happens next—whether they will find another life, eternal peace, or torment. If that's the case then I will do everything I can to help my mother, to comfort her to sleep as she has done so many times for me. If there is such a thing as heaven or nirvana or eternal peace, I want her to have it. And if there's not, then, at least I'll have done what I can so I won't feel guilty later.

Hindus believe that we keep being reincarnated until we are no longer afraid of death, until we know the truth about our immortal souls. Once we reach the core of our own True Self, there is no death in death.

I don't get that at all.

Everything to me today seems so final; I have a hard time imagining how my mother will still be alive in any form when she leaves her body. I only know for sure what is right ahead of me. I can only imagine the warmth of her hands going cold; I cannot at all conceive her limitless soul warmed in peace. When I look inside myself, I sense a vast emptiness where my soul should be. My body seems a vulnerable shell. If Hindus are right, I guess I have a lot of lives to go before this all makes sense to me.

If Mom's really going to die, I want her to have a good death. That is something I can do for her. I read somewhere about the Chinese belief of a five-blossom death being a good death. Mom has a chance at that, she's gotten four out of five so far. The five blossoms represent the best things that can happen in life: my mother has a long marriage, two sons, the respect of her family and friends, and two grandsons. Dying peacefully in her sleep would be the last blossom.

I want her to have a good death. In a sick, twisted way, it's sort of like her wanting us to have a good Christmas when we were little kids. I don't know where she got the money for it all. She must have scrimped all year. Maybe we just didn't ask for too much, but it always seemed that we all got exactly what we asked for. Sugar, Randy and I would sit for hours with the Sears catalog, taking turns marking the pages and making our lists. After a month of deep meditation on the ideal, Christmas morning would arrive and we'd be transported to kid heaven. Mom always made it possible, so I guess that's what I have to do for her. Check all my pockets for whatever currency I can trade so that her death can be everything she dreamed of.

-whb

William closed his journal and considered its usefulness from seat 2D on United Airlines flight 1482 to the East Coast. He'd slept only an hour or two all night, even with the extra leg room in the first class cabin. Maybe he was too uncomfortable to sleep. Maybe he was too upset. He couldn't be sure because he was still trying to focus on the facts of the situation and forget his emotions. He had thought that if he wrote them down, he could close the book and keep them inside.

But the feelings kept poking out, and despite his best efforts, tears formed in the corners of his eyes every time he tried to sleep. *Why am I feeling the loss of something I don't really have?* While he felt he knew his mother like the back of his hand, William was certain his mother didn't know him. She never had. He'd spent a lifetime trying to fit into a mold that had no relevance to his real shape and size. *If my mother dies now, I would be losing an icon in my life, not someone I was close to.*

William thought this was true, yet he was still uncomfortable that he was missing something. Something important about all of this. He was anxious to see his mother so he could figure it out.

"Ladies and gentlemen," the flight attendant announced. "We are making our initial descent into Philadelphia. Please make sure your seat trays are secured and your seat backs are returned to their original, upright, and locked positions."

William prepared himself for landing.

Randy Williams locked his New York apartment and headed downstairs to the garage. He had changed his name when he'd finished law school, dropping the last name of Baldwin and replacing it with his father's first name. He'd kept Randy, even though he thought it childish, because he was convinced he would never learn to answer to the more formal *Randall*, which his parents had apparently never thought of. And since he'd always wished his parents had christened him with a middle name, he added the name Ascher between his first and last and felt satisfied with his new moniker. Randy Ascher Williams was a much better name for an attorney.

He put his bag in the back seat, closed the door, and checked his image in his rearview mirror. Struck by the visible panic on his face, he reached into his pocket for a Valium. He brought a lot more with him, even though he only planned on staying one day. He didn't believe his mother would ever die, so he didn't really believe she was dying now.

She's too tough, he thought. *The bitch will never die. I'll probably die before she does.*

Since she was up early and had already gotten the boys off to school, Sugar headed to the hospital. William was coming today. As she walked heavily down the fluorescent hallway, her footsteps screamed the anger she would try to hide.

He didn't know their mother the way she did. He needed to be here to understand the impossible situation they were in. No, she couldn't let her mother die. Not by herself. She needed William to handle things. Maybe he would know something they could do to prevent what was going to happen. Sugar clenched her jaw. William had never borne the load in the family. He was always so independent, attuned to but never involved in the family's inner workings.

Because he'd grown up so close to his younger brother, William never took his role as the older one. He'd always acted as though he wasn't quite ready for whatever responsibility was appropriate for his age, aligning himself instead with Randy and friends less mature than he ought to have been. This had frustrated his parents to no end. Bill and Frances both had dreams for their eldest son, dreams that William had tried but inevitably failed to commit to, much like their mother's half-hearted attempt to meet her family's expectations that she live to a ripe old age.

Sugar tried to stuff her resentment back into her throat. It was going to be a long day.

Frances had been re-admitted the day before, and the tests confirmed the blood clot in her abdomen. The first course of treatment was to dissolve it, a relatively simple procedure.

Her new room was right off the elevator, on the second floor to the right. Sugar had left her there sleeping late last night.

But now the bed was empty.

For a moment Sugar's mind wandered to the worst case. Then, she tried the idea that she had the wrong room. No, she was sure this was it. Maybe she was off getting a test? No, the bed sheets were gone. The balloons and all of her mother's belongings were gone.

Just before Sugar's knees buckled, a nurse entered the room. Although she stopped Sugar from thinking the worst, she told her something that was, in fact, only slightly better.

"Your mother was moved to CCU, the cardiac critical care unit. Her heart rhythm went wild last night, and she'll have better monitoring there. Here, let me show you how to get in."

Dazed with an adrenaline rush, Sugar wished she wasn't alone, but her husband was gone and the boys were too young to help. Where was her father when she needed him? She followed the nurse down the silver hallway, her feet moving on the floor, her mind hovering somewhere above.

"First you stand here," the nurse indicated a place where two green adhesive footprints had been stuck to the floor. "Then you press this big red button on the wall."

The large steel double doors swung open fifteen feet ahead. The nurse held out her arm for Sugar to proceed. She passed into a chamber of all-powerful secrets, a shiny, secret place where she didn't belong. The door that required a magic combination closed firmly behind her. Sugar grew just a little calmer when she saw that the tile, the nurse's desk and all of the woodwork were pink; not the greasy green of the rest of the hospital. Actually, it was kind of nice. But this comfort quickly gave way to fear as her mind registered the stagnant smell of death.

"Can I help you?"

Sugar dreaded the days to come, when no one would ask her and the family if they could help. They would know everything that could be done had been done, that things had taken their course. But on this day, when everything still seemed possible, Nurse Pat introduced herself and directed Sugar to her mother's room. Sugar thought she looked vaguely familiar, and concluded Pat was one of the nurses who had taken care of her mother last week.

"Your mother's heartbeat was abnormal when she was admitted yesterday. We weren't worried because the beats were at a normal speed. Until last night." Nurse Pat ushered Sugar to the left side of the corridor.

"Last night she was going at over two hundred heartbeats per minute. That's way too fast, and she was feeling chest pain. When her lungs filled with fluid, we had to intervene."

Sugar didn't know what all that meant, but she suspected they had prevented her mother from dying. They'd saved her life. Again. For the second time.

She was desperate to see her mother alive. They reached the room, this time a private room, and Pat slipped away. Frances was awake.

"Baby. You're here. They've put me in intensive care."

"Momma."

Sugar headed to the bed and saw her mother attached to a floor-to-ceiling monitoring unit with cords and wires strung back and forth between it and the bed. She kissed her mother's cheek and tried to hug her. Frances stopped her, taking Sugar's hands in her IV-rigged left hand.

The clock hung straight in front of the bed. "I've been watching that second hand go around and around, Sugar. I don't have much time left."

Sugar sighed. She knew it was going to come to this. For the first time, she shared her mother's certainty that this was the end. The realization hit her hard. It gripped her at her ankles, seized her veins and arteries, numbed her lungs and her muscles and every organ so that her only reaction was the one tear that formed in the well of each eye then spat down her cheeks. She turned slowly and collapsed into the pink vinyl chair.

7

FRANCES had been up all night. Once the chest pain started and the night nurse took her pulse and blood pressure, things happened very quickly. One of the reasons she hated the medical system was that she felt like a piece of meat, on display for an endless trail of doctors, nurses and technicians. These were highly trained people, she knew, each doing their jobs in a way that must be good. But how could it be when no one asked her any questions?

As if *congestive heart failure* was all they needed to know, each had set about poking and prodding and listening and rolling her back and forth and up and down to get their perspective. In a few minutes, everyone was gone except the orderly who was transferring her to a gurney, a feat Frannie could have willingly participated in a day earlier. But now she was too weak and tired. He lifted her like she was a child.

Frances was the first of her family to make the trip down the hallway to see the secret button and the big double doors. She had an oxygen cup over her mouth and two people walking with her. She was covered neatly with a white cotton blanket.

In that moment, she felt important, like one of those people on the television shows she watched. She heard terms like "Stat," and "CCU" and "Ten CC's" that made her feel more like she was watching the drama instead of participating in it. She'd seen this a hundred times before. She waited for the good-looking male doctor to put her at ease when he was done flirting with the bright and beautiful female doctor who had admitted her to CCU. Where were they? She looked around, but all she saw were regular-looking people in pastel cutie-pie smocks and blue or green pants. And they all looked tired. It was the middle of the night.

The door to Room 223 was wider than the doors in the other rooms she'd had. Frances saw the nine-foot technology center next to her new bed and had a very bad feeling. She didn't want to be attached to machines. She'd given the okay for the IV drip, just a regular IV. Not this kind of machine with lights and sounds and five different display panels. She made up her mind then: if things were this critical, she wanted nature to take its course. Like it had for her father.

She thought again of her dad and his death from colon cancer. Back in the fifties there had been no fancy machines, and he hadn't had money for a hospital or a nurse. There'd been no place for him to do his dying except in his small, cramped apartment at the end of the train line with his daughter as his nurse.

Sugar and William had been only three and one at the time. Every day Frances put them on the train, and together they visited Grandpa. The children hadn't really ever even met him. He was more a concept than a person. They waved to him from his bedroom door once their mother had him all cleaned up. Until that good-bye ritual, they were content to stay together in the playpen in the living room, playing with their brightly colored plastic toys. They were good kids.

Frances shuddered at the memory of her dad's suffering.

They'd had no money for morphine. But she did now. She paid half her monthly Social Security check for the finest medical insurance a senior citizen could buy. She'd made up her mind a long time ago that she was never going to be stuck in the position he had been in, without anything but the cancer that ate him from the inside out and the daughter who watched it happen helplessly over the course of a year.

The blood. Oh God, there'd been so much blood. By the time Frances would arrive in the morning, his sheets would be laced with feces and blood, and he would be lying in it waiting for her to arrive. He moaned in pain as she rolled him over and back trying to clean him, trying to get the sheets out from under him.

The stench of his wasted body and the things that flowed out of it again filled her nostrils as she lay in her hospital bed. *It smells like death here, too*, she thought. She picked up her arm and put it to her nose to see if the odor was emanating from her or whether it was just part of what happened here behind the protective doors. She wasn't sure. Whatever, she was part of it now.

This is where I will die.

Frances watched the doctors and nurses and technicians install her to the monitor machine, set up the IVs and record critical metrics. Then they left her alone. She heard the clock ticking and panicked.

The clock ticked seconds, so many seconds. A night full of seconds. Hundreds of them, thousands of cruel, tortuous seconds. She looked up at the monitor. Her heart was racing again. She could not calm herself. The pain in her stomach had returned, but she bore it as she bore the labor pains of her three children. It was good pain. She waited.

She began to pray, deeply pray. She pleaded with her God for an answer. After many, many ticking seconds, she finally found peace. She knew her fears were over and that God was as ready for her as she was for Him.

By coincidence, or luck as William perceived it, he and Randy arrived at the hospital at the same time. He hadn't wanted to go to his mother's room alone.

"Hey, bro. How goes it? Started the job in Salt Lake yet?" William reached out to give his brother a hug.

"Next week. Bad timing on this Mom thing. I can't save her and the planet at the same time."

Randy stepped back to appraise his older brother. William did the same. The two were only a year apart. Growing up, they'd done everything together. Although they didn't look a bit alike, Randy tall and dark and William a stocky blond, they'd acted almost as twins, experiencing the world at the same time. They'd had the same friends and interests for all of their early years. It was still hard for William to imagine how one could have turned out to be a philosophical computer geek and the other an environmental attorney.

Neither brother spoke his assessment. They nodded to each other and kept walking across the shiny white linoleum toward the elevator. William could barely feel the floor when he walked; his senses dulled as his intellect took command.

"Well, bro, the whole thing's 'outta our hands. Gotta depend on the good Lord to call the shots here. If it's her time, it's her time."

William was still in the habit of turning to his religion of origin for the answers. Although he was not a practicing Catholic, he still found solace in the black-and-white nature of its teachings. As if God either left you alive or dead, with no choice or middle zone.

"But I'm glad we're here. Sugar said we'd be dealing with all of the issues, whatever that means. I'm not quite sure what to expect."

The men took the elevator to the second floor, got directions to the secret CCU entrance and saw their mother for the first time in years. It nearly took William's breath away. It was as shocking a turn of events as any plot twist in the thriller novels he read.

She was much different than he remembered, and by the look on Randy's face, William assumed he, too, had entered an alternate reality. This was not the indestructible woman of their memories, the much-taller woman whose voice could knock them over, whose gaze could melt their best defenses and whose judgment could send them to tears. They had not spent enough time around their mother as adults to have rewritten those childhood beliefs with any impression of her vulnerability, uncertainty or fear. Only their sister knew their mother in that way. Frances maintained a fierce façade before all men, including her husband and sons.

"My sons, my sons. All of my children here with me. This is good."

She was hoarse from the oxygen flowing into her nose and drying out her throat. She released Sugar's hand and raised it to welcome her boys. She introduced them to the nurse who was fidgeting with all of the gadgets on the technology center.

"Pat, these are my sons, come all the way from the West Coast and from New York."

There were feeble introductions. William had already absorbed enough information to disorient him. If his mother had either died or begun tap dancing, it would have met with an equal response.

Frances directed her comments now directly to her sons, who were still standing close to the doorway as if they might have to leave suddenly.

"Boys, come in here. I have something to tell you."

They had no choice. William went first with Randy lagging behind to kiss their mother on her right cheek. William embraced his sister and made small talk. She had a way of putting him at ease; and at that moment, he needed her as much as she needed him. Randy nodded in Sugar's direction and took his place along the wall, at the foot of the bed. Sugar kept staring at him. William knew exactly what she was thinking, as he'd thought the same thing when Randy had first appeared. *What have you done with my brother*? Randy looked so different than when they'd seen him last. Sugar stared at Randy as if she were struggling to see the troublesome little brother she'd always known: the rebellious teenager, the twenty-something perpetual student, the thirty-something Peter Pan. Nearly forty now, he looked so much older. William looked again at his brother. *Who are you now*?

"Where's Dad?" the stranger who sounded like Randy asked, trying to make conversation.

William looked around and sincerely wanted to find him. He was looking for someone else who might direct what was going on here, someone to confront Frances if confrontation was required. Someone to make all this a bit more normal.

"I don't know where your father is. He's never here when I need him." Frances exaggerated, but it felt true when she said it. "I can't wait for him. I have to tell you something, and you have to understand."

Their mother, tethered to her greatest nightmare, began her story—a story Sugar and William both knew but one Randy, long protected as his mother's youngest, had never fully heard before. He listened with a combination of dread, anger and disinterest. He needed each emotion to balance out the others.

"They've broken up the blood clot but I still need surgery. The clot stopped the blood flow to my intestines, and now a section of it is dead. The only way to fix it is to take out the dead part and hope it all heals up." She watched their faces turn from fear to dread.

"I don't want the surgery." She paused a moment to let it sink in. "And I don't want any of this."

Frances pointed to the contraption beside her. It was monitoring her heart rate, blood pressure, oxygen and other things none of them could identify. "I had heart failure again last night, and they brought me to the cardiac critical care unit. No one asked me if I wanted to be here or if I wanted their treatment. I don't. They just brought me down the hall and expected me to take all of this. And I don't want it."

"I know, Mom." Sugar moved closer, as if her nearness might make her mother reconsider. Sugar and her brothers all understood the gravity of the moment, but Frances seemed to be floating, weightless, in it.

"And I don't want these." Frances pointed to the IV tower that now held five bags of clear liquid.

"What are they?" Randy was for a moment curious if his mother was getting better drugs than he had.

"I don't know," she wheezed. "But I don't want them."

Sugar whispered, "Last night there was only one bag, filled with glucose water and something to keep more blood clots from forming. I don't know what all this is now."

"I don't want this," Frances lifted the arm that bore the IV site, the blood pressure cuff and the oxygen sensor. "Or this," pointing to the oxygen tube across her cheeks. "I don't want any of it. You know what I want." She looked deeply into each of her children's eyes to be sure they understood exactly what she was saying.

"I know what you want, Mom." It was William's turn to speak. "But—"

She cut him off.

"I want to die, William. I am ready. No more shots or medicines. Sweet Jesus, I'm ready." She put her head back on the pillow and closed her eyes. Her speech came in short bursts now that she'd expended what little energy she'd saved up.

"I tried. I did what they said. But it's not working. My heart is still wild. And I still can't breathe." She paused, then added, "And my gut still hurts. Now I've got this thing—" she motioned to the catheter in her groin into which they had been injecting medicine to dissolve the clot, "this damn tube sticking out of me." She rested a moment. "That's enough, please."

Their mother's voice grew softer, losing its insistence. "I asked them to put me down," she shifted her eyes around, looking for anyone who might be listening, "but you know they're not allowed to do that."

Her eyes twinkled in a familiar way and she had the suggestion of a wry smile.

Her children looked at each other, their brows contorted at the possibility that their mother was making a joke.

"You asked them to kill you?" Randy laughed out loud, the first to see the humor. "Put you down like a dog? Ha! Mom, that's hysterical."

He could imagine the whole thing and hoped the doctors and nurses laughed. He didn't want anyone to think his mother was crazy, even though he himself often suspected it.

"It's called euthanasia when they do it to humans, Randy. Don't laugh at me." She held up a finger to scold him but he couldn't stop laughing. He could picture the whole thing, like a scene from a movie.

"Stop laughing," she insisted. "I know they can't give me a shot to end it all but I asked them anyway. I did it so they know what I want. I keep telling all of them, but no one listens. I don't want any more saving. You've got to help me."

Randy looked to his sister for an answer but she made no reply. None of the three knew what to say.

Frances took their silence for agreement.

"Good. Then you'll go along with it."

William jumped in, relieving Randy and Sugar of any responsibility.

"Mom, I don't know what you're talking about. This isn't your decision. God has something in mind for all of us. You can't go telling Him when it's your time." William, again quoting Catholicism 101.

"He's calling me, Son. I can hear the call. They've already kept me from God twice now."

"When the time comes, Mom, you won't have a choice. You don't get to decide." He stuck to his position.

Frances was growing noticeably upset. She and William had never agreed on anything, Randy remembered. Why would they now? Clearly, she needed an ally.

"And you, Randy, what do you have to say?" she asked. "Will you go along with it?"

At the heart of the matter, Randy believed he didn't care much if his mother lived or died. He'd long since repressed his feelings about her. He'd been a sickly child who'd had to fight for independence. Against her will, he moved out when he was eighteen to fend for himself in the world. He'd known it was the only way he could have his own life, a life where he wasn't sick first and a man second. If he clung now to his mother, he would have to question everything he had decided was true about her and himself.

"It's your life, Ma. You gotta do what you gotta do. I'll support you."

Randy wasn't sure if this was the right answer for his mother but he knew it was the best answer for him. He had just gotten his life in order again and he wasn't going to let her shake it up. Again.

"I want to talk to the doctor." William was taking charge and Frances didn't like it. "From what I hear from Dad and Sugar, I'm not convinced you can't be cured, Mom."

He headed to the nurse's station to ask for a report on his mother's condition and to request a consult with the doctor. Sugar wandered down the hallway in the opposite direction.

Frances choked back the pain in her stomach; she couldn't remember when she last had morphine.

"Now tell me all about the new job, Randy. I don't want you hanging around this hospital and missing your first day. You can have a visit, but then you're going home to get ready for your new life. I'm so proud of you." She closed her eyes and listened.

Randy made mental note of his mother's approval, relaxed and poured out his story. When it was finished, she opened her eyes and smiled at him to show she'd been listening the whole time.

"I'm glad you're here, Randy. You always make me feel good, Baby Boy."

She still called him that after all the years. Randy was thirty-nine. She reached for him, and he put his hand in hers.

"Now tell me a poem. You know. A funny one."

Randy thought for a moment, remembering the first time he'd written a poem for his mother. It had been about the poor chicken she was cutting up for dinner, and she'd laughed so hard she'd cried. She'd swooped him up in her arms and held him tightly as she kissed his face. He had tried many times since then to get the same response. He tried again:

"There once was a girl who said 'I'm done,'
And welcomed the blood clots she could die from.
But along came the docs
And they broke up those rocks
And she said, 'That sure hurt like a bitch, son.'"

Frances smiled through her pain. She didn't laugh because she couldn't. "You're just like me, son," she said. "More than the others."

"How? Last time you called me your 'wayward son.' I thought that was a better description." He withdrew his hand from under hers and put it on top.

Frances pulled her hand away completely.

"You are my wayward son. But you always say things like they are. You're not afraid of the truth and that's important now. I like that about you."

"Is there anything else you like about me?" He was doubtful.

"You have an amazing ability to rhyme on cue."

8

"I wouldn't let my mother do this."

Doctor Al-Biruni was indignant. Her straight, black hair was tied back tightly, and her white jacket was crisp and clean. Her name was embroidered over her left breast in yellow thread that complimented her dark gold skirt.

"How is it a matter of my *letting* her do anything, Doctor?" William asked. "It's her life. Shouldn't she get to make her own decisions about how she is going to die?"

"She isn't dying."

"You don't know my mother. If she says she's dying, she's dying."

"But she's not. We can fix everything that is wrong with her."

"Fix her, doctor? You can make her whole? What, exactly, can you fix?"

William stood in the hallway outside the visitor's lounge. His shirt and pants were rumpled from the red-eye flight, his eyes burned and his hair was cowlicked in about eight places. He stood leaning on one hip with his arms folded in front of him.

"We can fix the damage from the blood clot. We can convert her heart so it beats normally again. I can't fix the COPD—

if you wanted that fixed you should have stopped her from smoking a long time ago."

The doctor paused for effect, and William bristled at the accusation. She shook her head back, and he saw the bands of muscle tense in her neck.

"But we can give her medications and oxygen so she can get around. She's got years left to live."

"On oxygen and medication. With limited mobility while the disease progresses."

"Yes, lots of people do it. These days they even have motor carts at the food store. Oxygen machines are portable."

"And if she says no?" William suspected she would.

"She'll die. A painful and ugly death."

William found what he'd been looking for. "She's dying, then. You just admitted it. Without treatment, she will die now. With treatment, she'll die later because you can't stop the disease's progression."

He wasn't really trying to be difficult. He just wanted clarity. He thought this was the heart of the matter.

"But she doesn't have to die now." The doctor sighed with impatience.

"But if she wants to…."

The doctor rolled her eyes and shook her head. "Listen, if she wants to get healed, she stays at the hospital. That's what hospitals are for. If she doesn't want to be healed, then I won't be part of it. She'll have to go home to die."

They remained in the hallway about three feet apart, arms folded in front of their chests. Squared off, positions established. William well understood the principles of healing in the Hippocratic Oath, only he hadn't found many doctors who really understood the humanistic aspects of it.

"I don't know if I can talk her into living, Doctor. She hates medicines, she just won't take them. Up until a few weeks ago, she wouldn't even take an aspirin for a headache. And she doesn't want to live attached to machines." There wasn't going to be a happily ever after, he knew.

"Is she depressed? Why doesn't she want to live?"

The doctor appeared concerned for the first time. William wanted to keep her from latching on to another thing she could heal.

"Doctor, my mother has had her death in mind as long as my sister and I can remember. It's part of who she is. Mom has strong faith and she's not afraid."

"I wouldn't let my mother do it."

Dr. Al-Biruni ended where she'd begun. She turned on her heel. William assumed she had just then remembered something very important she had to do down the hall, something that did not involve arguing patients' rights.

He stood in his place for several minutes as orderlies and wheelchairs and other people's conversations passed him by. His thoughts stood perfectly still. He hoped for some inspiration, for some answer to the riddle his mother was posing: *When is life not a life?*

He looked down the hall, and saw Sugar's back to him as she tried to pull herself together. He looked diagonally into his mother's room. His father had arrived and was sitting in a chair next to the window, looking out, lost somewhere in the pages of his life. William doubted he would be of much help going forward. Randy was leaning over his mother's bed, talking quietly. He couldn't see his mother at all.

He knew they were all waiting for him. Waiting for him to know something or to do something. He had even fewer answers now that he understood the questions. Like his medical training, William's religion only served him to a certain point. When the questions got tougher, he lost his focus and looked for absolutes. If they existed, he never found them.

"Well, Mom, it's like this," William began. "If you want to get healed, you can stay at the hospital and they'll heal you."

"And insurance is paying the whole thing, right?" His father finally spoke from the window.

"Right, Dad. You have good insurance. As far as I can tell, most everything in the hospital is paid for. But if you go home, you'll require more nursing than insurance will cover."

"If I go home, I go home to die, right?"

Frances was sitting up straight despite the discomfort in her belly. She was eager for information. Her eyes were suddenly bright. Finally, someone was engaging the conversation she'd been waiting to have.

"Yes, Mom, you can go home to die. Or you could go home and recuperate. It all depends on whether or not you have the surgery." He paused, giving her every chance to change her mind. She didn't budge.

"I told you, I'm not having the surgery, William."

"The doctors feel you have a good chance of surviving this, Mom. The surgery should fix everything, and they can do a procedure to fix your heart so it beats normally again."

"And then I can go home? I'll be okay?" She was doubtful

but she was carefully considering what he'd said. After a long moment she'd decided.

"I don't believe it. They already fixed this heart thing once, and then it happened all over again. All I was doing was lying in bed, and it happened all over again." She relaxed against the pillow. "I'm not going through this again. You all are just going to have to let me go. Get on with your lives." She waved her hand, dismissing them and the idea in one motion.

A nurse entered the room with a syringe and walked behind the family over to the IV drip. She dispensed a medication into the tube then said, "I'm sorry, Mrs. Baldwin needs to have some privacy right now. Can you all wait in the hallway?"

"Take your father to get something to eat. Make sure he gets something good," Frances instructed.

The four of them followed instructions and left the room, walking toward the big metal doors and the cafeteria beyond. Sugar explained the hospital's many routines, and they all assumed it was time for Frannie's sponge bath.

"What are you getting, Sugar?" Randy came up behind her and Bill with his tray.

"A bagel, French fries, chocolate pudding and a Coke," she declared with a guilty smile. "I've had everything this cafeteria has to offer, and these are definitely the best. The burger-in-a-bag is like freeze-dried astronaut food. All the ketchup in the universe can't help. The pizza is okay, sort of like movie pizza. It may be bad but it's still pizza. But stay away from the Swedish meatballs. They're evil."

Randy headed for the salad bar, appeased his conscience

with a cursory look, then took a pretzel, fries and the apple pie. With spring water.

"The apple pie is terrible. Take my word for it. Plastic fruit." Sugar made an effort to warn him but he stayed pat.

"What are you getting, Dad?"

"The Swedish meatballs."

Randy and Sugar laughed. "I like them," he defended. "You won't know until you try them."

William came up behind them with a tray of fries and pizza. "Tomorrow we get fast food. There are all kinds of places right down the road."

"Deal." The thought of a greasy burger made Bill's mouth water. "Something's wrong with the world when the food they serve at a place where you're supposed to be healed isn't as wholesome as a burger joint. How do they expect people to get well?"

They laughed as they approached the register. Randy made an exaggerated effort to pick up the check, and although Sugar looked skeptical, she allowed it. Bill approved by putting his hand on the taller son's shoulder.

"Thanks, buddy."

Bill thought it was a nice lunch, really, even though the whole family struggled not to talk about the impending implosion of its nucleus. They did a great job at faking normal. They talked of the growing-up years, years Bill remembered as clearly as if they were stored on DVDs on the bookshelf. Sugar talked about her boys, and her brothers listened politely even though they barely knew their nephews. They all made the same jokes they'd made for the last thirty years.

"Sugar, your soda looks disgusting," Randy said. "Since when do sodas have floaters?"

Sugar recognized the floater as a piece of Randy's pretzel. "Scumbag." She turned directly toward him and opened her mouth so he could see her chewed food.

"Gross."

For a moment, everyone forgot that an argument had kept Sugar and Randy apart for almost five years. Bill sat back in his chair and smiled. Things were just the way he'd remembered them. In this foreign landscape in which he had found himself, he'd finally come across others who spoke his language.

The social worker, Marialena DeFrancesco, extended her hand to Frances in introduction.

"Thank you for taking the time to talk with me." Frances made an attempt to make the social worker comfortable while she tried to remember her name. She was horrible with names. "But in the long run, Mrs. DeFreckle, it won't matter."

The caseworker almost laughed but kept her professional demeanor as she corrected Frances. "My name is Mrs. DeFrancesco," she said kindly. "What do you mean, Frances, that my being here won't matter?"

"I mean there's nothing you can really say to change my mind."

"Frances, I understand you've denied any further medical care. Do you understand what's at stake?"

Frances was aware that this was going to be a very important discussion. She found herself relaxing in spite of the fact that this would be the moment where she took control of her life, for perhaps the first time. She found herself speaking more slowly than she normally would, and she struggled to make sure her words were clear. She didn't want anyone to think she was a loony bird. Her inability to remember the proper names of people and places was a longstanding family joke; she didn't want it to appear that she was just now losing her mind. What had she said her name was? Marta DaFiasco? Mary DeMolition? Frances decided not to address the social worker directly so her sanity wouldn't be questioned.

"I understand I am refusing surgery to repair the damage that was caused by the blood clot in my artery, and that means I will die. I also know that I've had heart failure and that it's still not ticking right. I am refusing to have my heart fixed. I am also refusing all of this." She motioned toward the IVs and monitors. "I am ready to die."

Satisfied, Frances rearranged her covers so they were nice and neat. Caught between shock and deep respect, it took the social worker a moment to find an approach.

"So you wish to return home to die? We can't keep you in the hospital if you don't want to recover. You know that, don't you, Frances? Hospitals are for sick people to get well."

Frances hadn't really thought that detail through and hesitated. She didn't think Bill would like her dying at home. No, that would never do.

The social worker took Frances' hesitation as an opportunity.

"You know, Frances, you have very good medical insurance. It will cover all the costs of your recovery. But it does not provide you with hospice care."

"What is hospice care?" Frances was relaxing against the pillow.

"Hospice refers to the care of nurses and other professionals who help you between the time you leave the hospital and the time you actually die. Hospice nurses assure your comfort, cleanliness and administration of medications to ease your suffering. People who don't have professional hospice service need to have their families and friends take care of them. And you are going to need a lot of care because you are bedridden. Can your family provide that?"

Frances didn't want to be a burden on everyone. This was exactly what she'd been trying to avoid. Just before she asked if she could just go to a nursing home, she realized that nursing homes were expensive. She knew that from when her uncle had lived in that nice place with the big windows and private rooms. She didn't have that kind of money. She also realized, selfishly, that dying in a marginal place with dark corridors and outdated facilities like the ones she saw on news reports was not in her plan. She wanted a dignified death.

"So let me get this straight," Frances summarized for Melanoma DeMessco, "If I stay here and consent to surgery and procedures, my insurance will pay for everything—even if it costs millions of dollars."

"That's correct."

"But if I chose to die and not incur any more medical bills, my insurance won't pay for my hospice care, even though dying doesn't amount to a fraction of the cost of living."

"That's correct."

Frances thought a moment then smiled. "Isn't that sort of short-sighted on the insurance company's part? Why don't they pay for hospice care and save themselves a lot of money? That just makes good business sense. They're wasting their money on people like me who don't want to live. This is what's wrong with the medical system."

Now the social worker had to laugh. She appreciated her sense of humor at such a time.

"That's not the way the system works, Frances, and I guess that's a good thing."

"Marlina, here's the thing. Bill and I don't have much money, and I don't want to burn up his savings on my dying. Then he won't have anything much to live on after I'm gone."

"I understand your situation, and I can see you do, too."

Frances thought a moment, as if the situation were suddenly clear.

"Okay, I've decided to live. I'm not going to leave Bill destitute." Frances shook her head in agreement with herself. "Yes. I'll do it. Will you tell my doctor that I'll have the surgery? I want to get this going as soon as possible."

"Thank you, Mrs. Baldwin. I think you're making a good choice." Marialena DeFrancesco stood to leave, her mission accomplished.

"Thank you for explaining all of this to me. I almost made a big mistake, Mrs...."

Frances paused, having gotten herself into something she wasn't sure she could get out of. She felt a flash of brilliance.

"DeFresco," she finished.

Frances felt relieved. She had made herself perfectly clear.

"It's a miracle," Bill said when he heard the news. Tears ran down his cheeks, and his face registered emotion for the first time. He hugged Sugar closely and wiped his eyes. She patted her father's back to signal for him to release the hug as her mother looked up peacefully from the pillow.

"I want the surgery as soon as possible. No reason to delay."

William was relieved but skeptical. What did this mean? He wanted to talk to the doctor along with Sugar and find out more about the aftermath of the surgery and make sure his sister understood what their mother's life would be like going forward. After all, she would remain closest to their parents after he and Randy went their own ways.

"Let me go see if I can find the doctor," Sugar volunteered.

William followed her, and the two of them found Dr. Al-Biruni at the nurse's station as if she'd been waiting for them.

"I gave your mother an anti-anxiety medication in her IV drip. It seems to have made all of the difference in the world." Dr. Al-Biruni was smiling and her shoulders were relaxed. "We can continue that in her regimen going forward."

The blood rose up into William's face. Dr. Al-Biruni had stopped seeing his mother as an individual woman; she saw her only as a life to be saved at all costs. That was her calling. *This is why I am not a doctor*, he fumed inwardly.

"She didn't say she wanted to live," he choked. "She said she didn't want to spend the money to die. It was a financial decision." He knew the reality of the statement would not diminish the doctor's feeling of success.

"But it doesn't matter, does it? She's going to try. If we can save her life, it's worth it."

Sugar discussed the particulars of the surgery with Dr. Al-Biruni, who presented it in boiled-down, nontechnical terms, as if that was all Sugar would need to understand. She explained it to her mother in the same terms, and Frances didn't even flinch. It sounded easy enough.

"Well, if that's what I have to do, I'll do it."

William knew by her tone of voice that his mother was determined now to live through the operation. Her mind was made up. And once she had set things in motion, Frances was not the kind of person to look back. He'd been an army marching in the wrong direction, fumbling now for a way to stop his momentum and pivot.

"Now tell me what you had to eat for lunch. Bill, did you have something good?" Frances was already on to the next thing on her mind.

"Swedish meatballs."

"Potatoes?"

"Mashed."

"Gravy?"

"Yes."

William could not believe she was talking about lunch, as if the whole thing was settled now.

"Randy, what did you have? You've lost a lot of weight since I saw you last. I hope you're eating well."

"I had fries, a pretzel and apple pie. And the pie wasn't too good." He rubbed at his esophagus, identifying the current location of his dessert.

"You're gonna get fat. That's a terrible lunch," Frances scolded with a smile.

William now sat in the chair by the window and considered the last hour's events. They hadn't told his mother the truth. First, while it was true that her insurance didn't cover hospice, Medicare would. It could have been worked out, William was sure. But no one had mentioned that because once they thought she would agree to surgery, they stopped considering hospice as an option.

Second, no one had told his mother that after the surgery she would be in the hospital for up to four more weeks. At home, she'd be in bed and unable to get up for the bathroom for at least two more. No one had told her she'd need physical therapy to strengthen her muscles and her heart and her lungs once she got home; she would be months as an invalid with only a visiting nurse. And Sugar.

No one had detailed the numerous medications she'd need to take at all hours of the day, and no one had told her she'd probably need to be hooked up to an oxygen tank for the remainder of her life. Even if the surgery was completely effective, there was tissue damage to her heart and lungs that could not be repaired. She would never again be as good as she was just last week.

Life as his mother knew it was over. Without having any idea, she'd just committed to living only a portion of the life she'd once known, and to adopting a whole new identity as a person she'd never wanted to become.

When is life not a life?

"It's a miracle," Bill repeated.

William wanted to smack him.

9

"I'VE been playing doctor," William said. "I might as well have a plastic stethoscope."

"What do you mean?" Diane was being careful not to say the wrong thing. Her voice was soft.

William had called her because, frankly, he had no one else to call. Sugar was falling apart. Randy wasn't going to help. And his father—well, his father was still out to lunch.

"Until today, my mother's hospitalization has only been a concept. I dealt with it by putting on my make-pretend doctor's uniform and carrying my plastic stethoscope. It was a two-thousand-mile-away game I played by my rules. But actually being at the hospital the way Sugar has been, at my mother's side, seeing her in pain, seeing her so small and weak but so determined… Shit, Diane, I would have made a terrible doctor."

"You're a brilliant network designer. The world needs those, too."

He relaxed a little, convinced he'd made the right decision to call her. He needed her, he realized.

"Do you know what 'the issues' are yet? You were afraid there were things you didn't know." Diane had been listening, after all.

"I don't even know where to begin with that." After a full description of the hospital cafeteria, William found a way to tell her how his mother had boomeranged her way to the surgery schedule.

"I can't believe it. That's great! I hoped she would come around." Diane couldn't resist the "I told you so." She never could. William bristled inwardly and kept talking.

"The surgery itself will be pretty straightforward. They're going to remove the necrified tissue then sew up the parts of the intestine that weren't damaged by the clot."

"Will, these things are done all the time without complications. I'll bet she'll be just fine."

William wished that were true, but it wasn't.

"Stop trying to humor me, Di. You know the problem. The question is whether she's strong enough to come out of the anesthesia and recuperate afterward. Even though she's always made us promise not to hook her up to a ventilator, she'll need to be on one for twenty-four hours after surgery. If all goes well, she'll wake up afterward and breathe on her own."

"She must be weak. If she doesn't come out of it…." Diane stumbled on the idea.

"We'll have to decide whether to pull the plug." William finished her sentence.

Diane didn't answer. Finally, she said, "Yeah. Wow."

William's mind was lighting up with all kinds of connections, none of which were useful. He had a lot of information but none of it came in the form of how to deal with his own mother dying.

Diane spoke again while he grappled with his thoughts, as always, getting right to the point. "You know" she said, "in med school death was failure. We were always left to wonder why we weren't smart enough to find the answer to outwit it. If we healed, we were brilliant. If we couldn't, we still tried to feel brilliant by saying it was all out of our hands. The goal was to win against death regardless of the quality of life it produced."

"Remember Arnold Blatz?"

"The eighty-seven-year-old man you resuscitated."

Obviously, Diane remembered the story. But William liked to bring it up anyway from time to time to illustrate his point.

"I broke three of his ribs performing CPR when he came through the ER with a heart attack. He lived, with a punctured lung and internal damage that would take him months or a year to recover from. I don't even know if that's what he wanted. And little Joey James? Remember him?"

"The ten-year-old kid."

"Yeah.

"Left brain damaged, unable to walk or talk. His parents will have to care for him the rest of their lives."

Diane didn't need to be illuminated. She already understood, but William was on a roll.

"Right. Just like that, I changed their lives in a split second. Without ever asking them. A few minutes later, and both those people would have died. Is this what God had intended for those people? Or is it all just an accident of timing? I had to make the decision. For them."

"And you couldn't come to terms with that."

"No. Because I, myself, don't think I'd want to live in the state I'd left some of my patients. I know my mother wouldn't."

"But she might have to now."

"Right. I feel like I'm the only person who knows my mother's decision to live was ill-informed. It's based on lies and half-truths. What do you think, Di? Was her doctor right though, that it doesn't matter?" He wanted another opinion. Hospital ethics were tough enough when it wasn't your parent being treated.

"I don't know. I'm a dermatologist, remember?" She laughed.

William appreciated that for once, her humor was self-depreciating. She hadn't let her guard down like that for some time.

"Right. I guess you're no better at this than I am," William conceded. "But, what do you think? If they can save her tomorrow in surgery, will it all be worth it?"

"You know what I think, Will. That's what doctors are supposed to do: protect life at all cost."

William was still uncomfortable with the answer. "At all cost, right. Including truth?"

Diane hesitated. "We take the Oath, Will."

"I only remember the part of the Hippocratic Oath where we physicians promise not to play God. When doctors don't ask, they maintain control over the decision. If more patients decided they would prefer to die rather than live the quality of life medical intervention might leave them, a lot of doctors would be out of jobs."

"Not me. People still need to have their lesions burned off."

Diane's second attempt at levity was her way of telling William the conversation was over. He took the cue and tried to back his intensity off a few notches on the Richter Scale.

"Good, because I don't want to have to support us both."

Bad choice of words. The idea hung in the air because that was one of the reasons William always fought the idea of having children. Neither acknowledged its relation aloud, but his unfortunate response made William feel even worse.

"I'm a coward."

Diane didn't answer. He was grateful.

"I am a coward for not telling her all of this. No one else has had the cruel courage to tell her. Not even the doctor. That's the way things are done these days—we think we're sparing the patient something by sharing their ordeal. We know the truth and bear it for them. It's all spin. We've only given her enough information to decide one thing. Are we sparing her the added burden of her emotion, or are we sparing ourselves the unbearable consequence of her decision?"

The question, like so many other things, hung between them.

"I don't know, Will. How could I? But I do know you're doing your best. And so are the doctors. It's not going to be easy. You knew that."

"Yeah. I knew."

William realized that she didn't have the answers he was looking for. He felt alone again with the burden.

"Listen, thanks for talking to me. It was good to hear your voice. I've got to go now." He didn't know where he was going, only that he needed to be alone for a while.

"Sure. Fine. Call whenever you want. I'll help if I can." Her tone was getting more formal. "Sorry I couldn't be more help."

The door was closing again between them. William grabbed the handle and closed it quietly.

"I'm not sure anyone can help."

WILLIAM'S JOURNAL

AUGUST 25, 2005. "The issues." The issues of life and death—I'm having trouble processing it all according to my conceptual rules. Rules? Ha! There's so much more to it than science. Even the religion I've propped myself up on all these years doesn't seem to give any clear direction. And med school left me with more questions than answers.

I live with those questions every day of my life.

Most times I decide I did the right thing.

The other times I think I saved them because of my own fear of dying.

And worse, a few times a year I allow that I didn't save them at all. I condemned them to live in a way I wouldn't want to live myself.

As a society, we are always trying to make certain life is happy, or that it seems to be, anyway. Sickness and death are embarrassing and ugly by our standards. Their presence in the middle of our otherwise happy lives is intolerable.

I think that's why I wanted to be a doctor in the first place. To save people from having to face their mortality, not to help them face it. I wanted to be their hero.

If we *cheat* death, we are champions. We dodge the bullet—life won by a quick move in the nick of time. And if we lose, we are death's *victims*, as if we had nothing to do with it when we had everything to do with it!

When we are born, we invite death into our lives. It's the natural endpoint of our whole purpose here. And there's no easy way out. That's the fact. But our society's got us running scared; we don't know anything about death anymore. Our whole focus is on life and living. I can't tell you how many books I've read about how to have a happy life. I've never even seen one on the shelf that would tell me how to have a good death. If I knew that, maybe I wouldn't be so afraid.

It used to be that life and death were part of everyone's lives. Death dwelt in every fiber of a family. Until a few centuries ago, children were always part the deathbed scene—both in art and in reality. Children learned at an early age because they were included in death's rituals; they learned how it was done the same way they learned to feed and dress themselves. Death was truth, and truth was plain. It was what it was.

Death happened. Brothers and sisters died in sickness and accidents; mothers died in birth; fathers worked themselves to early graves. It was normal and sad at the same time, and life went on with that understanding. Now, the only normal state is happiness. Grief has no place in our lives, so we fear it as we would any other wartime occupation.

I've been secretly grieving my mother's death since the first time she made me aware of its presence, sitting beside us at every dinner table, kissing me on the head a second time, saying goodbye again after I've hung up the telephone. She's been making a place for it for as long as I can remember. I always wanted a mother who would want to live, a mother who would love each day and never grow tired, one who wouldn't be resigned to a certain death and take the easy way out.

When she said she would have the surgery, I saw a glimpse of that woman. A woman who would meet this head-on and fight. Fight for the people she loved—fight for *me*. I want to believe it's true. I know my mother, and if she decides to do something, she's going to give it her all and make it happen. That's the kind of person she is.

But what if she dies on the table tomorrow? What if she starts clinging to life, and it's brutally snatched from her? That's much worse. Then I would wish I had become a doctor after all, so I could save her. Maybe that's why she insisted I go to med school: to save her in the end. To save her from herself. Is that what I'm supposed to do now?

I write this and see that maybe Mom's way of thinking is much farther along than I originally considered. Maybe not fighting death is not the same as giving up. She's accepted the pain of dying the same as she accepted the pain of giving birth to us. I watched her today, I saw it. She only asked for medicine when she really needed it. She's going to work hard at death, she won't flinch. God, I love her. She never flinches. She's not afraid because she's got her faith. She thinks she knows what comes next.

The Grim Reaper isn't a villain to her at all. He is *God.*
-whb

10

WILLIAM left his hotel early. He was staying at a hotel instead of his parents' house in order to have some time to himself; he didn't want to watch over his father while he was so overwhelmed with his own issues. Besides, he considered himself a rather private person, even within his own family. His grief was personal.

Having spent the night in contemplation, William now saw the issues Sugar had invited him home to deal with. He could see both sides of the argument and was waiting for a sign. When exhausted of his philosophy and logic, he let himself believe in synchronicity. Meaningful coincidences. He liked to believe that coincidences sometimes amounted to divine intervention. *Just give me a sign and I will do what I'm supposed to do.*

He got in his rental car and turned on the ignition. The satellite radio sprung to life as soon as the engine turned over. It was set to the Christian rock station, certainly not a choice William would have made. In fact, he didn't remember it being on at all the night before as he'd driven back from the hospital, but it was playing at normal volume now. He glanced down to the display panel and saw the song and artist currently playing:

Something To Believe In *By FM Static*

Oh, dear Lord, William thought to himself, goose bumps on his arms. *Just give me a sign. I'll believe.*

"Mom, do you have a living will?" William asked after the morning pleasantries had been exchanged.

Frances was in good spirits and still optimistic about her surgery. He was hoping they wouldn't need a written copy of her advance care directive. But his practical side told him that if they were faced with having to take her off the respirator, he wanted the decision to be hers instead of his. He knew it was important for people to specify how they wanted their care to be handled if they were unable to make the decision themselves. The acceptable format of those documents varied from state to state, and William knew it would take a well-written document to be legally binding.

The events of the prior day had not allowed anyone time to discuss what had happened. Frances' wishes were obviously opposed to those of her family, and her wish to let her die was fresh in William's mind. He wasn't sure his father would be able to put his mother's position before his own needs if he was called on to make the decision. Frankly, William was afraid he couldn't trust himself to do so, either.

"Yes," Frances said. "It's at home. Tell your father it's in the safe and he needs to bring it. I almost forgot about that. I don't want them bringing me back anymore if I'm going to die. And remember, I won't live connected to machines. Promise me."

Relieved that her living will would make the decisions he himself did not want to face, he made the promise. Then he left the room to call his dad.

Sugar was already at the hospital by the time Bill and Randy arrived. While Sugar and Randy tried to catch some of their mother's good cheer, William took his father aside to take care of the paperwork.

"Did you bring it?"

"No."

William was confused. "Couldn't you find it? She said it was in the safe."

"It's there. I didn't bring it because it isn't time." Bill's face was turning red and he was noticeably uncomfortable.

"Dad, she's going into surgery and might not make it out. She's going to be on a respirator, and we don't know if she'll regain consciousness. You know how she feels about being hooked to machines. She'd rather die."

"I've never heard her say that."

William realized for the first time that his father hadn't been in the room yesterday when Frances had asked to die. Was there a possibility Frances had never told Bill about her end-of-life plan? Taken aback, William looked at his father's face, appreciating for the first time that it was frozen and his eyes were glassy. He looked like he was in shock even though he seemed to be functioning normally.

William softened. "Dad, we have to be prepared. They've already saved her from dying twice now. She doesn't want to be saved anymore."

"I've never heard my wife say that. I don't know what you're talking about."

Bill did not appear to be trying to understand, only to be understood. William could tell by his tone of voice that his father was not going to change his view. Exasperated, William pressed on.

"Dad, she's going into surgery soon. They'll come in a few

minutes to start medicating her with a relaxation injection. There's no time. I can't believe you're doing this to her."

"I can't believe you are saying this. Do you really want your mother dead?" Bill's voice was as flat as his denial.

"No, Dad, but it's not my decision to make. It's hers. You weren't here yesterday. You didn't hear her."

"It was the medicine talking. Must be. She would never want to die. She would never leave me."

So that was it. William knew people made the best choices they could for their loved ones' care, but those decisions were almost always based on selfish needs. It didn't seem fair to have to fight against his father for his mother's right to die, especially when every cell in his body agreed with his dad. While William could clearly see what was motivating his father, he couldn't imagine what would motivate his mother to keep such a secret. No, he couldn't, for one minute, believe his mother had never told his father what she had told her children over and over.

William looked at his watch and realized he didn't have much time left. He went to the nurse's station and had them page Dr. Al-Biruni. She arrived within minutes.

"Doctor, I want a DNR."

He knew a written Do Not Resuscitate order document was needed to prevent the hospital from taking heroic measures should his mother's heart stop beating. No defibrillators, no injections, no CPR. All other arguments regarding a hastened death aside, his mother would not want to be brought back if her heart had already stopped beating. She would want to stay dead, peacefully, at that point.

Dr. Al-Biruni glared back at William and said sarcastically, "If you are worried about us resuscitating you, Mr. Baldwin,

I'll be happy to get you the proper forms that would be legal in our state. If you are trying to get a DNR on behalf of your mother, you should be well aware that it doesn't matter what you personally want for your mother unless you have a legal power of attorney or if she is incapacitated and you are legally designated her health care surrogate. These are legal matters that cannot be compromised."

"Doctor, I want my mother to live. Believe me, I do. But you know she doesn't want to. She's already looked you right in the eye and told you that. Now she's having this surgery because you slipped her some Xanax, and no one has told her the whole truth. She's decided to live to save money instead of having a peaceful death, and you have let that happen." He paused to let her consider the moral and legal implications of this.

"You know the whole thing is against her principles. The least you can do is let nature take its course if she dies. Please, Doctor. Do the right thing." William never broke eye contact with her.

She looked away. "I will get the paperwork done immediately."

When the social worker came in to have Frances sign the DNR forms, her husband stood and left the room.

"I can't breathe," Bill said, but William suspected his father didn't want to start being witness to his mother's wishes. Afterward, a nurse came in to give Frances the first injection to relax her before surgery. The three siblings kissed their mother and said goodbye. None of them seemed to believe it was final.

"Randy, tell me a poem. Make me smile. This is what I want to remember." Frances closed her eyes.

"Close your eyes now and sleep through the day,
Here's Demerol and ether to take you away.
They'll slice you and dice you and sew you back up,
And when you wake up you'll be a sick pup.
But don't worry Momma, you'll be yourself soon
Bossing us around when you're back in your room."

11

FOUR hours later, a nurse came out and told the family that Frances had made it through the heart conversion and the surgery without incident. Twenty-four hours later, she was taken off of the ventilator. Doctor Watson, the tall, middle-aged surgeon who'd operated on Frances, was telling the family about how she started breathing on her own. As far as he was concerned, the operation was successful.

"She woke up when she was supposed to, looked around at the faces in the recovery room, and was surprised. I guess she expected angels. 'Well, I guess I didn't die!' she said loud enough that all of us in the other corner of the room could hear her. 'I thought I would die—I wanted to—but I didn't!'

Your mother is a hoot," he laughed, looking at the William and his siblings. "She entertained us all for about half an hour before she fell asleep again. Some people are like that with the anesthesia and all. I told her, 'Welcome back, Mrs. Baldwin. You did just fine. Everything went just as it was supposed to.' And you know what she said? She said, 'Well, I guess I'll just have to make the best of it now. When can I go home?' What a woman!"

"Yeah, that's our mom," William said, not sure what they were going to do next.

"It's a miracle," said his father.

William drove Randy from the hospital back to their parents' house. While he'd turned the volume down on the radio (he really couldn't tolerate anything but jazz), William wanted to see if there were any other messages from God when he started the car.

Not Ready to Die By Demon Hunter

Randy never asked and William never said, but the reason William smiled and felt happy was more due to the message than any relief over Frances' awakening. That had been a near non-event because there was so much ahead. Turning off the radio, he started singing the first song that came into his mind, which happened to be a TV show theme. Randy joined in. They'd always harmonized well, and the song led them to a discussion of the movies the TV star had appeared in until they reached the house.

It was a celebratory night at the Baldwin's. Sugar brought her boys Jason and Eric over, and they ordered thirteen cartons of Chinese food, counting the white rice. Any tension between her and Randy wasn't palpable; they all seemed to relax into the roles they'd played when they'd last lived together.

"I brought a surprise," Randy teased as he put his fork down on the kitchen table. None of the Baldwins used chopsticks. "If you can figure out what it is, it's yours." A familiar game.

"Animal, vegetable or mineral?" William started as he served himself the last of the moo goo gai pan.

Randy twisted his face. "Hmm. It's made by animals but made of plastic. Is that a mineral or a vegetable?"

William shot back, "Neither. This game was invented

too long ago. I rephrase my question. Animal, vegetable or technosubstance?"

"Technosubstance."

"Bigger than a beer can?" Bill asked.

"No. Not in total mass."

Sugar asked, "Can I wear it?"

"Well, you could, but it would serve no purpose."

"Does it need refrigeration?" Jason, Sugar's youngest, came into the room. Of the two kids, Jason enjoyed games the most.

"No."

He followed up with another question while his older brother looked on. Eric's straight hair curled at the ends, his mouth hung straight. It was the look of a bored thirteen-year-old; life ceased to be fun somewhere around twelve and a-half.

"Can I sit on it?"

"You can sit on it. Sure, why not? But why would you?"

Jason shrugged.

"Does it make a noise?" Sugar asked.

She was getting closer. When they'd been kids, she'd usually won the game because she was older and smarter. Nothing had changed.

"If used properly."

"You brought a CD. One of your own recordings?"

Randy looked surprised that Sugar even knew about his recordings. Their mother must have mentioned it to her. He didn't just write stupid rhyming poems. He wrote songs. Randy was tentative, doubting whether he should have brought anything at all.

"No. It's not my music. Something else."

"Oh good! Put it on." She was excited.

Randy liked making his sister smile. "First you have to find it." He sat back in his chair and returned the grin.

"It's on top of the refrigerator, right?"

She had already stood to fetch it. Crossing the kitchen in five steps, she patted around on the top of the once-fashionable olive appliance before anyone else could get up.

Randy was disappointed. How could he have forgotten that was the first place she always guessed? He wanted to carry his little game on for a while longer to keep her engaged.

Sugar went to the stereo and inserted the CD while their father started clearing dishes and boxes. When Jason and his brother heard the music, they rolled their eyes and left to play video games in the den.

Oldies. Sappy ballads from the seventies and eighties. Songs about being left at the altar and crying over lost love. Songs with hints of forbidden sex. And early disco— the worst. All of Sugar's favorites. Favorite songs she would never admit to now, but she somehow knew every word. And although he tried to hide it, William knew the words too.

"I had to listen to Sugar's music. We all did. I hated it." William said.

"Yeah, me, too," Randy agreed.

"And that's why you have all these songs in your collection, because you hate them?"

"I downloaded them all for Sugar."

William laughed and made a face. Sugar accepted the explanation without question and bounced up and down to the music.

"I mixed it up just for you," Randy quipped a little too anxiously.

Sugar knew it was his peace offering, and it was about as straightforward as she could handle. Any direct conversation about their differences would be too intense given everything else that was going on. They each opened another beer and sang along with songs nearly forgotten, regressing to another time.

The singer was a whiny cross-dresser with bad makeup. He was singing about some evil woman. All three sang along.

"This reminds me of Billy Overbrook," Sugar said dreamily.

"Billy. Yeah. He wore the same kind of eyeliner."

"Stop it. He did not. He just had those deep, dark, mysterious eyes naturally." Sugar tried to remember if that was true. Maybe he had worn makeup.

"Didn't you lose your virginity to him?"

"Shhh! William! The boys are in the other room. Be good." She slapped at his leg and folded her arms and legs across her body. "Yes. I got him before Tracy did, but apparently not before he got half the girls in our junior class."

They laughed. The next song was a pledge to rock and roll, the song of the faithful.

"We played this over and over when we went to North Carolina on vacation. On the tape recorder in the car. Do you remember that?" Randy had always been a big fan of the band along with Sugar.

"Yup, I remember. Once we got there, Mom and Dad went out and we had a party. Where did you guys get that beer? You couldn't have been more than sixteen."

"I was fourteen." Randy reminded her that he was younger than William.

"Fourteen? You kill me, Randy. I never told Dad. I was supposed to be in charge that night."

"He's listening in the other room. Dad?" Randy called.

"I didn't hear a thing."

Sugar whispered, "Oh, shit. He must have heard about Billy, too. Dad still thinks I'm a virgin. Oh, well, I guess all our family secrets are out now." She paused for effect. "But no one is to talk about what happened on my senior class trip. Promise me." She looked back and forth at her brothers and shook her finger with her eyebrows raised.

The brothers agreed aloud but all of them knew that when the time was right, they would betray her.

"Anybody want another beer?"

As promised, Frances sent Randy back to New York so he could get ready for his new job. He was relieved, and William wondered who was luckier, the son who leaves or the son who stays. A week ago he would have known the answer. Now he wasn't sure.

Frances' body was noticeably drained of the energy that had so far sustained her. Each movement finished slowly after it began. But her voice still synchronized with her thoughts and she was, of course, giving instructions.

"Now, go, Randy. Get out of here. I don't want to see you again. Don't worry about me, just concentrate on the job. It's a lot of responsibility, and I don't want you screwing it up because your mother's in the hospital. There are more important things in life. This is your future we're talking about."

"Goodbye, Mom." He kissed her on the cheek, trying to make it look like he wasn't in a rush to leave.

"Call me. Let me know how things are going."

William wondered which of them was in the greater hurry.

"I will." Randy shook hands with his dad, who wished him luck on the new job.

"Now say goodbye to your brother and sister," Frances instructed.

"Goodbye, brother. Goodbye, sister."

He gave William a one-armed hug. Then Randy turned toward Sugar but hesitated; he wasn't sure how far to go.

She took a step toward him and gave the same kind of hug her brothers had given each other. Then she said earnestly, "Be good. I hope everything goes well in Salt Lake. And drive safely back to New York. The last thing we need is a calamity with you."

William walked Randy to the parking lot, happy to get some fresh air and a glimpse of the beautiful autumn afternoon. As Randy opened the car door, he turned and said, "Mom's caused me a lot of trouble in my life, Will. I have a lot of bad feelings about her, so this has been really hard on me, keeping them all covered up and pretending everything's okay. And Sugar hasn't made it any better with that stick up her ass. At this point, I don't even know what I did to offend her so much. It was too long ago.

"Anyway, whatever happens, I won't be back. I need to put this all behind me. Get on with my life." He paused while William grappled for an appropriate response, then added, "You know, I sort of hope it's really going to happen now. And I hope it happens sooner than later because I can't go through this again. I really can't take it anymore. Thank God I'm outta here."

Randy got into his car and started it up. He glanced at

himself in the rearview mirror as he adjusted it. His legs still hung out the side, and he looked to his brother for a reply.

William hardly knew what to say. It was just like Randy to have the last word and for the last word to be a stunner. He supposed that was what made Randy a good lawyer: his ability to say exactly the wrong thing at exactly the right time to leave the situation off-balance.

"You know, Randy, sometimes you can be a real asshole."

William immediately wished he'd had a better come-back, but Randy hadn't given him the time he needed to be witty. Sometimes things just weren't complicated enough to require a more detailed response.

"Yeah, well, you're a jerk-off. Love ya, bro. Take care of Mom."

The previous night, William had been so pleased at the equanimity between them, the camaraderie and laughter, the apparent peace between Sugar and his brother. But he should have known what Sugar knew: Randy could never be happy like that. He needed the tension, needed the conflict. And he always found a way to create it.

"So, uh, good luck in Salt Lake. Don't forget to call Ma. She loves you."

"Yeah."

Randy closed the door. He didn't even stop at the stop sign on his way out.

William turned toward the hospital. He considered that maybe it was Randy who needed the sign from God.

The next morning, William looked down at his satellite radio receiver.

Testing The Strong Ones By Copeland

What was that supposed to mean? William was tired of trying to figure things out. Maybe the answers weren't going to come from the satellite radio after all. He put his coffee in the cup holder and switched the thing off, embarrassed that he'd ever thought God could talk through a commercial broadcast. Disappointment was a bad way to start a day.

William made the drive to the hospital through the familiar roads of his youth, remembering bike rides and friends' cars and noticing how everything had changed. There seemed to be a strip mall or gas station on all four corners of every intersection, homes built in every open space. The suburbs used to have trees and quaint old roads with homes of character. Now his hometown resembled a planned community.

He felt like a stranger as he drove past his old high school, trying to remember the good times instead of the dread and doom that now shadowed him. He wished to be young again, before death and responsibility had converged to make him feel like the weight of justice and decision lay squarely with him.

Again, William was the first one at the hospital. Frances was neatly tucked in her bed, and it looked like she was asleep. He watched her for a moment at the doorway trying to restore a sense that everything could possibly turn out okay after all. Then she saw him and sprung to life.

"Look what they did to me." Her voice was uneven, her eyes like saucers, her breathing hoarse. Shock, William quickly concluded.

Frannie held out for his inspection a balloon inside of a light gauze wrapping, a balloon that had been her hand, a normal hand receiving an IV just twelve hours before. She looked for his reaction.

"They said the IV came out of the vein and it kept dripping under the skin until it blew up my hand. They blew up my hand!" She became louder as she saw the Williams face dissolve at the sight. Her lips were nearly white as the words spit out of her mouth.

Her hand didn't look human. It was double in size with a deep purple color running half-way up her arm. There were black spots all over it, and it looked like it would, in fact, blow up at any minute, oozing smelly, alien entrails across the sheet. The skin was stretched so tightly that the normal wrinkles were gone and it was so thin you could see through it.

A nurse in blue pants and a kitten-print smock walked in behind William.

"Time to take you down for some tests, Mrs. Baldwin." She began the blood pressure and temperature ritual.

"What happened to my mother's hand?" William asked quietly.

He knew what had happened. He'd seen it before. What he really wanted to know was *why* it had happened. It didn't have to have happened; it was carelessness on the part of the hospital. He wanted an answer. He needed to feel someone else was responsible for his mother's care because he couldn't be there twenty-four hours a day to guarantee it. He also knew that if Frannie was going to allow herself treatment, people were going to have to be honest with her.

"I wasn't here, Mr. Baldwin. Looks like the IV dripped under the skin for a while before they found it. Hon, it happens more than we'd like. It will take a while to go down. But it will go down."

"How could this happen?" William tried to invoke the arrogant attitude of a doctor fighting against a system that had failed him despite his brilliant care of the patient.

"She was sleeping and I guess the night nurse didn't notice."

William appeared scornful, but it was actually that he was repulsed by his mother's hand. He looked away, not knowing what to say. He could see his mother also had been profoundly affected by the incident.

"How long will it take to go down?" He tried to keep his voice dominant.

"A while." The nurse met William's eyes as if to discourage any more questions. *Not in front of the patient*, she seemed to say.

"How long is a while?" *I want her to know it will get better*, William tried to imply.

The nurse did not want to answer, but William held her gaze.

"A while. The doctor will be in to talk to her about it later." She finished the blood pressure reading and left.

"Does it hurt, Mom?" he asked softly. "You should elevate it so the swelling can go down."

He helped her position the pillows for comfort and ease.

"Do you think they'll have to amputate my hand?" The question was sudden and cruel, but it was the only question in her mind. "I don't want to live with only one hand, William. I won't do it. I can't."

She was drawing another line in the sand, bargaining the terms of her survival. Frances let a moment pass and found William's eyes.

"I know you'll help me. Please help me, William. I'm counting on you. Help me die."

The words, *help me die*, reverberated through the room, echoing off the corners and dancing in the middle of the floor.

"Please."

William looked out the window and considered jumping but there was no latch to open it, and the roof of the next building was only two floors down. Not high enough. He considered leaving but a cart blocked the door in the hallway and where would he really go anyway? He considered screaming at his mother but she looked too helpless, an innocent compromised in a bad system. In the end, he chose a light-hearted answer.

"I don't know, Mom. If this is not the big day, if this is just a minor setback and the doctors say everything is going to be okay, then I'm going to fight for you. I'm not going to let you go that easily." He smiled, as lovingly as he could in spite of the fact that his breakfast was in his throat and his coffee was burning its way back up.

Frances ignored the sentiment. "And if it isn't, you'll help me. Right? You'll make them all let me go."

"I haven't promised anything yet, Mom."

The orderly arrived with the gurney. Still wearing his doctor demeanor, William stood to his full height.

"Where are you taking her?"

"X-ray."

"Why?"

"I don't know. I'm not the doctor."

William looked at his mother. "While you're gone, I'll see what I can find out. Don't you go worrying about anything. You just concentrate on staying calm and getting well."

"I'm not going to get well, Son."

"Try. Just for today. You've had quite a shock to your system with the surgery, Mom, and now this." He repositioned her blankets so her gown was covered. "You don't need any more stress."

He looked at her, so small and frail, and knew that whatever spirit she had mustered and fought with now faced defeat. William put a pillow under his mother's hand to make her comfortable during her ride downstairs.

"I'll call Dad and tell him what's going on. Don't worry any more."

He stroked her hair back away from her face, and she reached up with her other hand to pull her bangs back down onto her forehead. She looked tired as the wheels started turning. The orderly didn't say a word as he maneuvered her through the door.

"Good," she said. "Find out where he is. He's never here when I need him."

William retraced his steps back past the stick-on feet, through the double doors, and back down the hall to the family lounge off the elevator. He longed for the time, which now seemed like long ago, when his mother's death had been just a concept.

12

BILL was waiting for Frances when she got back from her x-ray. She relived the trauma while telling him everything she knew about the situation. He couldn't look at his wife's distortion. His silence grew deeper, his face more like stone. His eyes were deep red from lack of sleep, from suppressed tears, and from the pressure of his thoughts pounding in his skull.

As the morning went by, Frannie's spirits seemed to lift and she made an effort to pick up the mood. She didn't like them all moping around her bedside. Her hand didn't really hurt anymore. Nothing hurt with the morphine. A loosely-folded hospital gown covered her hand so no one had to look at it, and it was elevated on its own pillow. In fact, she had nearly forgotten what had even happened to it. She was light-headed and energized by the oxygen coming in through her nose.

"They gave me food today," Frances told them all. "They gave me a boiled egg for breakfast." She paused long enough for effect, but not long enough for their reaction. Then she said, "It tasted like the crypt."

"Like you know what the crypt tastes like, Mom," William chuckled.

"I do now."

"Did you eat the egg?"

"I couldn't. It was death."

No one commented.

"They're going to try to get me out of bed to walk."

"That's important after an operation so you don't get pneumonia."

"I can't do it. I can hardly pick my head up off the pillow. My feet are so swollen I can't walk, and I can't breathe either. I can't stand up."

"Well, you've had a rough morning, Mom. A lot happened. Don't worry about it, just do your best and give it a try." William tried to be encouraging.

Bill did not speak.

Trying to draw her husband out of his funk, Frances asked, "What did you have to eat for breakfast, Bill?"

She hadn't had anything to eat in six days yet she wasn't hungry. But she was still curious as to what everyone else was eating.

"Cereal."

He was astounded. Her mood made no sense to him. Nothing made sense to him anymore except the deep fog of his mind.

"What did you have, Son?"

"I had a muffin and some coffee. The hotel puts out a free continental breakfast with all kinds of good things. The coffee was actually good."

"I had cereal and toast," Sugar said as she entered the room. She headed to her mother's bed and elected not to look at her mother's hand when it was offered. William had given her fair warning.

"Lunch? Bill, did you eat before you came?" Frannie closed

her eyes, and it seemed like she was imagining everything they told her. She was the only one in the room who was comfortable.

"No."

Bill was still confined to one-word answers. She opened her eyes to see if he was going to say any more, and when she realized he was not, closed them again.

"Did you finish the roast pork, Bill?"

"Yes."

"Don't eat the spaghetti sauce. It wasn't that good."

"I ate it last night. It was fine. Sugar and the boys came over."

"No, it wasn't. Don't eat it any more."

"It was good, Mom, really," Sugar said. "The boys love your spaghetti."

"Oh," Frances said half-heartedly, "you people never listen to me. You don't believe I'm dying, and you won't believe the spaghetti sauce is no good. Don't eat any more." Then she fell asleep.

Bill was convinced she was high on drugs, Sugar was confused because she'd come in late and still thought her mother wanted to live, and William, having seen it all transpire, was exasperated. His mother often left him that way.

An hour later, Frances was roused by a round woman with white shoes and a brightly flowered hospital smock.

"Hello, Frances. I'm Sheila Johnson, your physical therapist. The work we do together will help you function independently at home. This is our first of many visits."

"It's no use, Miss Jansen, it's not going to work. I can't breathe."

"Well, the first thing we're going to do," the therapist said, ignoring Frances' comment, "is to get you out of bed. Come on, I'm going to help you."

Bill, Sugar and William moved the chairs away from the bedside and stood near the doorway. Frances groaned loudly as she was forced to sit up.

"Oh, no, come on, Shayna. I can't do it. I'm too weak."

Sheila Johnson was already maneuvering her into a standing position. "Now all you have to do, Frances, is put one foot in front of the other and take a few steps. Your legs have atrophied from being in bed so long. But you can do it."

Frances took the few steps, but it came at great expense. She collapsed back onto the bed, which was painful with the drainage tubes in her stomach and her bruised hand. She struggled for breath.

The therapist lifted her back into position and adjusted her oxygen flow.

"See?" she said. "That wasn't too bad."

Frances still gasped for air. "I can't breathe."

"You're having a panic attack, Frances. You have enough oxygen coming from the tube. See, you can breathe. Now relax."

Frances tried but each breath was short and painful. The therapist taught her how to make those short breaths more productive by puffing and making her breathing more regular.

"Now we're going to have to help you handle your panic when breathing is difficult, Frances. You will have to learn how to do it because this will happen a lot now when you overexert yourself."

"I can't."

Sheila Johnson ignored the objection. "Now, what do you normally do to relieve stress?"

Frances and her family laughed.

"Smoke a cigarette," Sugar chimed.

"Well." Sheila Johnson didn't think it was so funny.

"Until a week ago, I smoked a cigarette to relieve my tension," Frances confessed. She coughed loudly.

"Well, you won't be doing any more of that."

"I know," Frannie replied obstinately. "I may be dumb, but I'm not stupid, Miss Jackson."

So far, she didn't like this physical therapist at all. This was just one more person who wasn't listening to her.

Still trying, Sheila Johnson asked, "What else do you do to relieve tension?"

Frances chuckled low and deep in spite of herself. "Start an argument with my husband."

Everyone looked over at Bill, who was also smiling despite his gloomy mood.

"That's right. That's what she's always done."

It didn't seem right to get involved in family arguments, so the therapist stopped asking questions and started giving Frances some breathing exercises and visualizations to help calm her when she needed it.

"You try to practice those, Mrs. Baldwin, and I'll be back tomorrow for another round. Remember, when you can't breathe, you must relax."

"Thank you, Sheera. But don't bother coming back," Frances replied.

Sheila Johnson shook hands with Bill and nodded in Sugar and William's direction.

"Tough customer," she said to them.

Then she smiled for the first time and left for the nurse's station to write a note in Frances' chart.

In the days to come, William, Sugar and Bill would develop a routine for sitting around Frances' bedside while she slept. But on that day, there was only the awkward awareness that they were duty-bound to sit inside on a beautiful summer afternoon playing Frances' game. They tried not to stare at each other or talk about what was happening. Instead they paced the floor, skimmed the newspaper headlines passively, and in Bill's case, stared out the window absently as if this waiting were the most normal thing in the world.

After an hour, William suggested lunch. They all agreed and left Frances sleeping peacefully.

Frances' brother, Holden Mayfield, stormed down the hall of the hospital. This was the first he'd heard that Frances was ill. When Bill had called him last night, he said Frances was in the hospital again. Again? Holden hadn't been aware that his sister had ever been in the hospital. She'd always been as healthy as a bear. Bill said the doctor thought they'd fixed the problem, and she didn't want visitors.

Holden wasn't a visitor, he was her brother goddamnit, and he was going to see what was going on here. Since the phone call he'd been fighting a menacing feeling that unsettled his sleep. He'd replayed the conversation with Bill over and over in his mind, looking for evidence that he was overreacting. And now this hospital was giving him the creeps. They'd told him how to get to the Coronary Care Unit, but he'd come face-to-face with the metal door. He pounded on it for a moment before he was asked to stop.

"Sir, please stop pounding, it upsets the patients. Let me show you how to proceed."

Impatiently, Holden listened to the woman's instructions, backtracked down the hall, placed his feet on the decals, pressed the red button, and walked through quickly before the doors could close. But being on the inside of the heavy armor disturbed him even more. He didn't like this, not one bit.

He turned right and saw his sister in the room straight ahead. Her eyes were closed and she looked just like he'd imagined. Really sick. His intestines tightened. There was no one else in her room, and he wondered where Bill and the kids were. Certainly, if this were really serious, Fran would have more attention, wouldn't she? But why all the monitors and tubes? What was wrong with her, anyway? Trying to maintain his composure, Holden shook Frannie's leg.

"Hey, Sis, wake up. It's me." He was calm and gentle despite the fact that his blood pressure had risen thirty points.

As if waking into a terrible dream, Frances began to scream, "Get out. Leave me alone!"

He knew about her bad dreams and night terrors. She'd had them since she was a child. He touched her softly and put the flowers he'd bought in the lobby store on her tray. Her outburst had drawn some attention from the nurse's station. Pat came in to see what was going on with her favorite patient.

"Frances, is everything all right?" She reacted protectively to the expression on her patient's face. "Honey, don't be so upset. We've got to keep you calm." She began to fuss with Frances' pillows and smooth her hair.

"Then get this asshole out of my room."

"Fran, it's me, your brother Holden." He assumed,

incorrectly, that for a moment she hadn't known who he was and had woken to find a stranger beside her.

"I know who the hell you are. And I want you out. I didn't invite you here. You only show up when rich people are dying so you can inherit their money. I have nothing, Holden, and what I do have I leave for Bill." She closed her eyes and said, more calmly now, "Get out."

"Sir, you will have to leave and take the flowers with you. This is a cardiac intensive care unit and the patient has emphysema. Flowers are not allowed." Pat carried them out to the nurse's station so they wouldn't sit next to Frances while she negotiated Holden's departure.

"What are you talking about, Fran? You're not dying and I don't want your money. I'm here because I love you."

In reality, Holden wasn't sure at all why he'd come. And the answer was getting less clear as he began to suspect that his sister really didn't want him there.

"I am dying, little brother, and if you don't want my money you must be here for something else. Like mom's ring or her antiques. How about the house? You know it belonged to her. You want your rightful share, don't you? Well, forget it, Holden. The paperwork is all in place so you get nothing. Just the way mother wanted it."

"Frannie, you have to admit Mother was a bit nuts before she died." He was beginning to see the similarities in his sister. "The will leaving everything to you was questionable, but I never said a word."

Holden was a businessman, and he had taken pride in his composure when his mother's will was read. It was true, he had not contested it.

"No, you never said a word. You just started to hang around our two rich uncles and convinced them to leave everything to you. It was supposed to be split between all of the heirs, Holden, yet somehow you ended up with most of it. What a coincidence, huh?" Frances wasn't even out of breath. This argument filled her lungs with the resentment of many years' reserves. "You didn't even know those men! And you weren't there when they died, either. I was there."

"I was called away on business."

"You didn't care about them. I took care of them for years, like I cared for our dying parents, Holden. Where were you?"

"I'm here now. With you. I want to take care of you if you're dying. I want to help you get better if I can."

Holden felt this was the truth—yes, this is why he had come. He'd known instinctively that something was really wrong. The truth of the matter was that he did want Frances to recover; he wasn't ready to be an orphan who had lost both siblings. He had no anchor in the world without her.

"You didn't help our brother get better. Maybe if you had, he'd be alive today." Frances wasn't about to let him relieve his guilt now.

"Arthur drank himself to death, Fran. No one could have saved him." He kept his voice low and controlled, in contrast with her escalating emotion.

Her bitterness spewed out. "Why was he a drunk, Holden? Do you even know? You didn't know Arthur, and you sure never tried to help him when he fell on hard times. At least I tried. I tried to save him." Frances turned her head away in righteous indignation.

Holden thought for a moment. "I want to save you."

Looking back at him, she laughed. "Forget it. I don't need saving. Anyway, it looks more like you're trying to kill me with those flowers. You don't even know how to help. I want you out of here, Holden."

"Why do you hate me all of a sudden? I've never seen you act like this."

That wasn't completely true. They used to argue like this all the time, both of them equally at fault. But things had changed as they got older. He'd done what it had taken to feel closer to her, avoided her alienation by strategically visiting her on holidays and sharing the events of their children's lives.

"Why are you saying all of this now?"

Frances smiled in a way that made him more uncomfortable than the idea of death itself. "Because I can. I have nothing left to lose."

He sensed the power of her certainty and it left him weak. He asked quietly, "What can I do?"

"You can leave. And you can pray. Talk to your God and ask him to forgive you. And while you've got him on the line, ask him to save me a place in heaven. I'm going to be knocking at his door very soon." Frances was calm now that she'd said all she'd needed to say.

"Sir," Nurse Pat had been listening outside the door and chose the moment of her interruption, "I'm going to have to ask you to leave now. You're upsetting the patient, and we have orders to keep her calm. We do not want to have to give her any additional medication if we can avoid it."

"Frances?"

"Leave, Holden. It's over. Give me a kiss on the cheek and send my best to the girls. Tell them I love them."

Holden tried again to convince her of his good intentions; Frances again raised her voice in response. The nurse escorted him down the hallway with a reprimand not to return unless invited.

Sugar had waited in the hallway, listening. She remembered a conversation she'd had with Uncle Holden about six months ago. *It's not like he wasn't warned*, she thought.

"I'm worried about your mother, Sugar," he had said. "You saw her last week. She looks thin and tired."

Uncle Holden had never singled her out to have a conversation before, so she hadn't known what to make of it. Did he really care about his sister or did he have another motive? She'd had to wonder. Mom and Uncle Holden had that kind of relationship, one of deep attachment despite the distrust and loathing between them. She'd felt the need to defend her mother because Frances would have been furious if she'd known Uncle Holden was talking behind her back.

"I saw her, but I didn't notice. We had a really nice visit." Sugar had said as she'd tried to remember the details.

"You didn't notice?" His normally quiet and punctuated voice had grown sharp and rapid. "How could you not notice? Her eyes were tired, her skin looks terrible. It looks like she's lost about ten or twenty pounds."

The truth was, she hadn't noticed. Her mother looked like her mother, getting older every time Sugar saw her. Like parents generally do. When you see someone frequently, it was hard to notice subtle changes.

"Well, since she started having trouble with her teeth, my mother hasn't had much interest in eating. Eating is just not fun any more if you can't really chew. She even stopped liking her tuna fish sandwiches, and you know how much she loved those." Had he?

Uncle Holden really struck out then. "I would think you would be as concerned about your mother as I am."

Sugar had tried to remember the last time Uncle Holden had been concerned about her mother. It must have occurred sometime between his Easter and Christmas visits. Anyway, if he was so concerned, why hadn't he had this conversation with her instead?

"Well, I'm not worried about her, Uncle Holden. You'll have to accept the fact that my mother just doesn't want to live that long. If there is something wrong with her, she probably hopes it's bad enough to kill her."

The normally staid Uncle Holden had grown angry, like he was today. It was a side of him Sugar had never seen before, but knew her mother must have.

"How can you say that? Of course she wants to live. My doctor says everyone who thinks they want to die changes their tune when they really get sick."

"Well, if that's actually true, Uncle Holden, then don't you think she would have stopped smoking once they told her she had COPD?" Sugar's trump card.

"COPD?" Uncle Holden squinted, trying to see the situation more clearly with this new information.

Sugar helped him out. "Heart and lung disease. Chronic emphysema and bronchitis. She was diagnosed recently, and yet she keeps on smoking. That's her choice. She knows what she's doing."

He had stumbled, physically knocked off-balance. "I didn't

know. I can't believe she didn't tell me." Uncle Holden had looked hurt.

Actually, Frances had never told Sugar, either. She had learned about it through her father. Frances had told only her husband.

"Well, Uncle Holden, I respect my mother's wishes. If she doesn't want to be around that long, I can't stand in her way. I've been living with this for a long time. It's her life and she gets to decide how to live it. I love her, but I can't stand in the way of her and her destiny."

Sugar had believed her own words then, but now, though, she was closer to her uncle's opinion.

"That's bullshit."

Uncle Holden had used a curse word. Sugar had never heard him do that before, not in front of her, anyway. He'd turned his back and stormed off. She hadn't seen him again until today at the hospital and had hid in the hallway because she just wasn't up to another confrontation.

He's so smug about this, Sugar thought. *He just walks in and thinks he knows what's best for my mother.*

But she also felt her uncle's disapproval and had struggled with it from then until now. He had implied that she didn't love her mother enough to try to keep her alive.

13

WILLIAM needed a break but had nowhere to go. He drove around the neighborhood again, but his car brought him right back to the hospital parking lot. But it couldn't make him go in. He sat, windows down, sun on his arm, trying to enjoy the lone ash tree that had already begun turning yellow next to the small outpost building at the end of the asphalt.

He checked his watch. Eleven a.m. in California. He checked his cell phone. Three bars of power.

He waited. The events of the morning bore down on him, blocking the sun, blocking any kind of clear thought except one: *She wants me to help her die.*

He dialed the telephone. Diane answered.

"How can I let go?" he asked.

"I don't know, honey, but you have to."

He didn't say what he'd been thinking, *She is my mother, she was my first thought. She's the person who has known me the longest in this world, since the first time I turned in the tide inside her. She knew my first breath.*

Instead, he intellectualized. "In fighting my mother's death, I am fighting my own. Death is the universal foe, our ultimate conqueror. It's winner-take-all. A zero-sum proposition, and I know I can't win."

"You make it sound like a video game."

"I don't mean it that way. I just mean that she stands between me and death, and without her I am next in line. I want her to fight for me, but she's defenseless. It's not a war she believes in any longer. It's mine."

"It's a futile war, Will."

"I know, but does she have to lose so easily? I just don't understand how she can walk right into death as if it is her savior instead of her slayer."

Diane didn't say anything. She listened.

"But how can I deny her? She gave me life in the first place, and now she asks me to let go of the only part of me I have ever known for certain." He came to the core of the truth, and it had already begun burning him in its heat. "I've struggled for years to find myself, Di. Yet she's always been there, a constant. We are each other. I've been trying to find what part of myself exists outside my mother."

Diane found her spot. "That's what it's all about, Will. Children create a mother from an ordinary woman. You defined her destiny as surely as she defined yours. Some women are meant for that. But it's both your destinies to find your own ways. That's what happens."

William let the personal reference slip but noted it for another time. "I suppose only she has the right to ask. And I suppose I don't have the right to deny her. But it's almost like she isn't thinking of me at all. That's the hardest part."

"Her death isn't about you, Will."

"If that's the case, then why doesn't she do it alone? She says it's her spiritual path. If so, then why does she need me? She's made it about me—she is drawing me into it, making me a part of it. She asks that it be something we do together."

"You and your mother never seem able to do things together. It's always your way or her way." Diane had said that a lot over the years. "There's never a compromise."

"It wasn't always like that. I remember once I took her for a ride around the block on my new black banana seat bike."

"The kind with the sissy bar?" Diane laughed with the memory. "I used to have one of those, too. Mine was pink."

"Well, mine was black with a big sissy bar. And I finally talked my mom into letting me take her for a ride. The wind was in her hair as she held my waist, laughing behind me, and holding her legs straight out beside her so she wouldn't scrape her toes. I was her chariot driver that day. I pedaled standing straight up, as fast and as hard as I could. I knew we wouldn't fall even when I jumped up and down the curbs. And she trusted me. She never once said slow down or stop, you're going to kill us. I was a nine-year-old king of the world."

"Maybe it will be better if you think about it like that. You're just going to take your mother for another ride."

"That's the problem. I can't make her laugh and she won't just to go along for the ride. This is more like Monopoly where she holds Park Place and Boardwalk. With hotels. And when I pay up, I am not sure what I'll have left. She's going to bankrupt me."

Diane let the silence speak before she did.

"When you come home," she said, "it will be like passing GO. I'll be there for the next round."

Frances had been right. The surgery hadn't fixed her.

Late the next evening, she and Bill were sitting alone playing cards when the surgeon came in to tell them. He said her digestive system was still not working. Despite all the tests, he couldn't seem to pinpoint why. Doctor Watson suggested exploratory surgery anyway, but he couldn't guarantee she was strong enough to survive it or that it would be fruitful.

"But I am willing to try it if you are. What do you think, Mrs. Baldwin? Shall we schedule you for tomorrow morning? There's no time to wait." Dr. Watson paused for an answer. He'd already cleared his calendar anticipating her approval.

Frances folded her hand, placing her cards on the table. "No."

"No? I can't really give you any more time to decide, Mrs. Baldwin. Frankly, you don't have much time left."

"No. I will not have surgery."

The doctor argued for almost ten minutes, thinking she simply didn't understand the consequence of her decision. He'd already heard from Dr. Al-Biruni that Frances would be difficult yet he was disbelieving. He'd never had a patient who chose certain death over a chance at life. Her chance of living was twenty-five percent. That represented reasonable odds.

Frances stood her ground.

Bill remained silent, meekly shuffling his cards. After Dr. Watson left, he asked, "What do you want to play, Fran?"

"Hearts."

"It's not called Hearts, Fran. It's called Gin Rummy."

She always called it the wrong thing. He dealt the hand and moved his cards around. They played their turns, Bill squinting and fiddling with his cards. He played to win, holding ruthlessly onto the card she needed, and won the first hand.

"Again, Bill."

Confidently, he dealt again. This time, his hand was mismatched with little promise but the draws he took gave him hope. He needed one more card to win again: either a king of spades or a two of hearts. He maintained a poker face to hide his position. Frannie discarded the two and laid the fan of her cards before her.

"Gin, Bill. That's all for tonight."

When he reached his car, Bill sat inside for forty minutes before starting it up and driving away. He did not think to call his children to alert them to the events of the evening; in fact, he was doing all he could do to forget them all.

Back at the Pennstead Inn, one of the many restored 1960s-built motels that lined the main access to his hometown, William spent a sleepless night. Unaware of the change in his mother's condition, he nevertheless was plagued by sadness and doubt. His exhausted brain was bombarded with medical terms, possible scenarios, and replays of his latest conversation with his mother.

As he finally drifted into involuntary unconsciousness at three in the morning, he was awakened by what he counted was six people—two mothers and four children—arriving in the room next door. The motel had been half-empty until then, and William hadn't been aware of how thin the walls were. The connecting door between his and the next room might well have been open, for it seemed to conduct instead of block the sound. For fifteen minutes the children whined and the mothers scolded, and suitcases and bags were dropped and slammed. William called the front desk.

"There's nothing we can really do, Mr. Baldwin, except give them a call. I am sure they will settle down soon."

William heard the phone ring on the other side of the wall. The woman who answered it had a bad attitude.

"This is our room," she said. "We've been driving all night and now our children have to get settled in. There is nothing more we can do. Tell whoever called to go to hell." She hung up the phone. William could hear it as clearly as if she were standing right beside him. He didn't need the receptionist to call him back.

"People in this hotel are so ignorant!" The woman recounted the conversation to her friend in a tone even louder than the one she'd used before.

"Hey, Buddy, why don't you turn the television on?" she called. Buddy did as she said, and then the woman turned it louder. "See how they like that!" she shouted.

William was unaware of ever having been so angry. His mother was dying and this woman was playing games with him. She was making herself the center of the universe, demanding the right to take up space in William's life, while William's mother was demanding the right to slowly fade out of it. It wasn't fair that he should have no say about either. This woman—whoever she was—didn't care what William thought. She didn't care how hard she was making it, how tired he was, or what he was going through. He was just supposed to ignore his own needs and pretend what she was doing was okay.

Blind with rage, shredded by the unfairness of grief, William walked to the connecting door and pounded his fists as loudly as he could.

"Shut up! Shut up! You selfish bitch! There are people trying to sleep here!"

He pounded until his hands hurt, until his energy was gone, until he stood motionless with his head against the door. The television sound went down. William tried to recover himself. *Quiet. Peace. Oh, please.*

Breaking the silence, the woman said, "You should be ashamed of yourself." The sound to the television went back up. The conversation started again. The smallest of the children began to cry.

William, shaking with rage and impotence, packed his bags and left the hotel. He got into his car and turned the radio off before starting the engine. He couldn't take in one more piece of information, he didn't need anything else to think about. And he certainly didn't want to know if God had a comment on what had just happened. He felt like his head was about to explode.

He drove the five miles to his father's house, let himself in with the key under the mat, went back to his old bedroom, and fell deeply asleep.

Still, he was up the next morning before his father. His father's door was still closed, so he left a note and got into the car. He stared at the satellite radio receiver. Should he turn it on?

Falling Upon Deaf Ears *By As I Lay Dying*

14

I don't think it's a question of why I want to die. That's what Sugar wants to know. As usual, she—like the rest of them—never quite sees me straight, and actually that is the whole point.

What she should have asked was, "Why don't you want to live?" Two different questions.

I don't want to die, not necessarily. But I really am just damn tired of living. I'm done. I don't have anything else to give. I'm ready to see what else might be in store for me.

I know what's going on in the world. I watch the news and read the papers. The confidence I have lost in my fellow man over the years has transformed into a stronger belief that there must be a God and a Heaven to save us from ourselves. So I don't really believe I'm going to die, exactly.

I think I'm still a Catholic, but I'm keeping my mind open to what else God can be. I somehow have the feeling there's a lot more to it than The One Holy Catholic And Apostolic Church has told us. The more I pray, the more I feel this is true. And the more I pray, the more I can hear God calling for me.

I am not running from Him. I am not turning my back. I am walking to Him with my arms open wide, unafraid of my physical death. Is this not the deepest faith?

I don't believe my spirit will die. And this poor tired façade is ready. This body is old before its time; it never served me especially well except to cocoon my babies. It never brought me much pleasure, never brought me the pride of a beautiful woman, was never cherished by anyone—not my parents, not my husband and certainly not myself. I won't be sorry to see it go. It's been shutting down on me little by little, and now I feel it is time. I am willing to let me go.

They're all concerned about the death of my body. I suppose they all expect me to fight—to make every effort to keep the meaningless organs and tissues alive. No one was ever that concerned about my spirit, which has been dying a slow death as long as I can remember. And there is no cure for that in their medicine bags. Only God can save my soul. It just doesn't seem right to preserve the flesh when my spirit has moved on.

Sometimes I feel so empty inside that I feel I'm already good and dead. I sense no beat to my heart, no circulation to my emotions. I go through periods when the void has opened and the bright white light consumes my every waking thought. I lose my sense of color: nothing excites me or calms me or soothes me. I lose my sense of taste: there is no sweetness in life or even sour. Everything I'm supposed to like or love seems bland. My temperature drops from the heat of the moment into cold indifference. There is nothing left to define me. My substance fades and I become invisible even to myself. Is this not death? I believe it is.

But until now I have held on in the moment when letting go would bring me release. I hold on for my life. I hold on for them. I call to God and ask Him for help and get angry when I hear no answer. On the outside, all they see is my argument, my temper, my moods and my withdrawal. I throw words and act in ways that are not me. Just as a soldier might kill just to keep himself alive—because he must. Those I love the most become my torturers. They become benevolent captors imprisoning me in a life I no longer want or need. I strike out at them; I hurt and stab and bleed and maim them because I must. They don't understand why I hurt them, but the very action brings me back alive. It gives me substance.

This twisted circle of love and hate and need and detachment has been at my core for some time. It's not really living. It's barely staying alive. Not even my husband knows me well enough to understand this.

So, have I not died and survived a thousand deaths before this one? That is why I am not afraid. I have planned for this, planned for the day when I could be at peace. Now I seek the dying from which there is no death, the dying that will bring me to God.

The struggle is over. I cannot and will not do it again. I am through. I have tried to find inside myself one last bit of strength, one little bit of fight. But there is none. I have survived for them—for those who think I have no right to leave, for those who hold onto me as if the world will stop revolving without me, yet who put me on the front line to fight all their battles. Protecting them from the fear of their own deaths and the uncertainty of mine. But that is not my cause. It is theirs.

There's nothing else I want to do here, nothing more I need to say.

I decided last year that I'd seen my last Christmas and blown out the candles for the last time. I've been everywhere I want to go. I've met more people than could ever make a difference to me or I to them. When I was young, I created three of my own human beings, grew them inside me and prepared them for the world the best I could. An amazing feat when you think of it. And I've seen my grandchildren born...one of my greatest joys. God, I loved them when they were babies. I still love them. But they're older now—just two more people to negotiate with.

I'm always negotiating to be seen, always negotiating for a small corner of my own in everyone else's life. And frankly, I'm just tired of it. I'm ready to fade away as I've been threatening to do my whole life. There must be another place for me.

At one time I felt like I belonged to my husband and he to me. But I was wrong about that. At one time I thought my children belonged to me and I to them. But I was wrong about that, too. I am fiercely protective of them, and that is largely the nature of the bond between us, but there is no real connection. They belong to the world now.

Still, I cannot see myself living without any of them. Not the boys or Sugar or even Bill. If any of them were to die before me, I—I can't even think of it. I couldn't go on. I would die then in a pool of contemptuous self-pity. What could be worse?

So I am determined to go first, for all of these reasons. My concern now is how I will leave.

My kids are grown and living their own lives. I am a burden to them when I need them, and I need them more than ever. That scares me. If I live with this illness, this COPD, I will definitely need them and my husband more and more over time. They'll grow to resent me, as I did my father when I took care of his dying, cancer-ridden body. I love my kids too much to put them through that. I am determined to protect them.

Sick people are ugly and needy and helpless; believe me, I know. I cared for both my parents, my brother, and four aunts and uncles as they've lived with progressive diseases. Sick people don't want to be sick. Miserable, they make demands. Medicines and procedures just keep them around longer, miserable and demanding. They lean on others and are pathetic in their inability to make their own way in life. And I will grow bitter like my uncle, who threw obscenities at me whenever I interfered to get him better nursing or comfort.

I've always made my own way. I only know how to be in charge. The things I've learned always made me stronger. Why would I want to learn how to be weak at this point? I would need to learn to be dependent if I am going to live with this illness. That just doesn't seem right. I can't imagine anyone would want that for me.

I've never considered myself a proud woman, but I guess that's what I am. I've always associated pride with vice. But to maintain my pride, my dignity, in death seems virtuous now. To die a proud death is the best I can give to all of them. To do otherwise would be to become someone else. So what else can I do, really?

When I was sick this summer, I made sure I didn't burden any of them. I wouldn't let Sugar or the kids see my skin peeling away so they wouldn't have to worry about me. So I wouldn't repulse them. I let Bill do whatever he wanted with his friends so he didn't feel tied to me. I couldn't fix the rash and I couldn't bolster my spirit, so I used the time for us all to practice my dying. To get them used to the idea that I wouldn't always be around, participating. It was pretty easy for me, really, to separate. Most days I was ready. I used the other days, the days when I longed for their voices and concern, to strengthen my resolve.

My firstborn son William understands all of this better than anyone. I pushed him away from me for a long time and he let it happen, so he understands we are separate. I lashed out at him in rage and said horrible things to him when he didn't finish his medical training, trying to provoke in him the same level of emotion I had felt in my disappointment. He lashed out right back.

I loved him for that, even though I couldn't tell him. He loves me both for my rage and my kindness; he doesn't pretend I am only capable of one or the other because he knows of both in himself. And, like me, he struggles to know the meaning of his mortality. I hope when his time comes, he knows the peace I have found and sees it as clearly as I can now.

The surgeon still won't admit I'm dying. He thinks a twenty-five percent chance of staying alive is enough of an incentive for me to risk spending it as a vegetable or worse, a fully conscious but incapacitated shell. The doctors don't see the big picture—I left my life a few months ago.

And they're not in this body. I've had the procedures, I've come out of the operation, and still I knew I wasn't fixed. I've taken their medicine and I'm on their IVs, but they can't heal what is really wrong. The doctors seem disappointed, as if I am failing them somehow. They want to tell me to try harder but they can't. They keep sending me for tests as if a test might tell them something different than what I keep saying: I am dying and it's okay. It's my time.

I might agree that maybe I'm depressed and that's why I can't find a reason to live. If I thought I could be helped, I might give it a try. I could talk to a shrink, and I would detail a life history of loss and grief and pain, and you could say I was running away from a bad childhood and years of bad luck. And you might be right. And ten years ago it might have mattered.

But what does it matter now if my body is done? When I close my eyes, I feel my awareness and identity on their own trajectory, away from this body. There is nothing I can do to reconnect. And as I've been trying to tell them—I don't want to.

Everyone is just going to have to let me go.

15

NURSE Pat fussed around the bed. She looked forward to her morning routine with Frances, helping her bathe and feel comfortable. After the first week, she'd finally learned how to draw eyebrows just as Frances wanted and lately had been doing it even though she hadn't been asked. She distributed medicines and checked all the vital signs and mechanical connections. She liked to tuck the blankets in just so, sides tight and feet loose. That way, Frances would feel that someone had taken care of her and her family wouldn't worry about her. Since her hand had been damaged, Pat had been especially vigilant when it came to her patient. She wasn't going to let anything like that happen again.

"You remind me of my daughter, Pat. Always fussing about and taking care of me. You make a good nurse. Did you always want to be a nurse?"

Pat smiled wistfully. "No. For years I thought I wanted to be a princess. Then I became a Girl Scout. One day our scout leader took us for a hike, and I fell into the stream and fractured my ankle. She gathered the girls around, and they all did first aid on me. Then my scout leader carried me on her back out of the woods and took me to the hospital."

Frances laughed aloud. Her eyes twinkled with the delight of an unexpected gift. "Pat. Patty?"

"Yes."

"Patty Trexler!"

Nurse Pat smiled. She had originally thought it best not to disclose the personal connection between herself and her patient. But she had grown even more attached to Frances since she'd arrived and was upset to learn from Dr. Watson that Frances had denied further treatment. Now she needed to make a connection.

"Momma?" Sugar arrived at the door. "How are you today?"

"Sugar, you'll never guess who this is." Frances had her head back against the pillow, exhausted from the morning's routine. "It's Patty Trexler. Remember her from Girl Scouts?"

"Patty Weingarten now. I'm married."

"I knew you looked familiar!" The two women eyed each other, trying to make out the crayon traces of the ten-year-olds they remembered.

It was May 1973. The Girls Scouts of Troop 563 were snug in their tents that chilly morning on the Pennsylvania side of the river at Washington's Crossing State Park. The dew covered the canvas and the grass and the picnic tables and everything that had been left out to meet the sunrise. A circle of eight tents had been set in the clearing, inside the protection of tall oak and elm trees. At the center was a big fire pit for cooking. Behind the tents were the cars of the troop leaders and their husbands.

Frances had not slept well; she had lain awake listening to the sounds of the nighttime and the breathing of her husband and young sons beside her. When light first appeared, she moved quietly so they wouldn't hear her leave for her morning cigarette. Outside, she enjoyed the heat inside her lungs, enjoyed the smoke swirling with the dew and mist, the look of the camp and the sensation of being in charge of this little army. When she began to hear the murmur of voices and giggles from the tents, she blew out the last of her mentholated breakfast and stomped the butt into the dirt. She was very careful about forest fires. When she turned, she saw that Sugar had crept up silently behind her.

"We'd better get the girls up now, Sweetie. We have a long day ahead of us, a hike to the nature center over in New Jersey. I'll start the fire so we can cook up some breakfast. Nothing better than eggs and bacon while you're camping." She took a deep breath of the morning air. "You go rouse the troops, baby."

Frances jumped up from the tabletop on which she'd been sitting, leaving an imprint of her rear end in the dew. Sugar decided to sit at another table for breakfast.

The crackle of the firewood blended with the sound of canvas unzippering, and the sounds of humans mingled with the smoke drifting straight up to the treetops.

"What should I be doing, Frances?" Dolly, the senior troop leader rubbed her eyes and puffed her hair with her fingertips. "I've never been camping before, and I need coffee. Where's the coffee?"

Dolly and Frances didn't really get along, mostly for reasons like this. Dolly's obliviousness was reliable and unremarkable, so Frances avoided small talk and explanations. Instead, she just walked away. As usual, Frances managed on her own.

"Okay, girls, where's Patrol One?"

Six hands raised on the far end of the circle.

"You are in charge of making the orange juice. Patrol Two?"

Five girls volunteered to butter bread for the toast. Patrol

Three began breaking eggs, and Frances asked Dolly to work with Patrol Four to supervise the bacon frying. Frances never trusted children around hot fat.

"And remember, Dolly, put dish soap around the frying pan so the fire doesn't leave burn marks on the stainless."

The pan in question had come from Frances' kitchen at home, and it was an heirloom classic. Dolly was confused and resentful that Frances acted like she was in charge. She, after all, was the true leader and Frances was her assistant. Of course she knew how to fry bacon.

"Here's the dish soap, Mrs. Bellamy." Ruth Griffin handed her a plastic squirt bottle.

Dolly hesitated, then went right ahead and squirted the soap right into the center of the pan and tilted it right and left so it covered the bottom. Of course she knew how to fry bacon. She just never knew bacon needed anything extra in the pan. She carefully set the bacon strips in the soap and put the frying pan on the grate over the fire.

"Eeewww. Mrs. Bellamy, what are you doing? That's disgusting!" The girls of Patrol Four were already objecting.

Frances rolled her eyes and mourned the loss of a pound of bacon.

"The soap goes on the *outside* of the pan, Dolly."

It was going to be a long day.

According to Frances' maps and the advice of the park ranger, the hike across the bridge to the Titusville Nature Center would take about an hour, assuming they would stop now and then and do the things Girl Scouts do on a hike. It was only about two miles, but ten-year-old girls don't move very quickly—unlike Frances, who could probably cover the two miles in about forty-five minutes at a brisk pace.

They filled their canteens at the water pump and headed out, leaving the fathers and siblings behind. Frances chose the Gristmill Trail. According to the map, it went past the Thompson-Neely House, a historic site she would show the girls. It appeared to be about a fifteen-minute walk.

"Girls, pay attention. We'll be going to the Franklin Mealy house first, then we'll go over to the Taterville Nature Center."

The girls agreed. At one point they left the trail to identify some wildflowers. They saw signs of small animals, probably chipmunks, and the girls searched through the leaves and brush for walking sticks. After half an hour, the Thompson-Neely house still had not appeared. Without a landmark, Frances found the map useless. If they weren't on the right trail, she had no real idea where they were.

"Okay, girls, if you have a compass, take it out now. Let's see what we find out." The girls complied.

"Which direction are we going?"

"Southwest."

Frances was confused. They should have been heading southeast. They moved in that direction at the first opportunity; Frances did not make any explanation. A bridge appeared, and they took it. She re-calculated their location on the map and they weren't far from where she had originally fixed their position.

"We should reach the Taylor-McFeely house soon!" she said.

"And then we'll be in Taterville!" The girls teased her now.

"It's called Titusville, Mrs. Baldwin." Mary Callan addressed Frances respectfully.

"Thank you, Mary. I've always had trouble with names. Okay, girls, let's stop for lunch."

Troop 563 sat in the grassy clearing eating their sandwiches while Frances studied the map. She let the girls rest a few minutes more while she tried to make a plan. Then they headed east.

The lively group, undaunted by the disappearance of the Thompson-Neely House, sang songs as they walked. Frances led the chorus one line at a time, and the girls repeated the song about a poor little goat who ate the revengeful farmer's shirts and got his head chopped off by an oncoming train. It had a catchy tune and a melodic finale as the goat reaches his place in heaven.

As the girls laughed and danced along the trail, Patty Trexler stepped too close to the slope and slid clumsily on the leaves, down a short hill into the stream. It was one of those things that happens in slow motion: the girls all watched as Patty tried to stay upright, grasping at saplings to retain her balance but falling and splashing into the water nevertheless. It was chilly but not cold, and the sight brought more of a laugh than concern from her friends.

Frances left the trail and went after the girl. It was steepest where she'd fallen. From farther down the path, it was easier to access the stream. One by one, the whole troop followed except for Leader Dolly. She remained on the path in her white Keds, not seeing a real reason to dirty them.

Patty had not gotten up from where she landed. She was still laughing but was unable to put weight on her foot. The pain was beginning to set in. Frances knew immediately the girl wouldn't be walking.

"Okay, girls, take out your first-aid guides. Tell me what we do for someone who's hurt her ankle."

Frances went into her own pack and took out the first-aid kit. Six girls got their feet wet carrying Patty out of the water. They all gathered around and talked about how to wrap the ankle as Frances held Patty in her lap. She kept her arms wrapped around the girl to warm her. Patty winced several times but all in all, she was quite brave.

The scouts did the wrapping and unwrapping and rewrapping until they finally got it right, and Frances took off her jacket to put around the wet girl. They helped her stand, and Frances carried her piggy-back style. They walked twenty minutes more without any sign that they were headed in the right direction.

Sugar was now looking at the map. "Mommy, I don't think this map makes any sense. We should have seen Bowman's Tower by now, and we sure haven't seen that."

Frances had no idea where they were. She'd never had a good sense of direction, but had undertaken a hike in the woods because the map made it look easy. She wanted to cry. Leader Dolly was sweeping pieces of the forest off her shoulders and pants and shoes. The girls were all proud of themselves for being prepared and were marching along in formation, even after three hours. Certainly, they would all get the first aid merit badge for this.

I wonder when they'll start looking for us, Frances wondered. They had no choice but to walk on. Luckily, Patty was not a big girl but any girl on your back for an hour was still too heavy.

"There it is!" one of the girls cried. "A building!"

Expecting the Thompson-Neely house, they instead saw a zoo-like structure with a guide giving a tour to some children.

"The Taterville Nature Center!" they all cheered.

Frances didn't even care that they were making fun of her. She walked to a picnic table, put Patty down, and collapsed with her head in her arms.

"That was so much fun," Nurse Patty said, laughing aloud after they all volunteered the details they remembered until the whole story emerged.

"Mom, did you have any idea where we were going?" Sugar asked.

"Of course, I did," Frances lied. "I was the leader. It was my job to know."

She was feeling exhausted. *Where did I ever find the energy? That seems like a different Frances, so long ago.*

"You were great, Mrs. Baldwin. I've told that story so many times in my life. I had the best time in Girl Scouts. After you left, it wasn't the same so I quit." Pat turned to Sugar. "Your mom is awesome."

Frances couldn't help but to smile.

"The best part was that we always did so many things. We were a very busy troop," Pat said.

"We went to the circus, and the Ice Capades," Sugar volunteered. "And we sold cookies at the shopping center, remember that? I swear, these days the parents sell the cookies, not the Scouts. The girls just stand on the side while their moms do all the work. I think the parents are afraid to let their kids handle the money or talk to strangers or something. It's just not the same. Girl Scouts is where you're supposed to learn how to be competent, not reinforce how inept you are."

"Another thing that really left an impression on me, Mrs. Baldwin, was when you took us to the nursing home," Pat said.

Frances remembered, and the thought sent a chill up her spine.

Pat continued, "We made those little bunnies out of a bar of soap and a wash cloth, and we each gave one to a sick person. I remember how lonely the people were and how their faces lit up when we walked into their rooms. I learned a lot that day. I learned that a lot of people are alone when they're sick." She glanced at Sugar. "You're very lucky, Frances."

"Yes, you're right. I am. My family is very good to me."

Sugar remembered the nursing home. She remembered it well. She remembered that when they had come home, her mother had begun to cry and panicked. Frances had lit a cigarette and described the worst of what she'd seen in a loud voice so Sugar had a hard time focusing on her positive feeling of having done a good deed. Frances had always done that to Sugar, mixed the bad into the good. No good feeling was allowed to exist very long without being tempered. Frances called it realism.

Thirty years ago, when she was about Sugar's age, Frances had said, "I never want to be like one of those people in the home, Sugar. I do not want to live that long. Did you see how unhappy they were? That was horrible. I'm sorry I took you girls there. I shouldn't have done it."

Sugar nodded, knowing that the rest of her friends would be remembering a different lesson from that day. Her memory of the white-haired woman who'd smiled had all but disappeared.

"I will never go to a home like that. So you don't have to worry about me."

Yes, Sugar remembered. There would be no soap bunnies for her mother.

Nurse Pat held Frances' hand at her bedside and spoke quietly. "You were always so resourceful, Mrs. Baldwin. You were my role model. You could do anything; you always knew how to handle things. That's why I'm so surprised about your decision. Don't you think you could just give it a try?"

"Your decision?"

Sugar was still unaware of the surgeon's diagnosis the night before. Bill had not informed his children, he'd just gone home to bed.

"We'll talk later, Pat. For now, let me visit with my daughter."

Pat smoothed the blankets on Frances' feet. "Okay, Mrs. Baldwin. You relax and get some rest. I'll be in later." She held up the Girl Scout hand sign: three fingers extended with her thumb across her palm holding her bent pinky. "On my honor."

Frances smiled.

Sugar was unsure what to do. She tried to make small talk and her mother went along without any further explanation.

Frances was pleased when William soon arrived. She was afraid to face Sugar alone, but with William on her side she could do it. Sugar was pleased with his arrival, too. She could handle anything if he was there.

16

SUGAR found it hard to face the truth.

"I'll never forgive you, mother. If you don't do everything you can to live, I will never forgive you. It's like you're committing suicide, and I will never condone it. Don't ask me to. It's against everything I believe in." The words sat like heated oil, splattering, and ready to fry anything that came near.

Frances was tired and she didn't want to argue. "William," she implored. "Talk to your sister."

"You talk to me, mother," Sugar insisted. "Why are you so intent on dying? Why won't you try to live? For us? For your grandchildren?"

"I did everything you wanted, Sugar. If it was up to me, I would have given up a long time ago. I just can't do any more."

"You're killing yourself, Mom. They said the surgery worked, didn't they? Last night you told me maybe you would try to eat something again. So I brought you some rice pudding this morning." She threw her hands in the air. "But no. Now you want to kill yourself again."

Frances answered kindly but firmly. "I am not killing myself, Sugar. My body is tired. It's old. It's failing. And now, all this."

She held up her bad hand, which now harbored a neat surgeon's incision to relieve the pressure, and then pointed to the tubes draining her abdomen. She left her hand open and extended, imploring her daughter.

"Please, honey. Let me die my way. You're going to have to realize that it's my time. And you're going to have to get used to living without me. I've done all I can do to prepare you. But you have to let me go, sweetheart. Let me go."

She reached for Sugar's hand, but she turned and left the room. Now it was Sugar's turn to need oxygen. She couldn't breathe. With a nod to his mother, William followed her out.

"She's committing suicide."

Sugar was so tired she could hardly stand. With her back against the wall, she began to slide down toward the floor. William picked her up by the arm and took her to another waiting room down a new hallway, which he had found yesterday on one of his own pressure-relieving walks outside his mother's room. It was brighter with multi-colored padded chairs, new carpeting and a big window.

"How? How can you say she's committing suicide?" he asked.

"Medical help is available and she's denying it. God wants her to utilize all help humans can give before she dies."

"How do you know what God wants?"

"Why would he give people the intelligence to become doctors if he didn't want them to save people?"

"That's a bad argument, Sugar. We can't know what God wants." He snickered. "Obviously."

"Well, that's what I believe. I believe she's killing herself."

"Is there a difference between jumping off a balcony when you're perfectly healthy versus jumping when you're terminally ill?" He'd been wrestling with the same questions all night.

"No. I just don't see it. It's the same thing. When God wants her, he'll call her."

"Sugar, she says she can hear the call and the doctors are drowning it out. She's met with a priest for counseling. He told her it was okay to let go if that's what she thought God wanted."

"I don't believe her. If God wants her, he'll take her. But he hasn't. He let her live through the operation."

"Sugar, they've saved Mom's life three times now. If she hadn't been in the hospital she'd already be gone."

"But she *is* in the hospital, and she should be doing everything she can to stay alive."

She got up and walked over to the window. She stared at the side of the next building as if it had the depth and detail of a landscape. When she spoke again, her lips barely moved.

"William, I can't lose her now. She's all I have. Please, don't take her from me." She turned to him, "You'll leave, and I'll be alone with just Dad and the boys. It's more than I can face right now. I've just gotten over David leaving us. Mom was so good to us after the divorce. We're closer than ever. Don't make me and the boys lose her, too."

She spoke as if William was making the choices. As if this whole thing was in his hands, waiting for him to decide.

"They said she'd probably die on the operating table, Sugar. Is that how you want to lose her?" William implored her now as gently as he could.

"She didn't tell me that."

"She's even weaker now than after the first operation. Do you want us to have to make the decision to disconnect her from machines because she never regains consciousness? Is that the way you want to lose her? Or do you want her to end up a vegetable? Is that better for the boys?"

"I didn't think about that. That would be terrible." Sugar began to cry. Angrily, she asked, "Where is God? Why doesn't he just take her?"

She looked upward, as if God was somewhere on the third floor making choices. William put his arm around his sister.

"Sugar, she's doing the only thing she can do. She's giving us time with her before she dies. She's trying to make it peaceful instead of upsetting for us. Maybe *that's* where we'll find God."

Sugar sniffed and considered it. "What does Dad think?"

"Who knows? I assume he knows about this. He's not here yet, and his door was closed to his room at ten this morning. That's not like him. He's surely not taking it well. He says he's never heard her say she wanted to die."

Sugar stood up straight and snapped her head toward him. "You're kidding, right? He didn't know she was going to do this the first chance she got?"

"He says no. He says his wife would never feel that way. Apparently, according to him, they've never talked about it."

"Then why did she tell us so many times over the years?" Sugar was amazed by the possibility that he really didn't know.

"If it's true, it's probably because she thought he'd never go along with it and she'd need us to fight the battle. He says it's the medicine talking. He doesn't believe his wife would want to leave him."

"Well, he'd better get used to the fact that if she won't live for her children or her grandchildren, if she doesn't want to live for herself or because of her religious beliefs, then she is sure as hell is not going to want to live just to take care of him. If we have to get used to the idea then he'd better get used to it, too.

"Oh, how I would have loved to have had a few years where I didn't have to live with the fact that my mother was ready to die and would take the first road out. How I would have loved the ignorant bliss he seems to be living in. What a lucky man."

She spoke for them both. Then there was nothing left to say except, "I love her, but I don't know if I can forgive her."

"I hope you can forgive me for helping her. She's asked me and I'm going to say yes. I have to do it, Sugar. Please understand."

She didn't, but she hugged him as if she did. She knew Frances was asking something different from him. More than acceptance, she wanted his cooperation. He was in an impossible position. Sugar was afraid to ask him how he really felt about it because it didn't matter. They all knew he would follow his mother's wishes.

William found his mother with her eyes half open, perhaps watching the antiques show on the little television swung close to her bed, perhaps pondering her fate, perhaps thinking nothing at all.

"Well?" she asked simply, without taking her eyes off the screen. She winced in mental and physical anguish; the morphine was wearing off.

"I've been thinking a lot about this, Mom."

"Help me, Son. Let me go."

He sat on the edge of the bed and took her good hand in his.

"Mom," he began, trying to think of the words to express

what he wanted to say, what he knew he had to say, was supposed to say, was destined to say since the day he was born. Still, he tried to get some distance by invoking his best, most disinterested bedside manner.

"Mom, if it is your time to go then I won't stand in your way. I won't lecture you, and I'll do everything I can to make it peaceful for you."

Frances relaxed. She'd known she could count on William. Above all of them, she could count on him. William had the guts to do it. Not like the others.

"This is it, William," she said as honestly as she knew it. "This is my time. There's a lot to do. We need to get my affairs in order and deal with the hospital and the family. Take the rest of the day off. I'm going to need you tomorrow."

17

William's Journal

AUGUST 31, 2005. I did it. I've agreed to help her die. But I'm still not sure if I'm hastening her death or causing it. It isn't clear to me. I can live with the first concept. I can live peacefully knowing I helped my mother on her unavoidable life path. But I will struggle for the rest of my life if it turns out that I've helped her kill herself.

Sugar thinks Mom is committing suicide, and I don't think she's alone in that opinion. People are against suicide because they believe a life doesn't belong to the person living it—that it cannot be claimed like any other possession, and it cannot be terminated like any other contract. Religious people believe each individual life belongs to God; and if we end it voluntarily, we are taking something away from him. Or we are disrespecting a gift he gave us, or we have disobeyed the commandment to respect the sanctity of life. Non-religious people even generally believe it's wrong. It's against the human basic instinct to perpetuate, against the instinct rooted deeply in our brains and in whatever other physical mechanisms work to keep us alive despite the odds.

But people are not totally against death as a choice. Some claim martyrdom or just cause by killing others and/or themselves in the name of God. If we believe in that same God, we believe self-extermination and murder is acceptable if it's done with holy intentions. Likewise, it's okay to give up one's life for one's country—honorable even.

We also believe it's justified to take the life of someone who is trying to kill us. Self-defense is a valid argument in a court of law. Millions believe in capital punishment, a jury-approved murder in retaliation for heinous acts. Millions believe in abortion, which terminates the beginning of a life. Yet there is a near-universal public policy of unwillingness to terminate the end of a life. The logic that dictates pro-choice at the beginning doesn't seem to cover pro-choice at the end.

So all in all, I figure we've found many ways for death to be deemed acceptable—except at the end of life when it comes along naturally.

If a person isn't wealthy enough or doesn't live in a place where medical help is available, we believe it's okay for them to die unattended. No one makes much of a fuss about it. Happens tens of thousands of times a day, all over the world. Too bad. But if a person lives in a country of privilege, and they happen to be sick in a hospital before dying, the rules change. We seem to believe that there are no longer choices for that life.

That life no longer belongs to the individual or even to God. That life belongs to the doctors and nurses and hospital boards, to drug manufacturers and insurance companies and ethics committees. When did we turn over our deaths to institutions?

For thousands of years, right up until the twentieth century, death was a ritual of our species—an unavoidable crossing each generation experienced and the next generations witnessed. It was treated with the respect of any significant passage, just like births, puberty and marriages were. Death was attended by neighbors, friends and relatives as a matter of course—it was unexaggerated, unglorified. It was accepted with appropriate solemnity. It belonged to and, most times, was orchestrated by the dying person.

Then during the first three decades of the Twentieth Century, Americans began the trend toward depersonalizing death. Death was an inconvenient truth in the pursuit of happiness, so we set out to separate it from everyday life. Dying at home became an imposition on the lives of the living; it upset the normal routine.

So in America and other Western countries, our deaths began their migrations to institutions…where the final responsibility for dying was turned over to doctors, where the unknown territory of death was governed by the rules of those who paid the expense. This, supposedly, makes it easier on everyone concerned. The dying can do so without the encumbrance of responsibility; the living can go home and live ordinary, happy lives while the process occurs. And physicians and hospitals are paid handsomely for their trouble.

How convenient.

This might have solved the problem of death's unpleasantness, but it has created another issue entirely. It has left a hole into which all things spiritual fall and never find a landing. In a sterile hospital environment, with its science and protocol, there is no place left for our spiritual beliefs, no private place for religious rituals and prayer, literally no room for personal growth or understanding to occur as we learn from the evolution of an individual life. We no longer have individual participation in the natural order of life and death, or in the cycles of the universe. We have contrived in its place an institutional process for physical death that demands one-size-fits-all compliance.

Medicine and technology are its enforcers. The capabilities of doctors and the effectiveness of their techniques now define the choices available to a dying person. If it's possible, it should be done. No questions asked. Most people believe that a proposal put forth by a physician acting in your best interest should be consented to. Compliance is your best chance at living, which of course is now our ultimate goal. All of our choices are destined to be about our bodies, not our souls.

I was raised in the Catholic faith, and I've never seen any reason to change. But I have to admit I don't practice its rituals anymore; my religion barely touches my life unless a crisis occurs. I know the Church is very vocal about its position on the sanctity of life, but I also know that Catholics are not obliged to utilize every available medical intervention as a way to preserve life. We believe that the afterlife is more meaningful than the physical body. While euthanasia is against the law and the beliefs of most organized religions, taking control of one's death is not. And my mother's plan for a quality ending is already in place.

I knew my mother was dying before I left California. Before I even saw her. I am witness to the gradual decline of her body and her spirit. I didn't need the surgeon telling me Mom would probably die on the operating table to appreciate how weak she is. I did not need to consider the blood clots to know that what ails my mother is spreading through her body. I see the individual parts of her shutting down—her breathing, her digestion, her circulation. Medicine can treat each individual organ, but without the will to live her body and spirit will never work together again.

Maybe her spirit has already died a natural death. If there's a God, perhaps God has recalled her will and her spirit already. I don't know; I don't claim to know God or his will. But what if it really is her mission to turn to God willingly, to turn away from all things earthly? To detach from her loved ones and give herself freely to whatever comes next? We have no way of knowing for sure. We can only go on what we believe.

Buddhists believe that a clear state of mind, undisturbed by emotion for the living world and its events, is the goal of the dying person. Non-attachment is the key to ending a physical life. Perhaps my mother knows this instinctively.

The increasing effectiveness of all this medicine and all these procedures only prolongs the inevitable. It keeps a body attached to the earth, often torturing the spirit and preventing it from being at peace. Sugar believes Mom should live—she needs her to live—and the surgeon agrees it's worth a try.

There's no chance she'll recover. There's a small chance she'll live. What percent chance is acceptable? If Mom makes it through, they think what will remain of her will be satisfactory even though they don't know exactly what will be left. Maybe then she won't even have the capacity to make her own decisions about care, and it will actually become harder and harder for her to die.

I came here thinking this was all up to God, but he sends mixed messages. I don't know what to believe now. So I put my faith in the doctors, and they betrayed us by dealing only with her physical care. Now something has to be done: a life or death decision needs to be made. They're all looking at me to approve or disapprove of what Mom's doing, and there is no obvious answer.

Seeing her like this, a shadow of her real self, I've come to believe in my mother's right to choose her care. She is the only one who knows her body. She is the only one who hears her God, whoever he is, and what he is asking of her.

If my mother believes she is dying, she is. And she will. I can either deny it and hope for a miracle like my father, or fight against it like Sugar, or try to avoid it like Randy. I can do what the surgeon wants and talk my mother into playing roulette with whatever time she has left.

Or I can help Mom by carving out a little place for her to own her death and take whatever time is left to get her affairs in order. I can advocate her right to pursue happiness—which will mean making some of our own rules in an institutional system.

It will be the hardest thing I've ever done. Not because

of any philosophical stance on whether this is suicide or an argument over who owns her life. My philosophy isn't original, and my argument is debatable.

My concern is more basic.

I just don't want to lose her yet.

She might be ready but I'm not. And I don't know how to slow down this process. It's way out of my control, and I can't find a way to put it on my own terms.

So her death is about me, after all. Her death is about my life. When she is gone, I will be a portion of who I was. I will be reborn without a mother. No more protector, no more excuses. I will finally be responsible for my own life. And I will be closer than ever to losing what remains.

-whb

18

FRANCES waited all night for morning. Now that she was sure William would take care of things, she wanted to get started. She had her sights set to heaven and planned to rely on William to tie up the loose ends of what was left of this life. That was why she had always wanted him to be a doctor, so he would know what to do when the time came.

Frances watched the clock. As the minutes that made up her longest night spun by worthlessly, she finally lapsed into sleep.

The dream. It was happening all over again.

The whole house shook, the sound like lightning cracking as the plaster wall in the dining room split down the center. The floor boards in Frannie's house buckled with the explosion, and the smell of smoke began to burn her nose.

She and Bill had the same thought at the same time: *The babies*. The babies were upstairs.

Terrified, they ran to the living room and looked up the stairs. Some boards were missing and the whole staircase leaned to one side.

Frannie edged toward it but Bill pushed her back. "I'll get the children," he said. "You stay here."

"Mommy?" Sugar stood at the top of the stairs in her footed pajamas. "Mommy, what's happening?"

"Get William," she said. "Wake him up and bring him to the stairs. Daddy will bring you down. The house is on fire and we have to get out of here. Now."

But Sugar was barely five, hardly old enough to follow instructions and help with her brother while the house was burning down around her. She began to cry.

Bill took the stairs, in three long strides, stepping over the missing treads. Sugar held onto his legs, but he made her sit at the top of the stairs as he headed for the baby's room.

Unable to wait, Frannie climbed, past little Sugar who was now curled up in a ball, in search of William. He wasn't in his bed. She called for him, going from room to room, as the smoke grew thicker and the flames seeped from the cracks in the walls. She heard Bill with the crying baby in his arms. She heard him guiding Sugar down the stairs.

"I've got Randy and Sugar. Where's William?" Bill was picking up his daughter in his free arm.

"William! Baby, come to Mommy!" She called again. The flames licked at her face, her hair.

She found him there, in the midst of the fire and his face burned beyond recognition, as she, too, was consumed.

The night nurse rushed in. "Frances, Frances, honey, wake up, dear. You're having a dream."

Frances was covered in sweat, her breath was heavy and her heart beat wildly on the monitor. She tore at her face with her hands.

"Honey, you've got to calm down. It was just a dream."

"It wasn't a dream. It really happened."

"It was just a dream."

"The fire, the smoke, my babies…" She was panting, her chest and stomach moving up and down so fast she thought she might simply lift right off the bed.

Another nurse came in and injected a sedative into Frances' IV line. "You rest now, Mrs. Baldwin," she said. "Everything is going to be okay. I saw all your children. They're just fine."

Frances remembered the night of the real fire, the night she'd almost lost her first-born son. When she had found three-year-old William, he was unconscious at the foot of her bed, where he'd gone looking for her but hadn't found her. They took the boy away in an ambulance with Frances still clinging to him, and he was in the hospital with shock and smoke inhalation for days. Throughout the ordeal, he'd worn a glazed expression that scared her.

She'd seen the same expression earlier that evening on William's whisker-shadowed face as he'd sat at her bedside.

Now she knew what she had to do. He was still her son, even though he was forty, and she was not going to let him be alone with all of this. In trying to avoid the details of her own death, she had thrown him into the fire she had started.

Newly overcome by guilt, Frannie revised her plan. She was going to protect her son. She remembered this as she drifted peacefully to sleep.

The sun was streaming in the window on a beautiful fall day when Frances awoke. Her surgeon was standing beside her. She was lucid and as clear as the sunlight.

"Good," she said, "I'm glad you're here."

"Mrs. Baldwin, I've been thinking about your decision. I would like a chance to talk to you about it again. I've reevaluated your medical records, and—"

Frances waved her hand to cut him off. "Doctor, my decision stands. I do not want surgery. I don't want to die on the table and I'm not going to spend my last days on earth in a coma. And I sure don't want to take the chance that my family won't pull the plug on me."

He looked down on her. "Frances, I'm not sure you understand. Without the surgery, you will definitely die."

"I understand. I understand just fine."

"It will be a painful death."

"I am ready." She smiled at him to show that she wasn't afraid.

He grew animated. "Why? Why won't you give me a chance to save you? I just don't understand this. I've never seen anyone accept a death sentence with a smile."

"Doctor, if I deny the treatment, how long do I have to live?"

"A week, maybe two. Not long."

He hoped this information might frighten her into agreement. When faced with the absolute of death, most patients chose life.

"And what are the chances I'll live through the operation?"

"I don't like to quote odds, Mrs. Baldwin. Each patient is different and I can't be sure."

He knew it was low, but everything was relative. At what statistical value does a life become not worth the effort? He didn't know where Frances would draw the line so he avoided the question. Frances accepted his answer.

"What are the factors working against me?" she asked.

He sighed. "Well, your age, for one. The condition of your lungs, the extent to which you've been weakened by the attacks you've suffered. You've been through a lot. But it's possible, Frances. It is possible you could have the surgery, I'll fix what's wrong in your digestive tract, and you will recover. Isn't that worth taking a chance for? To live maybe five or ten more years?"

"You mean to live maybe five or ten more years while I die of COPD and congestive heart failure."

Dr. Watson didn't know her well enough to know that once she'd made up her mind, it didn't change. She'd been blessed with a powerful combination of intuition, common sense and intelligence, and she'd learned early on that her decisions were usually right. She wasn't a woman who spent much time second-guessing herself, and this logical explanation to Dr. Watson was very laborious. Still, she tried.

"If you call that living, it might be worth the chance. But it's not what I call life. The answer is, and will remain, no, Doctor." She added, "But I thank you for your enthusiasm and your efforts. Right now I just want all of these machines disconnected so I can be at peace."

Dr. Watson knew that not having the operation and disconnecting the machines were two different things. He was only the surgeon. Frances could deny his intervention, but the question of her medication and monitoring were not his responsibility.

"You will have to talk to Dr. Al-Biruni about that. She's your primary physician."

"She's not my primary physician; my primary physician is Dr. Marcus and I haven't even seen that character. I guess he doesn't do hospitals. Dr. Ali-Baba is my hospital-appointed attending physician, my case manager, the one who is supposed to attend to my needs and care. And I don't like her. She doesn't listen to me."

"She's a very qualified cardiologist."

"She's a ninny."

Dr. Ninny walked into the room making her early morning rounds. Dr. Al-Biruni suspected they were talking about her by the look on Dr. Watson's face.

"Good morning, Jim. Good morning, Frances. How are you today?"

"I'm tired. I'm tired of all of this. I was just telling Dr. Watson I'm through with treatment. No more operations and no more medicine. It's my responsibility to make those decisions, and it's my decision to just say no. That's what we tell the young ones, isn't it? 'Just say no to drugs.' Now, disconnect everything."

The doctors looked at each other. *See what I have to deal with,* their eyes tried to tell each other.

"Okay, Frances," Dr. Al-Biruni said patronizingly, "I see we're back here again. I thought you'd changed your mind about all that."

"No, I didn't really change my mind. But I was willing to give it a try. I tried to do what everyone wanted. You, my daughter, my son, my husband. But you're right, we're right back here again. Nothing is helping and the situation is only getting worse.

"No, no. I'm through with all of those questions, and I'm through with all of you. I want you to stop trying to talk me into things and do what I want done. Doc Watson says I have two weeks left. I have enough money and insurance to live that long. I really am dying this time. I'm the patient and it's my choice.

I'm of sound mind and this is what I've decided. You don't have to like it. Just do it."

Dr. Al-Biruni was ready. "Okay, Frances. But first we're sending in a psychiatrist just to confirm that 'sound mind' part. We can't take any chances."

After what she'd seen with the Xanax prescription, she wasn't convinced that this wasn't all due to a case of anxiety and depression.

Frances closed her eyes. "Yeah, I know, you might get sued. Go ahead, protect yourselves. I'll talk to the psychiatrist."

And she did. Frances talked to the psychiatrist for almost an hour, answering all of his questions about hallucinations and suicidal tendencies and her family's mental health history. She told him everything she'd been telling her other doctors, nurses, family and anyone else she thought might listen. And the psychiatrist did listen, noting that this was a patient he wished he could spend more time with so he could learn more from her about how she was preparing for death. He had a number of other patients who could benefit from her insights. People who were still in denial and suffering emotionally when the situation was beyond all hope. People who would die in mental agony instead of peace.

At the end of the hour, the psychiatrist signed the papers testifying that, in his professional opinion, Frances Baldwin was of sound mind and capable of making her own decisions. He shook Frannie's hand as he left, commended her on her spirit and courage, and wished that he had more patients who thought as clearly as she did.

19

MEANWHILE, William and his father were on the back patio having coffee, watching the sparrows and the starlings poke in the grass. Squirrels were picking up acorns from beneath the big oak tree and had already begun hiding them behind the planters and in little holes dug in the soft garden dirt. It was early fall in the Northeast, and every living thing seemed to know that winter was coming. Brown leaves were already scattered in the yard from the wind overnight, and the tomatoes were rotting on the vines. Bill was still focusing on days like this, the Indian summer that always came right before the cold weather hit. The last days of warmth and growth.

"Dad, Mom needs your help."

"I can't help. Don't ask me."

"You know Mom wants to stop treatment. We have to make some plans. They're going to make her leave the hospital. We have to find a place for her."

"If you bring her here to die, I'll have to move after she's gone." He looked at William with tears in his eyes.

"What are we supposed to do?" This was his last chance to get his father to help.

"I don't know. I can't think. It's like my brain can't think past this cup of coffee." He held it up and looked at it. "I can't think past yesterday. My life is flashing before my eyes. I can't speak. I have this lump in my throat and nothing comes out."

"Dad, this is about Mom. I really can't—"

"I told you I can't help."

"She's going to need hospice care."

William thought if he kept explaining the reality of the situation, his father might come around. This was his responsibility, the husband's responsibility, yet he refused to take it on.

"I don't want anything to do with it."

"That's not fair, Dad." William didn't want to be angry, yet his father left him no choice.

"The whole thing's not fair, Son. You and your mother seem to have some kind of agreement that I knew nothing about. I never knew she felt this way. I thought she was like me. I want to live no matter what."

"I know you do, Dad. And when the time comes, we'll honor your wishes, just like we'll honor Mom's now," William said.

"I don't understand it. This thing, this other thing that she's doing—I don't know about it and I don't want to know."

"But it's what we have to deal with."

"I can't help you, William. I just can't. You're the doctor—"

William stood and went inside. He went to his parents' bedroom and opened the safe where his mother had placed her living will. His father didn't understand that Frances was the one making the choices. He was only helping her do what she'd already decided. Bill was implying that his son was influencing her somehow, that he was *suggesting* she undertake her dying process now.

Despite the fact that he knew the truth, William felt guilty for his compliance. He hoped that his mother's living will, or advance care directive as it was officially called, would help. He hoped it would prove that this had been all in motion before he'd ever even come to town.

There was a plain white envelope under his parents' life insurance policies. William opened it and saw a common piece of lined paper with his mother's handwriting showing through the back. Unfolding the document, he read what his mother had written:

THE LIVING WILL OF FRANCES BALDWIN

I, Frances Baldwin, being of sound mind and body, want to make my wishes known regarding my end-of-life care so that my family will know how to decide if the time comes. I do NOT want to be kept alive by machines or by any other unnatural or extraordinary means.

Frances Baldwin
March 15, 1997

William's hopes were crushed. This was not a legal document. It would never be accepted by the hospital as proof of his mother's wishes if she were ever unable to speak herself. Even he had to admit he didn't know what his mother meant by "machines," or "any other unnatural or extraordinary means." She had already consented to be kept alive by a ventilator after her operation. She had an IV drip with sugar water to keep her hydrated. Technically, without it she would die of dehydration. That was kind of unnatural, wasn't it? Was a shock of electricity to her heart extraordinary? Because she'd had that twice now to convert her heart to normal rhythm.

A legally acceptable, clearly articulated advance care directive did not exist. William placed the envelope back under the life insurance policies and locked the safe. The document was useless. He made a mental note to talk to the social worker at the hospital to see what form was legal in Pennsylvania. He would get his mother to sign one as soon as possible. He didn't know how much longer she would be at the hospital, and he wanted to make sure the spirit of her wishes was properly known by everyone who provided her care.

"Dad?" William went back out on the porch.

"Yes." Bill was still watching the squirrels.

"I know this is really hard on you. It's hard on all of us. Mom said you have some Valium in the medicine chest. Maybe you ought to take some. It might help you deal with things."

"I don't want it."

"Maybe you should just carry some in your pocket, just in case something happens and you feel you need it. The last thing we need is for you to have a heart attack or something. Are you taking your blood pressure meds?"

"I'm taking my medicine. But I don't want Valium."

"Okay." William made a mental note to get a couple out of the bottle and keep them with him, just in case.

"William?"

"Yes, Dad."

"I thought we were happy." Bill took a sip of his coffee to choke back the emotion rising in his throat. "I used to sit out here every morning with your mother. I thought we were happy."

William looked at the satellite radio as soon as he turned on the car.

I Am Free By *Newsboys*

As he drove, he searched for meaning in the title, imagining what he might find when he got to the hospital. He hoped she wasn't gone already.

He almost looked forward to having some control, to being in charge of the fight. He was prepared to fight with the doctors. He was prepared to fight with his father and his sister. He was prepared for the hospital ethics committee and the social worker. He'd called an old friend, an attorney, and had him on stand-by if needed.

William had a plan, and he needed to carry it out for his mother. Overnight, he'd done some research on the internet about Medicare and his mother's supplemental insurance. He developed an understanding of how they would both be needed to pay for a nursing facility or hospice. He was ready to put into motion everything that needed to be done so his mother would be at peace. He drove slowly and carefully to the hospital, reserving his energy for what lay ahead.

"Good morning, William." Pat looked up from the nurse's station when he got off the elevator. "We moved your mother down the hall out of the CCU. She'll be glad to see you. She's got a surprise for you." Pat smiled.

William was confused but followed her directions to Room 212.

20

DESPITE his preparation the previous night, William was in no way prepared for what he saw.

A quarantine sign on the door warned of his mother's blood infection. He knew what MRSA was: *Methicillin-resistant Staphylococcus aureus.* A super-bug, a drug-resistant bacterium that people can contract in hospitals. Some people died from MRSA because it doesn't respond to normal antibiotics.

William sighed. Another complication.

Inside, it was quiet and still. His mother was sitting there smiling, just waiting for him as if she'd known he would arrive at any moment.

"Look at me, William."

He did. She was propped up on her pillows, the sheets and her nightgown were noticeably clean and crisp. Her skin was bright and clear with a blush of pink in her cheeks, and her blue eyes were radiant. She was lovely. He caught his breath, entranced, and struggled to make sense of it.

"Look, William. It's all gone."

She's well again? Adrenaline surged through his body and he felt dizzy. What was going on?

His mother's left hand was neatly bandaged. Her right hand had no needles or tape. His eyes wandered in the direction where the IV tubes used to run, but there were none. There was no monitoring machine in this new room, no beeps, no clicks, no hum. The only sound was the quiet rattle of his mother's breathing and the steady swoosh of oxygen through the tube at her nose.

"I'm at peace, William. I've made it happen, all by myself. No more treatment." Her smile lit her face from within.

"But how—"

"I got my doctors to agree this morning. It's all taken care of, honey, I did this by myself. I didn't need to rely on you after all. I can see now that wasn't fair. I feel so good. Now I can die peacefully."

William wanted to feel the same peace, but he had so many questions.

"Mom." He exhaled and sat down to consider the situation. He didn't know what to say, so he said, "Mom, you've got a blood infection. There's a quarantine sign on the door. I guess you got it through your hand."

Frances only laughed. Her eyes twinkled as she held up her hand. "Isn't it ironic that the one thing I was the most afraid of is now the thing that will give me what I want? The Lord works in mysterious ways, Son."

William was clearly confounded. She gave him a minute to process the morning's events.

"Listen, Son. I'm getting tired but I need you to help with one thing." Her voice was slowing down, and she was obviously uncomfortable. She shifted her weight in the bed.

"Anything."

"I met with the social worker this morning, Mrs. DeMessa, I think her name is. She's sending the hospice people here later. I'll need to sign some papers." She coughed hard to clear her airways and finish the rest of what she had to say. William noticed for the first time that she was sweating.

"The best part of all, William, is that I don't have to go home. Your father doesn't want me there. He said if I died in the house, it would be too upsetting and he would have to move."

"I know. I talked to him about it." William wondered where this was all going.

"I don't want him to have to do that. It's his home. So they're going to let me stay in the hospital, in this room, but I'll get hospice care instead of curing care. It's a new thing they have going with the hospice organization for people who are going to die soon. Sit with me William, while I sleep, and wait for them to come in. Thank God, this is all working out."

She patted the bed and reached for his hand. William offered it and found himself tracing the lines in her palm, as he had when he'd been a young child. It was hot from her fever and she trembled slightly.

"I'm so cold," his mother said quietly. William checked her blankets. There were four of them.

When her breathing slowed, William put her hand beneath the covers. This was how he'd hoped it would come out, but it threw him off balance because it had been so easy. He hadn't had to fight for her, after all. She'd fought for herself.

Just like her, he thought, *always taking me off-guard.*

He chuckled to himself and turned on the television, found the music channel and selected the elevator music over the Sinatra station. Something to keep them both calm. No more inputs. He needed some time to process. Absently, he read the morning paper as she slept. She opened her eyes a half-hour later.

"Turn that music off. It's driving me crazy." She smiled softly and her eyelids were heavy with the promise of relief. "I guess we missed the game shows. See if you can find that antiques program or something."

He chuckled again, this time with the pleasure of not knowing his mother as well as he thought he did.

The hospice representative arrived just before noon and introduced herself as Kristen Swift. Unsure of whether his mother was awake or asleep, William took the young woman down the hall to the family lounge. He paged through the pamphlets and watched as she flipped through a hard-cover loose leaf binder with plastic pages. The presentation answered all of his questions from a business point of view. He knew his mother would be pleased to learn that Medicare would cover the hospice care.

"But how exactly will my mother be cared for?"

If the hospital wasn't going to be taking care of her, he wanted to know who was. Kristen smiled, anticipating his approval.

"Actually, Mr. Baldwin, her care will be provided by the same doctors and nurses who care for her now. She'll have what we call 'comfort care.' Oxygen and whatever medication she needs so that she's not afraid or in pain. The nurses will keep her comfortable and dispense the medications. Her attending physician will check on her every day to record her vital signs and assess how she's doing with the medications. In addition, we'll have a visiting nurse from our staff act as a case supervisor. His name is Timothy Tyler. He'll evaluate her condition and ensure that the hospital is doing everything possible to make your mother comfortable."

William liked the program, especially since it sounded like his mother would be getting more care than ever. He liked the hospital's nursing staff, and they all seemed to like Frances. The best part was that she wouldn't have to experience the anxiety of an ambulance ride or acclimatizing to a new location and routine. Her last weeks would be free of worry. It was everything he'd wanted.

"Well, okay, where do we sign up?" He didn't see the need to talk to his father or to his sister or brother. He knew what they thought already. He was his mother's representative, a job he took seriously and now willingly.

"We'll need your mother to sign some forms. Is she able?"

"And willing," William replied.

They went down the hall to wake Frances. As they walked, William told her a little about his mother and the family's situation.

"If your family would like some counseling, we do that, too," Kristen said. "We are here to support you however you need. We have people your father can talk to. It sounds like he's having a tough time. Denial can rob people of the opportunity to get close to the dying."

"He'd never do it," William said. He just couldn't imagine his father letting the wraps off with a stranger. "But I'll mention it to my sister."

They reached the room again just as a nurse was coming through the door with a squeaky blood pressure machine on wheels. William smiled at her, knocked on the door and motioned Kristen inside.

"Mom, the hospice person is here. This is Kristen Swift, and she has some papers for you to sign."

Frances woke immediately, as if she had already been in the middle of a conversation with them. "That's good, William. Thank you. Just give me the forms."

"Mom, I want Ms. Swift to know that you understand what you're signing up for."

Frances repeated her intention, demonstrating that she understood what hospice care was and affirming that was ready to participate. Having a witness somehow relieved William of the guilt associated with not having the approval of his family. If they weren't going to listen to Frances, then he was glad someone else besides himself would.

It didn't hurt that Kristen was pretty and seemed really interested in him and his mother. For a moment he imagined himself calling her up to talk sometime. Then he caught himself in this thought and mentally smacked himself. He missed Diane.

Frances signed all of the papers and closed her eyes again. Kristen completed the paperwork and gave William a folder containing informational materials and copies of everything they had signed.

"Read through it all later, Mr. Baldwin. There's some really good information in the brochure."

As he walked her to the elevator, Kristen said, "Here's my card with my twenty-four hour telephone number. Call me anytime with any concerns you may have. I'm here to help."

"I hope I'll never have to use it." William meant it.

When he returned to his mother, the nurse was giving her a dose of morphine. As she settled back down and closed her eyes, she breathed slowly and her chest rattled. She was obviously in pain yet she seemed contented. She was peaceful, almost happy, and a smile crossed her lips as she fell asleep.

There was a blue pamphlet about the dying experience in the folder Kristen left. William read it carefully. Some of it was a med-school refresher, some of it things he already knew about dying but now read in a new context, and some of it was new information he had never known but was glad to have. He knew a dying person went through stages of separation, but he only remembered learning about the physical changes. He now read about the emotional withdrawal and the spiritual transition of a person who had one foot in this world and one foot out of it. It was a complete description of his mother, and his heart quickened as he read it. *This is normal*, he realized. *What my mother is experiencing is completely normal. She was right. She really has been dying.* Learning this changed everything.

This had always been his way, reading a book to understand how things worked. He had never been one for the chaos of hands-on experiments or experience. He preferred to read about something and reason out the details. That's why he liked his work so much. Designing computer networks was all rational and logical with a fixed number of outcomes; there were no messy human variables.

When he'd been in med school, he'd read a lot of books about death and about the cultural aspects of the transition. He had sought to understand the logic and traditions behind the emotions and behavior he witnessed. In the process, he'd collected in his intellectual reserve many concepts and theories to explain grief and suffering. As a student, everything had been conceptual or theoretical. This was entirely different.

He stared at the television screen and tried to piece together everything that had happened. He'd arrived in Philadelphia literally ignorant of the issues, but he'd somehow become the expert on his mother's physical and emotional state. It had taken every bit of knowledge and courage he had.

William realized that participating in his mother's death was the most emotionally authentic thing he'd ever done. While it was novel and kept his interest, it nevertheless made him very uneasy. And exhausted. It had required all of his energy just to keep up with the changes over the last few weeks. With every subtle shift in her condition, his opinion of his mother's circumstance had changed, and his feelings seemed to ricochet from corner to corner of his belief system.

He wanted to sleep for days, yet he wanted to have every minute with his mother. Being with her made him feel in control of an uncontrollable situation.

Frances was clearly happy with the turn of events. She looked like a sleeping angel; there was no other way to describe her. As William watched, her face took on a porcelain glow. Her eyelashes lifted in perfect waves against her cheeks. Her clean hair had been combed and lay in soft curls against the crisp sheet. She looked the picture of peace.

The grace that filled her then would carry them all through the weeks to come. Her tranquility, a quality he had never before associated with his mother, would bring them all peace.

With the children gone for the evening, Bill broke his silence.

"I love you, Frannie. But I don't understand why you're doing this."

Frances turned her head away from him. As much as she knew he was suffering, she didn't feel she owed him an explanation. He had never given her one.

"Why are you giving up? Don't we have a good life together?"

Bill was choking on his words already. There was only one answer he was prepared to hear, and he knew those were the words Frances would not speak. He suddenly regretted asking a question he didn't want the answer to.

While Frances felt a sudden surge of compassion, she'd thought about this too hard and too long to feel differently. It was impossible for her to extend herself and deal with his feelings. After all, it hadn't even occurred to Bill that she had many of her own feelings about her demise. *But what did I expect*, she thought, *my feelings are no more important to him on my deathbed than they have been at any other time in our marriage.* Too tired to start an argument, she let the silence hang in the air, dripping its contents slowly.

Something else was troubling Bill, even more than his wife's decision to leave him. Finally he said what he had been thinking for the last week.

"What am I supposed to do now?"

The silence grew juicier, more threatening. Either it would hang like a storm between them forever or it would break in one big burst. The light flashed. Frances decided to give him the truth they had both avoided for so long. This was no time for darkness.

Over the years, she'd found no reason to bring it up. Maybe she chose that moment because the shadow of Bill's selfishness had grown so dense. After all, there she was, facing the end of her life head-on, punctured and probed and enduring the pain and indignity of it all, and his main concern was about what he was going to do next week, next month, next year. And he was bringing it to her as if she was supposed to solve his problem.

Maybe she chose that moment because it was her last opportunity to clear out any confusion about exactly what he should feel sorry for after she was gone. It was something he obviously needed to be told, and something she had been meaning to tell him for years. Yes, that was it. Frances didn't have any more time for inaccuracies, for tomorrow she might lose consciousness, and Bill would live the rest of his life in his made-up world where he was the hapless victim of her desertion. The storm had to come now if it were to ever clear.

She shifted to a sitting position and winced in pain. She wasn't sure if it was from the incision in her stomach, or from the bedsores on her buttocks, or perhaps from the memory that clouded her vision.

"I know about Marion. I've known all along." She looked at Bill straight-on, facing him as best she could.

He stiffened and lost his breath. He looked down to the grey tile floor and noticed the discolored seams where the filth had collected between the squares of waxed vinyl. Frances took a deep breath of the oxygen offered at her nose, as deeply as she could expand her lungs. For the first time in over twenty years she exhaled the sadness that had constricted her.

Still Bill made no reply. He was fighting the tears that welled up in his eyes, fighting the urge to leave the room, fighting the urge to deny her knowledge of his infidelity. At that point Bill didn't even know for certain why he had loved this other woman, this Marion who had made him feel like the man he used to be—the man he had been before he married Frances and began making the millions of concessions that left him feeling emasculated and compromised, not himself at all. He couldn't even remember Marion's face, nor could he remember the exact words that had ended their passionate affair after more than ten years.

Bill was not a self-reflective man, and at this moment he was greatly confused. The individual compartments of his life had edged together with a simply spoken phrase and a thundering impact. He tried to stay focused. He couldn't see the whole picture, and would not if he could fight it.

"Bill, I know it went on for a while and that it stopped twelve years ago."

She paused and waited for him to react, to say something, anything. But he did not. Just as he had never said anything before.

She continued facing off with the demons that had sheltered in the family closet. "I knew when it was over. But I also know you never came back to me. You slept in my bed. We were intimate, but you were never again my husband." Her voice lowered to a whisper. It was not soft nor was it accusing. It was a voice speaking a painful truth that needed to be heard without being hammered into his head. She wanted him to understand, to feel her pain, but she was long past needing to hurt him back.

"Your heart just wasn't in it, Bill. So don't go acting now like you can't live without me."

The shame began as a kick in his gut; it spread quickly until it paralyzed his muscles. He had stopped breathing.

Frances wheezed as she drew oxygen. Her head relaxed against the pillow. For the first time, the muscles around her ribs softened, the clench in her intestines released. Her shoulders were warm with the blood that flowed through them, and her hands were no longer cold.

"I love you, Bill. But I don't know if I can forgive you. How can I when you never even asked me to?" Her face grew soft and she repeated, "I love you."

She tried to find his eyes while she waited for a reply. There was none, so she continued.

"The truth is—and I guess this is the time for the truth—you are not the man I married. I learned to live without him a long time ago. Imagine the loneliness."

She closed her eyes to feel it yet again—maybe for the last time. If she could conjure it into the room, Bill might feel it too and understand she could not bear it as an invalid. The loneliness had been hard enough when she had been a whole woman. Now that her health was gone, she could not stand strong against the isolation that shared their home.

"The greatest loneliness of all is when you are lonely with someone else, in the same house, in the same life. I've done it for over twenty years and I can't do it any more. How would you take care of me now, Bill? You couldn't. So you have to let me go. Let me go my own way." She folded her blanket around her chest.

"Now go home and come back tomorrow to see me. I'm not alone here. They take very good care of me."

Frances closed her eyes and fell immediately to sleep. Bill collected his jacket, carefully kissed her forehead, and walked to the car. It was a clear night and the autumn chill was descending with the dew. He had no real awareness as he drove home; Bill's thoughts were all caught at the dam of his denial.

I can't even begin to put this puzzle together, he thought to himself, *it's all too complicated.*

Already he had some sense that his wife's death was more than a resignation to illness or a spiritual pursuit. It was her way of divorcing him. It was a battle Bill didn't fight because he couldn't have won, he wouldn't have won, in the eyes of the law, their children, or anyone else. Frances' God was her attorney, and the jury had awarded everything to her in light of her pain and suffering.

21

SUGAR decided to go to work instead of the hospital. She had nothing more to say to her mother. William was able to handle it all now. *I've done all I could*, she thought.

She called her office, a local branch of a large temporary worker agency, and told the receptionist she would be in as soon as she got the kids off to school.

"Your mom's feeling better, then?" Olivia asked as the telephones rang incessantly in the background.

Sugar shook off her guilt. "She seems to have everything under control. Thanks."

As the recruiter with the longest service and best track record, she had more flexibility in her job than others might; she could do much of her work from home if she needed to care for a sick child or for any of the other minor emergencies that otherwise handicapped single mothers in the workplace. Most days, though, she was eager to get to her job. She found her self-worth there, a positive reflection of the woman she aspired to be. She wasn't anyone's daughter or mother or ex-wife; at work she offered just a sliver of her whole self. A polished sliver with the sparkle of a nice wardrobe, an even temper and an uncomplicated smile. And it was always enough. The one-dimensional Sugar was always valued and treated with respect.

The work itself was easy, and over the years she'd become an important part of the success of the business. While they were one of the smallest, they were also one of the top producing offices in the region, largely due to the relationships Sugar had built with the major corporations that had moved to the area over the years.

Emotionally wrung out by the past weeks, she was eager to regain her former identity. Slipping into her best fall suit, a blue pinstripe with a gathered waist, and a white blouse with a small ruffle at the end of the sleeve, she noticed she'd lost a few pounds. Well, one good thing had come out of this.

She heard the boys talking and knew they were in the kitchen.

"Mom, Jason just threw up." Eric said as he ate his large bowl of chocolate cereal.

Jason was sitting on the sofa watching television. He said nothing. He was only ten and Sugar had never left him home alone before, not even when he was well.

"Oh no. Jason, did you really throw up?"

"Yeah."

"Are you feeling any better now?"

"No. I might hurl again."

Of course. Sugar closed her eyes and tried not to cry. She'd just wanted to feel normal for one day before having to deal with sickness again.

"Baby, I was supposed to go to work today. I already called to tell them I was coming in."

"I'm sorry, Mom." He looked away from the cartoon, his face pale and his eyes half-closed.

That's not what Sugar wanted. Now she felt guilty for making a sick kid feel inconvenient.

"Maybe I can go to Dad's," he said.

David. Oh, that's just what she needed this morning. But she had no choice. With a sigh, she dialed his number, hoping he wouldn't answer the phone from a bed he was sharing with yet another woman. Even if he was alone, she hated to ask him for anything. She wanted him to think her life was going just fine without him. Even though it wasn't.

"Cindy?" He had never called her Sugar.

Unmasked by the caller ID, she admitted, "Yeah, it's me." She tried to sound casual and in control.

"Listen, Jason woke up sick this morning and I have an important day at work. Can you take him?"

It was a reasonable request. David ran a direct-mail business from his home office. Jason could stay in his bedroom there while his father worked.

The odds were against her, though. David had never made visitation very easy, so she was surprised when he said, "Sure." And then, "I'll be right over to get him. Give me twenty minutes." She wasn't even going to have to drop him off.

This was strange. Her stomach flipped, and for a moment she wondered whether she had the same bug as Eric. No, the only thing bothering her was David.

While she was getting Jason's things together and making sure Eric had everything he needed, she noticed how they were both beginning to look just like their father when he was young. She'd met David when they'd been in high school, and he'd been as lanky and as freckled as his sons were now. But that seemed like a very long time ago. They had married right after graduation and put off having kids for years while they traveled and focused on themselves and each other. She remembered feeling abandoned by David sometime after Jason was born, but she'd thought it normal, something men went through after their wives became mothers. It didn't seem to be of consequence at the time.

Sugar took a moment to fix her hair and makeup again before heading down the stairs. She brushed on a little more eye shadow and put another coat of gloss on her lips.

She had discovered David was sleeping around by accident. She'd trusted him completely up until the moment she'd seen the hotel bill on his credit card. When she'd looked back on his statements, she'd found hotel charges occurring at least twice a month. What had he been thinking, and why hadn't he just paid cash? If he had, Sugar might still be blissfully unaware that her high-school sweetheart had enacted the ultimate cliché: he'd slept with her best friend. When she'd confronted him, he hadn't argued. He'd simply left and never come back, except Wednesdays and every other weekend to spend time with the boys. Now he was standing at her door, looking through the glass at her. She let him in.

"God, do you look great, Cindy."

She bristled. She could only imagine where his eyes had been, and it felt unclean to have them on her.

"Jason's in the family room, David. Maybe you could give him a hand getting out to the car. He really doesn't look well but he doesn't seem to have a fever." She fussed about with her bag and a pile of papers as if they were very important.

"Before I do, I need to talk to you."

Sugar's knees weakened. She was sure she wasn't ready for whatever he was going to say. *I'm getting married. I have cancer. I'm moving to Oregon. I'm broke.* With David, she had to be ready for anything. She was never going to let him surprise her again. He closed the front door behind him and spoke softly.

"I've been thinking a lot about you lately. I can't get you off my mind. I miss you, Cyn. I close my eyes at night and there you are. I keep fighting the urge to call you up and just talk like we used to. I don't know what I'm trying to say, but nothing seems to feel right. I know I've been a real fool."

He took a step toward her, freckles and all. She took a step back.

She certainly wasn't ready for this. Of all the things he might have said, she never figured it would be the one thing she needed to hear. But she could barely hear it. Maybe he hadn't said it after all. It sounded like a movie playing on the television from another room. *I can't get you off my mind.* Static. She could hardly make out the words as her head swam with the implications.

"David, you can't do this to me."

"I know."

"No, you don't. You just can't walk in here and change my world like this. It's not fair. I have enough to handle. It's not fair." She moved as far away from him as she could. Her face flushed and her words came quickly and maniacally.

"Just take Jason and go. Please. Just go." Her arms crossed in front of her.

"But—"

She held up her hand. "Just go, David. Now."

When Eric left for school, Sugar took off her suit and hung it carefully in the closet. She combed out her hair and called in to work.

"I won't be in until this afternoon."

She took off her stockings and went back to bed.

Randy Williams looked in the mirror near the door. He leaned over and examined himself closely, then closed the door of his apartment. For the last time. He hadn't told Monica he was leaving. Monica, sweet Monica. He just couldn't do it. He'd planned to tell her before she left for her business trip, one of many business trips, but he just couldn't look her in the face and tell her he'd taken the job in Salt Lake City. Instead, he'd kissed her on the lips, a long passionate kiss, and carried her suitcase to the cab.

She'd been so nice to him. Monica had asked him to move in six months ago after his last girlfriend threw him out. He had nowhere to live and New York was not a good place to try to find a home on short notice. What had started as a hospitable gesture soon developed into romance and a devoted couple's lifestyle.

It had been an adventure for him. In six months he'd never stopped trying to sweep Monica off her feet. He loved to see the thrill on her face and loved even more the passion his efforts produced once they got in bed. Monica was uninhibited. When he said, "I love you," he thought he meant it, even though he suspected he was describing a more primal satisfaction. In reality he loved how he felt, and he wondered if he could ever see her clearly enough to know whether he loved her or not.

Randy had sought out the job in Salt Lake City. Knowing it was time to leave New York, he'd picked a place as far away as he could imagine. He did this from time to time, picking up and moving his life from one city to another in search of a new life, a new chance. New people and new places. New thrills and new chances to create himself.

While the legal position was not quite of the importance he'd led his mother to believe, it was nevertheless a respectable one that would afford him a better opportunity than the dead-end staff attorney position in Manhattan. And because the cost of living was so much lower, he'd even be able to afford a nice apartment.

He'd cleaned up Monica's place after he'd packed his bags so she wouldn't feel his absence. He removed the gourmet coffee from the shelf and fanned her six tea boxes out to fill the space. He put his granola, his vodka and his peanut butter in a bag and shoved it down the trash chute along with his magazine subscriptions. He left his sparkling water in case she might need it for guests.

With every intention of calling her once she got back from her trip, and with every intention of explaining himself, Randy took his two suitcases and three boxes down the elevator to his car.

After a short visit with his wife, Bill headed to a local bar. He hadn't been there in a long time, perhaps a year, but Mario was still glad to see him.

"Bill Baldwin. How the hell you been, man?" Mario was already pulling him a beer from the tap.

"Shit, Mario. Not good."

Bill sat down and took a long draw. Cold and clean. How long had it been since he'd had a drink? Not drinking had been an inconvenience rather than a problem for him. But it had been a lifestyle change, for sure. He'd stopped drinking because his doctor advised him not to mix alcohol with the blood pressure medicine. But Bill wasn't concerned about his blood pressure now. He just wanted a cold beer.

He liked this bar because he was his own person here. No one knew his wife. No one knew he had kids. He was just Bill from the neighborhood who occasionally came in to have a brew and a shuffleboard game or two with his buddies. Life was simple when he was simply Bill. But things hadn't been simple for such a long time. He'd always considered himself an independent man, a loner of sorts, but still a good-times kind of guy. As he sipped his second mug he began to get a sense, a vague feeling of disappointment, that Frannie was right. He was not the man he used to be.

In the years since he'd retired, he had spent nearly every moment with his wife. Now that he thought about it, he wondered why. He tried to remember the day she'd asked him to stay home, the exact words she'd used to convince him to give up his separateness. But he couldn't. The truth was that he'd given it all up out of convenience because as he got older, it had required too much effort. Frances had made his life easy.

While the kids were growing, he was responsible for bringing in the money but still managed to have his nights out as simply Bill. After he retired, though, he had no responsibility except to respond to Fran's requests and carry on arguments whenever she started them. That, and his chores, had consumed all his time. He'd spent the last ten years in just this way.

Now Bill was alone with himself. In a bar. With a beer.

And he liked it.

"Hey Mario. Did I ever tell you about the time we caught a forty-pound lobster off the coast?"

He hadn't. And he hadn't told Mario about his first girlfriend or his first job or about the time he spent the night in the brig when he'd been in the Army. Bill spent the afternoon teaching Mario all about the Bill he used to be. He drank a lot of beer, he laughed at his own jokes, and bought himself a roast beef sandwich.

"You know what, Mario?"

"What, Bill?"

"I gotta get me a woman. Damn."

It was April 1949. Bill Baldwin and his two friends sat in the diner smoking cigarettes and eating French fries. Bill was considered by most women, and most men, to be the best-looking one of their crowd. He had an athlete's physique with soft brown hair combed away from his face in waves, a perfect smile with clear white teeth, and dark brown eyes into which women lost themselves. Dreamy. That was the word women used to describe him.

Bill played baseball whenever he wasn't working at the paper factory doing physical labor. He had a good, secure job there and was liked by his supervisors and coworkers. Everybody liked Bill Baldwin. At twenty years old, he seemed to have everything.

"Damn, I gotta get me a woman." Bill Baldwin had everything except a steady girlfriend.

"Yeah, you sure do. What happened to MaryLou?"

"Cute, but she couldn't kiss worth a damn. I need me a *real* woman." The problem with MaryLou was that she'd been too meek, too slow in conversation. But Bill couldn't tell that to his friends. They wouldn't understand.

"You can buy one of those 'real women' downtown, Bill, if

that's what you're looking for." Charles raised his eyebrows to insinuate that he knew what he was talking about when it came to real women.

"Nah, I've had my share of those. My real woman's got to have class."

"Pearl jewelry and a good family?" Freddie teased.

"No. Wit and enough sass to keep me in line, that's what I mean. Besides, what would I do with a good family? Her daddy'd shoot me. And she better not be expecting any pearls. I'm a poor boy, Freddie, you know that. Just a poor working-class boy."

Frances Mayfield walked in the door of the diner with her cousin Mary, who lived in the neighborhood. Every male head turned and women put their heads down to gossip. Mary was beautiful, a gorgeous redhead with curls and white skin and long legs that made them all think of a wild young foal running free in the grass. She tossed her mane and looked for an empty booth, chatting up a few people along the way and leaving smiles in her wake. Bill rolled his eyes in appreciation.

"Look at that, boys. That's what I'm talking about. A real woman."

"She's out of your league, buddy. She's got much bigger fish to fry and you ain't more than a tadpole."

"How can you say that? She doesn't even know who I am." Bill put down his fork and leaned over for a better view.

"Hello? You dated her in high school, remember?"

"Mary?" It was Bill's turn to be confused.

"Yeah." Freddie laughed. "Mary."

"I wasn't talking about Mary. Jeez, she's a little girl playin' dress-up compared to the other one. Who's that she's with?"

He nodded in Frances' direction, with obvious appreciation and interest.

She was dressed plainly, but her clothes fit her well. Very well. Her dark hair was combed in a bob and she wore a touch of red lipstick. She was demure, movie-star classy. She didn't have a trace of Mary's pin-up girl beauty.

"That's Mary's cousin. Not sure about her name, Francine or Francie or something like that. She lives near the art museum, I think. Don't see her often but I understand she's a bit tough."

"Tough? Street tough? She don't look street tough to me. Anyway, I bet I could soften her up."

"Oh, yeah, I'm sure you could." Freddie winked at Charles. "Once the poor girl experiences the true depth of your charm and intelligence, she'll fall head over heels for you."

"Happens all the time, my boys. Just watch."

Bill stood tall, set his jaw and first stopped at a table with four women. He talked to them all, made them smile, and left them with a joke. All the while, he tried to catch Frances' eye. It worked. She was watching. It was hard not to notice Bill.

She watched him, and he watched her, as he worked his way past two more tables of attentive females. Finally, he slid onto the bench beside Mary.

"Hey, Mary. Long time, no see. You're as beautiful as ever. How's your Dad doin'?"

Bill had worked for Mary's dad at the gas station when he'd been in high school.

"He's holdin' up. You know he was sick last year."

"Yeah, I heard that. He's better?"

"Mostly." She didn't want to talk about her father so she

flirted with him. "Hey, Billy, what are you doing over here anyways? Come to buy me a shake?"

"Two lovely ladies like you shouldn't be here alone with no male escorts. It's a dangerous world, you know."

He tilted his chin down and looked at them through his eyebrows, trying to look dangerous. They giggled. He bought Mary a float and Frances a shake, and he did everything he could to get Mary to stop hanging on his arm. His plan was not working well at all. He tried to ask Frances about herself, and she tried to answer, but Mary repeatedly turned the conversation away from her cousin and back to the high school days when she and Bill had dated.

For a moment, Frances couldn't tell if he was flirting with her or with her cousin. *What am I thinking*, Frances thought harshly. *Everyone wants Mary.*

Suddenly self-conscious, Frances compared her own dark hair and faded sweater with Mary's shine and brilliance. She began to retreat. Her head grew lower and lower and her body smaller and smaller as she turned inward to a place where she was protected from Bill's probing eyes and Mary's superior ease. She stood and made an excuse.

"Gee. I just realized I have to get to work." She didn't mention that she had another hour before the start of her shift at the department store, but Frances would be more content walking around the block a few times than sitting there, invisible, as Mary and Bill relived their glory days.

"I appreciate the malted and your attention, Bill, but I'm sure you have more flirting to get done before dinner time. I'll be on my way so you can finish up."

Letting her sarcasm speak for her, Frances gave her cousin a little smile. Mary smiled back, glad to get Bill to herself. He tried for fifteen minutes to get away from Mary, eventually promising to call her again and take her out sometime. He nearly ran out of the diner, hoping that somehow Frances lingered outside. But she was gone.

His buddies followed him out, asking for a play-by-play. Just as he started to create a story about his brilliant success, he saw Frances rounding the corner away from the diner. He started after her.

"Boys, that's the woman I'm gonna marry," he said over his shoulder. He broke into a run.

Bill chased after Frances. He chased her for months—down the street, around her better judgment, through her suspicion and across her defenses—before she finally admitted she was in love with him. As soon as he heard this, with one of his world-famous smiles and an earnest promise of commitment, he asked Frances to be his wife. They were married three months later.

22

William tuned in for his daily message from God.

Alive By Rebecca St. James

He was relieved. He'd had a nagging feeling that his mother had died in the middle of the night and no one had called. He settled in for a normal day.

It was early September. He'd been measuring the advance of autumn by a large maple tree at the hospital's round-about. The plump, healthy green of summer had already begun to fade, and the leaves were taking on another, as-yet undefined color in their sharpening veins. If a big storm came, it would blow the green leaves right off before they aged. If the weather stayed too warm, they'd brown slowly without a colorful display at all. But if the nights turned cold the way they normally did this time of year, it wouldn't be long before the leaves caught fire in a blaze of yellow or red. William hoped to see a brilliant fall before he returned to the West Coast. He missed the Northeast autumn.

Inside the hospital, everything looked the same but Frances seemed more tired. Her voice was weaker, but her mind was obviously still sharp and active.

"Dad wants to know what to do with all the Get Well cards you've been receiving at home. He's got a big stack of them."

Frannie's book club, her neighbors, her oldest friends, her church group—all of them had been shut out. Every night there were messages from at least five people wondering whether they should visit her in the hospital. Every night, no one called them back.

"Oh, those poor people, still holding out hope I'll get well. I don't want the cards. Keep them at home."

"So what is he supposed to do with them?"

"I don't know. He'll figure it out. But I don't want them here." She thought for a moment and added, "Thank you."

"One more thing," William said. "Uncle Holden wants to visit you again. Dad thinks you ought to see him to make peace."

"Tell Holden I will see him, but only for twenty minutes. That's all I can do."

William would never understand the issues between his mother and her brother. He only hoped things never grew that tense between him and any of his relatives. Especially when it came time to die. He envisioned everything resolved before he left.

Sugar arrived then with two cups of coffee and handed one to William. She leaned over and kissed her mother on the cheek.

"Good, I'm glad you're both here," Frances said. "We need to talk about the funeral."

Sugar and William glanced at each other for support. They shrugged their shoulders, took a sip of coffee, and took their seats.

"Let's talk about the viewing first."

"I thought you wanted to be cremated." Sugar had heard it all before. At least she thought she had.

"I do."

"I thought you said, 'No wake.'"

"I did."

Frances explained the custom of an Irish wake, where mourning goes on for a few days before the funeral.

"It's barbaric. Too much sadness. But a short viewing is fine. And I want my funeral to be a celebration of my life. So here's how it will go."

She described the dress she wanted to wear for the viewing. She preferred a pastel color in which she looked best.

"You remember Aunt Bessie?" She turned to Sugar, expecting her to know exactly what she meant.

"Yes. We went to her funeral. That's the only time I ever met her. I guess I really didn't meet her, though. She was dead, after all."

"Right. Well, I remember that she looked like a princess in her casket. All sequins and pearls. That's the way I want to be. A princess. For one day."

Sugar laughed. "I'm not sure I can find glass slippers, Mom, on such short notice."

"Dyed to match will be just fine, size six-and-a-half. I want to be a princess." She handed Sugar the cosmetics from the storage compartment under her bedside tray, so the undertaker could make her look as realistic as possible. "Use the pink lipstick."

After a short, two-hour viewing, "Not too long, it's too depressing," she said, her body should be moved to St. Francis Church where she wanted a Mass for the Dead held for her. She wanted a lot of upbeat music, and told Sugar the songs she wanted sung, although she could not remember the names of any of them.

"You know," she said to Sugar, "the one about eagle wings." She hummed the tune and closed her eyes. "I love that one.

That's the way I want you to think of me. Free. Flying. On eagle wings."

"That's the name of it, Mom. 'On Eagles' Wings,'" Sugar knew the one.

"Okay, so you sing that, and then," Frances said, with a whoosh of her arms, "put me back in the hearse and whisk me away to the crematorium." She wiped her hands against each other as if finishing a job. "That's it."

William waited for Frances to finish but she didn't. She was closing her eyes again.

"Mom, what do you want us to do with your ashes?" He hoped she wasn't going to tell them to split them up and put them on the mantle.

"Oh, yes. My ashes. I want my brother Holden to let them go off the back of his boat in the Chesapeake Bay. I love it there. That's why I want to talk to him. Twenty minutes. You tell him only twenty minutes."

Her day's purpose completed, Frances fought off her drowsiness.

"Did I ever tell you about the rainbow?"

"What rainbow, Mom?" Sugar pulled her chair in to hear the story. There wouldn't be many more.

"The rainbow on my parents' grave."

"No, you never told us. Tell us about the rainbow."

Frances drew a long, rumbling breath and began her story.

"On the first anniversary of my mother's death, I asked your father to take me to my parents' grave. They're buried together. It was pouring rain the whole time we drove. Then it started letting up and we stopped at a flower stand and bought some flowers. The downpour started all over, and we had to stand under the awning for fifteen minutes until it slowed enough to get into the car. Rain, I mean you've never seen so much rain." She stopped and caught her breath.

"So we pull up to the cemetery to find the plot. By then, the rain had stopped. As we walked up we saw this rainbow. It ended right on my parents' grave. I mean *right on it.* Your father even has a picture of it. Ask him to show you sometime. The rainbow was *right on it.*

"We were both dumbfounded. Imagine it, will you? I wanted to cry but instead I said to your father, 'Good, they owed me a rainbow!'"

William and Sugar smiled, wondering if their mother really believed it.

"That's amazing, Mom," William said. "They *did* owe you a rainbow. You took care of them both while they died. You were a good daughter."

"Mom…" Sugar said. Her voice trailed off and it wasn't clear if she intended to finish. She had scrunched up her lips as if she were trying to hold something inside.

"What?" Frances turned toward her.

"Never mind."

"I don't have time, Sugar. Just tell me what's on your mind."

"Um, you and Daddy have burial plots together. Have you talked to him about that? You were supposed to be buried together."

A shadow of fear passed over Frances' face, as though a specter had just entered the room and made her, finally, afraid of death. "I can't."

"Mom, what is it?"

"I can't be buried alone. You know I'm claustrophobic. I can't do it. I just can't." Frances began to breath fast. Too fast.

Sugar stroked her mother's hand and smoothed her hair. Frances' face began to lose its contortion.

"It's okay, Mom. It's okay. Everything will be exactly as you want it. Don't worry about anything. You've done everything you need to do." Sugar's voice took on a sing-song tempo. "Now, rest. That's all you have to do. Your work here is done."

She began to sing softly, a song she had sung to her boys when they'd been small and sleepy.

When Frances had fallen again to sleep, William said, "You talk to her like she's a child. She won't let anyone else do that. You're the only one who can get away with it."

Surprised at what seemed like an accusation, Sugar frowned and defended herself. "I talk to her like I love her. That's the way you talk to someone you love when they need comfort."

William considered this as he left to call his uncle. There was so much he had to learn.

Frances stirred, whining in her sleep as if she were now in great pain. Her breathing was sharp, her face squeezed tight, her jaw set. Sugar knew she'd been given her medication only an hour before; they wouldn't give her another dose for a while. Since the antibiotics and breathing medication had been stopped, her mother had gradually worsened. The disease and infection were taking control of her body.

Sugar went back to singing and stroking. William heard her singing a Disney lullaby as he came back into the room. Frances was not asleep; she was obviously still suffering somewhere between wakefulness and the release that unconsciousness would soon offer her. He listened to Sugar sing two more songs before he relieved her with "Danny Boy." Frances sighed when she heard his voice.

"Daddy," she said. "I want to see my Daddy."

William had no way of knowing, but they'd sung the song at his grandfather's wake. Sung it maybe fifty times, and the tune had always reminded Frances of the sorrow when her father had finally passed. Still, Frances was smiling.

"I'll see my Daddy soon."

She sounded like a little girl. Tears spilled out of her closed eyes and down her temples onto the pillow. Sugar wiped them as she stroked her mother's hair and William stroked her arm.

"You're a dutiful son," she said to William, in appreciation of his comfort.

"I am a loving son," he answered back, and winked at Sugar to show what he had learned.

They sang to her for an hour more. They sang every peaceful song they knew: easy listening hits, church hymns, movie soundtracks. All of Frances' favorites. Once Sugar forgot the words at the same time William did. They hesitated, looked at each other, shrugged their shoulders and started humming. The next time it happened, they smiled at each other and made up some words. Frances still looked contented whenever she wasn't grimacing with waves of pain.

William and Sugar took turns leading and accompanying each other in song, all the while touching their mother as she had never let them touch her before. Except for the interruptions of agony when her whole body would squirm in the bed, they actually had a good time and enjoyed the intimacy as much as their mother did.

Sugar was singing the lead when William heard Uncle

Holden out at the nurse's station. He motioned to his sister then went to warn his Uncle about what he was likely to see.

"She's having a bad day, Uncle Holden. And now she's got a serious blood infection. This might be the end. I don't know how much longer she can go on like this."

Holden was noticeably stunned, as if he had just walked into someone else's life and had to answer to another person's name. He shook his head from side to side. He asked abruptly, "What's that music I hear coming from her room?" His tone implied that it just wasn't right.

"That's Sugar singing. We're trying to comfort Mom. She's in a lot of pain and the morphine doesn't seem to be helping."

Holden tried to take it all in; he looked confused and worried and nervous about being in the hospital where his sister's life was draining away, as if he thought whatever had hooked her might pull him into its grasp without him knowing. He took his nephew by the shoulders and looked him right in the eye.

"Well, I guess you're just loving her to death, then."

William smiled, although he was unsure of his uncle's intended meaning.

"Yes, Uncle Holden, that's exactly what we're doing. We're loving her to death."

Holden was afraid Frannie would start screaming at him again, so he looked over his shoulder to see who was around. That last time had made him feel like he'd been sent to the principal's office. No, last time he'd been stupid. He knew that now. He shouldn't have just shown up like that. This time she'd invited him. He belonged there now, as much as anybody else.

He regained his composure, stood taller and held his chin just a bit higher. He was prepared.

His sister opened her eyes when he came in then closed them again. Holden waited. Frances let him wait. The silence roared. He edged closer, minute by minute, until the quiet grew calmer between them and he was standing by her bedside. He sat. In the pink chair, the solemnity of the moment sank in. He looked around at her situation, then at his, understanding things for the first time but still not knowing what he was supposed to do.

In the long minutes while the sound of his own life faded to a whisper, Holden realized he had already lost her. There had been a time when he could wrestle his sister to the floor and make her cry uncle, but that time had long since passed. There were too many missed connections, too many words spoken and unspoken that separated them.

"Are you really dying, Fran?" He didn't know if she would hear him.

"Yes, Holden. When's the last time I lied to you? I think you were fourteen and I broke your guitar."

He remembered the day he'd come home and found a crack in his guitar. He was both angry at her and flattered that she would even play it. She'd never paid much attention to him until he got older. Holden began to feel sorry for himself and started to choke up.

"I'm not ready to lose you."

"Well, you are losing me, Holden. Maybe if you knew that a year ago, you would have been nicer. Maybe you would have taken care of me or shared the burden."

Neither said anything.

"It's over, Holden. Let it go." She moved a little sideways in the bed, shifting her weight, obviously in pain.

He thought of how the others had comforted her. Maybe that was the right thing. He was about to start humming, but he couldn't think of a song. He'd have to think of something else.

"What can I do for you?" He fluffed her pillow awkwardly, causing her head to fall to one side.

"One thing." She clenched her teeth and righted herself.

"Anything, Fran. Just tell me."

He wanted to be of some use now, maybe to make up for all of the times he hadn't. But Frances wasn't going to make it easy.

"I'm not going to let you relieve your conscience by holding my hand while I die. I'm not going to give you that chance. This is your twenty minutes. Then you go."

Holden's shoulders loosened. He had his out.

"So what can I do? Now?"

"Okay, here it is," she whispered. "I want you to put my ashes on your mantelpiece with a framed picture of me above it and say a prayer for me every night for the rest of your life."

Holden sank back into the chair. He imagined himself doing what she'd asked and wondered what would happen if he promised then didn't do it. She'd probably haunt him.

"And I want you to put me in the chair next to you at your table every night for dinner. I don't want you to forget me."

Holden didn't know what to do. This was weird, and he hated when she acted weird. He couldn't do what she was asking.

Could he?

"Holden?"

"Yes."

"Will you do what I'm asking?"

"Fran—"

"Yes?"

"Shit, Fran, is that what you really want?" He knew he'd promise her but he would be lying. She had to know that, too.

"Yes. And I want you to donate fifty thousand dollars to the SPCA."

"Now, that I'll do." His relief was obvious.

Frances laughed aloud, which led to a fit of coughing. She coughed out, "Hol—den."

"Yes?"

"You're such a shmuck. I only want one thing from you. Take me and the family out on your boat and let my ashes off into the bay." She settled down, opened her eyes and looked at her brother. "Will you do that for me?"

Holden smiled. "Yeah, Fran. I'll do that for you. I'll even play taps at sunset."

"You can be the one to let me go free. If you'll do that for me, I'll rest in peace."

It would break his heart. He would think of Fran every time he put his beloved *HoldenFast* into the water. But he would do it. For her.

"Do you forgive me, now, Fran?"

"No," she said, as she closed her eyes. The twenty minutes were up. "I'll never forgive you, Holden. But I do love you."

23

"SHE'S my favorite patient. I'm not going to abandon her." Pat explained to Sugar that Frances didn't want her morning grooming routine anymore.

"When she didn't want her eyebrows done anymore, I knew," Sugar said. Yesterday, her mother hadn't worried about her hair being combed, either.

"She told me, no, go take care of somebody else who needs you. But I still bathed her, changed her nightgown and put some powder on her so she smells nice. Don't you worry, Sugar. I'll take care of her."

Pat was as efficient as she was concerned. The men wouldn't worry about those things but Sugar did. She was glad for the help.

She went to her mother's room and was the first to arrive. It was the same room as it had been for weeks but it was becoming darker as Frances first had them close the shades against the sunlight, then turn off the fluorescents, and finally shut the door so she was alone much of the time.

"Are you awake, Momma?"

Frances opened her eyes and smiled at her daughter. "I really thought I had it there in the middle of the night, baby. But then I woke up this morning, as usual. I was very disappointed.

Another day. I feel like that movie, you know the one where it's Groundhog Day over and over.'"

Sugar knew the one. She was beginning to feel the same way. Another day. Same room, same routine, same words to choose from.

"That's why I was really trying to die in the middle of the night. Why is it taking so long?" Her voice was almost a whine. She was pained not by her body's trials, but because she wasn't getting what she wanted.

"You forgot the part where you're not God."

"Right. I remember now. His will be done, right?"

"Yes, so just settle in and enjoy the fact that we have another day together. That's His Plan." Sugar took her normal seat next to the bed. "So what shall we talk about today?"

"Tell me what you had for breakfast." Frances had no interest in eating food herself, yet she asked everyone who came through her door what they'd had for their last meal. She savored each word as if she'd taken a bite.

"I just had toast."

"You know what sounds really good? Toasted cheese. I love toasted cheese." Her eyes were still closed and she salivated at the thought. She smacked her lips.

Sugar was surprised. "I'll get you a toasted cheese, Mom. I'll go get you one." She started to get up.

"No, baby. I don't want to eat. I was just remembering how much I liked them. Ever since I was a little girl." She patted the bed to indicate she wanted her daughter closer. "I want to tell you about when I was little."

Sugar pulled the chair next to her mother, eager to know, hoping it wasn't a story she'd already heard. Maybe it was a story about how she'd ended up here, or maybe it was a story Sugar could tell the boys.

"My parents never cared where I went. Picture me about seven years old playing down near the Schuylkill River, probably a mile or so from my house. I would be gone all day. No one cared. I was very resourceful, you know. I made little boats out of sticks and leaves and paper, and launched them from the shoreline. I went into the water up to my knees and tried to catch fish with home-made fishing poles and bread on a bobby-pin.

"I had fun playing by myself. I knew a lot of people, and nothing bad ever happened to me. People were generally nice back then. I loved playing near the falls, you know, behind the Art Museum. I loved the sound." She closed her eyes as if she might fall asleep again. "I loved the water. That's why I want to be buried at sea."

Sugar stroked her mother's hand and waited. The words were slow, running like thick, muddy water between the women.

"I grew up as a loner, Sugar," her mother confided with her eyes half open. "I spent my whole childhood learning how to fend for myself. But I'm not complaining. That's how I grew so strong. Being alone isn't the worst thing in the world.

"And I was smart." As she continued her eyes were completely closed, as if she were far away. "I knew how to read before I went to school but I never told anyone. I was smart like your Jason. He knew how to read, too. I don't know if you knew that about him, but I knew it. He read me the soup labels. That's how I realized it. That kid's a genius."

She opened her eyes and nodded. Sugar knew Jason was gifted, but she wasn't sure about him reading before first grade. She made a mental note to ask him about that.

"Reading was my first secret. I had many more when I was a kid. When I was older, I was a hell raiser. Once I dropped a frog into a nun's veil. You know, that big white thing they used to wear on their heads."

"A wimple."

"Yes, that's it. The nun's wimple. Put the frog right inside as I walked by. They had a permanent seat reserved for me in detention. I never told you that, did I?" Frances' expression looked like a mischievous little girl.

"No, Mom. I always thought you held us to the same high standard you had for yourself." Sugar giggled. She'd heard the frog story many times before. Her mother's oldest friends still occasionally called her "Froggie."

"My kids were always good kids. But your Eric's going to be a hell raiser, Sugar. You have to watch him. He's very independent and secretive. I can see it because he's like me. He's always got something in his mind that you don't know he knows. And he's not going to tell you, especially now that he's a teenager."

Now Sugar was getting uncomfortable. She hadn't realized her mother knew her children so well. She had an urge to pick them up at school right now and ask them a lot of questions.

"You're a good mother, Sugar. You're doing a much better job raising those boys than I ever did raising mine. Girls are easy. You were easy."

Sugar was glad her mother thought so. It hadn't always seemed easy from her point of view.

"But the boys, especially when they're close in age, they're tough. I never knew how to get close to my boys. I was never close to them like you are with yours." Frances opened her eyes and took Sugar's hand. "I love those babies, Sugar. You take care of them."

"They want to see you, Momma. They want to say goodbye. They're very confused by all of this. Jason's been out of school for two days now, he's so upset. Please, Mom, let me bring them up."

Frances was suddenly stern. "No. I do not want them seeing me like this." She shook her head. "No." Then her words grew soft. "If you bring them here, I won't be able to do it, Sugar. Please, don't make me face them. I can't do it." She began to cry, for the first time. "I can't face those babies."

Sugar calmed her mother, soothing her hair and her face. "It's okay, Momma, I won't bring them."

"I need to die my way. I need to have some peace." She struggled to breathe.

"I know, Momma, I know." Sugar was crying, too.

Frances began to cough loudly, uncontrollably, and her face contorted as she leaned to one side. "I need a piece of ice," she rasped.

Sugar delivered a piece of chopped ice on a spoon. Frances dissolved it on her tongue and fell asleep. She was pale, as if there was no circulation in her face at all. Her lips were almost the color of her skin, her wrinkles were growing deeper and more pronounced. Her eyes looked sore. Frances had been nearly a week without anything to drink; she refused all food and water, and asked only for an occasional ice chip to wet her mouth. Sugar left her mother and went to the nurse's station.

"Shouldn't we make her drink? Please, Pat. I can't watch her be thirsty." Pat came around to put her arm around Sugar.

"She isn't thirsty, honey. This is normal."

"How can watching your mother die of hunger and thirst be normal? It's not normal. It's repulsive. It's gruesome."

Sugar was growing upset. The tracks of her tears wet her face without cleansing her soul. Pat led her to some chairs down the hall.

"Honey, I know it's hard to watch but this is the way it happens. This is what death is. Your mother's body is shutting down, one system at a time. Her eyes are often closed but she still listens to what's going on around her when she's interested. Part of her is still here but part of her is already gone. She sleeps a lot now. Little by little, she'll lose interest in all of you and she will move on. That's what happens."

"But she hasn't eaten in weeks."

"Food is part of the physical world, Sugar. So is water. So are words and television and all of us. Frances is being called away from all of it, and she's letting go in her own time. You're doing the right thing by letting her make her own decisions. She'll let you know what's important. Trust me."

"She told me I was a good mother. She's never said that before."

"She'll make her peace with her people."

"She always criticized me and how I was raising them, especially since I got divorced. She thought they spent too much time playing video games. They didn't eat right. They were getting sloppy." Sugar bounced her head back and forth as the ticked off her mother's complaints. "She had a whole list of criticisms about them. And now on her deathbed she tells me I'm doing a better job than she did." Sugar smiled, "Maybe death is a truth serum."

"Let's get some lunch, what do you think?" Pat said she was heading down for her break, anyway.

Sugar agreed. The two talked like old friends for an hour, bringing each other up to date on the thirty-odd years that had passed since they were Girl Scouts lost in the woods.

Sugar's mother sent her out to get two big bowls and a lot of candy and snacks. Sensing that her time was near, Frances wanted to leave a gift for the nurses. These people had been so kind to her, and she believed in thank you notes and appreciative gestures. So after lunch, Sugar did exactly as she was told.

It was sort of fun to go shopping for candy, more fun than Sugar had had for weeks, anyway. The selection was still new. Each bin was filled for Halloween, and Sugar loved the excess of it all.

She filled her cart with fifteen bags and boxes of nut bars, chocolate pieces, granola bars, chocolate wafer sandwich bars, caramel drops, peanut butter cups, gourmet cookies and those round hazelnut candies wrapped in gold foil. She added in some packs of gummy bears just in case there was anyone who didn't like chocolate. Someone who doesn't like chocolate?

Sugar put the candy on the conveyer belt at the checkout. "Hello, how are you today?" The checker, a woman in her early fifties with big teeth, a bigger hairdo and too much makeup, greeted her with a big smile. She looked like the kind of woman who could handle it, so Sugar exhaled the truth all at once.

"I'm pretty crappy, actually. My mother is in the hospital down the street, refusing to have an operation that will probably kill her but has a chance of saving her. And without the operation she'll definitely die in about a week or so. My father is acting like a jerk, my ex-husband wants to get back together again, and I haven't even told my kids their grandmother is dying." Tossing her head lightly to one side, she took a breath. "And my mom wants me to buy all this candy so she can give it all to the nurses who are taking care of her, as a sort of farewell thank you present because she doesn't have much time left. But hey, other than that, you know, things are going okay."

She took her wallet out of her purse. A tear rolled down her cheek and her chin trembled.

The woman behind the counter just stared. Sugar wished she would say something or come over and give her a hug, or anything that would let her know someone understood how miserable she was, how hard the situation had been on her. But it didn't happen. The woman behind the counter merely turned off the conveyer belt and said, "Seventy-four dollars and fourteen cents, please."

She left the store as quickly as she could and put the bags on the passenger seat. She did a quality control experiment with two bite-size candy bars and a nut cluster. And a cookie. Yes. Everything was in order, and things seemed better even if they weren't.

Back at the hospital Sugar divided the bags of candy, sampling a few from each bag for the boys at home. Frances decorated the outside of the two bowls with the stickers Sugar had bought. Her bandaged hand was clumsy and barely responsive, so she did everything left-handed. But it was a happy moment, like filling Easter baskets or trick-or-treat sacks.

"Did you get the cards?"

"I got the cards."

She opened the thank-you cards on the bedside tray and laid

them open so her mother could write her farewell message. She covered the bowls with cellophane and ribbons while Frances wrote in her feeble hand on the center of each card:

To My Guardian Angels:
I will never forget your kindness and friendship. Thank you for taking such good care of me and for being so nice to my family. I will never forget you.
Frances Baldwin

According to her mother's instructions, Sugar delivered one to the nurses in the CCU and one to the nurse's desk outside her current room. The treats were well received, and Sugar noticed the chocolate did, indeed, go first.

For the rest of the afternoon, Sugar sat at her mother's bedside while Frances went in and out of sleep. When Dr. Al-Biruni came in to check Frances' vital signs, she woke up.

"Thank you for the goodies, Frances!" The doctor had a cheery tone. "We're all enjoying them. That was very nice of you."

"Not as nice as all of the nurses have been to me. They are all sweethearts." Frances replied slowly. Her tongue stuck to the inside of her mouth, causing her words to slur. "I'll never forget it."

"We've got a girl who just got married, and we're going to send the bowls home with her when they're empty. Which, by the way, will probably be tomorrow. You should see everyone stopping by for a snack!"

A nurse whom Sugar recognized but could not name came in and echoed the doctor's sentiments. Clearly appreciative, she tucked Frannie's blankets around her, fluffed her pillow and cleared her tray.

"I'll get you some more ice, Mrs. Baldwin."

"Wait, there's something else," Frances asked. "Can I have a cherry cola?"

"A cherry cola?" Sugar smiled ear to ear.

"Yes, I would like a cherry cola, please."

It was the first thing to eat or drink that Frances had asked for since she'd entered the hospital.

"Of course, Mrs. Baldwin. I'll go downstairs and get it myself." The nurse smiled and stopped straightening the bed tray. She turned toward the door.

Dr. Al-Biruni took Frances' hand. "Frances, I know you and I have not always seen things eye-to-eye and that you have gotten angry with me."

"Yes, Doctor, I have. But now I know you were just doing your job."

"You see, Frances, I believe, both by my religion and my profession, that if someone is not dying, we should do all we can to save them."

"But you and I draw that line in different places, Doctor. You aren't in my body, so you couldn't tell that what I was saying was true all along."

"You're right, Frances. To me, it looked like we could fix what was wrong with you. That we could *prevent* your death with science and technology."

"But you see now that you weren't preventing it, you were interfering with it."

The doctor sighed. "Yes, Frances, but that's a fine line. I can only see it now that we've run out of options."

"Yes, it is a fine line, Doctor. Especially from your point of view."

"But I want you to know I understand now, and I am fully supportive of your decision. I'll do all I can to help you be comfortable. In fact, I am awed at your courage and spirit. You have taught me something I will not forget."

"Thank you, Doctor." Frances was satisfied. She conceded her position now that she had the upper hand. "And I will be more cooperative with you from now on. I know I haven't made your job very easy."

"No, you haven't, Frances." The doctor laughed, her face brightening. "But that's just part of your charm."

Dr. Al-Biruni left with a smile and a nod to Sugar just as the nurse came back in with a large cherry cola in a plastic cup. She held the straw to Frances' lips as Sugar looked on, clearly pleased.

"Oh, my," Frances put her head back on the pillow and rolled her eyes. "I can't begin to tell you how good that tastes. Another sip," she rasped as the bubbles froze her sandy throat. She rolled her eyes again and exhaled deeply, the sweetness curling her lips into a smile.

"Boy, that's so good, it's erotic." Frances opened her eyes, raised her eyebrows guiltily and looked over at Sugar. "I guess I shouldn't say that around my daughter, should I?"

Later in the afternoon, Sugar was still in the pink chair watching her mother sleep. She looked around the room and realized she knew it by heart—the chipped paint by the mirror, the stain on the third tile from the door, the corner of the center ceiling tile that was missing. She knew how to work the bed, the television, the call buttons and oxygen. It took hours to memorize these small details, time wasted because she would forget them soon enough.

She studied her mother's face, every line and freckle. She tried to imprint all of it in her brain so she would never forget her mother the way she would the room. She knew this might be the last time she ever sat next to her, the last time she saw her face. Tomorrow she might be gone. There came to Sugar an urgency, a need to put things in place. *If she died now, what will I wish I had said to her? What words need to be spoken?*

When Frances opened her eyes the next time, Sugar was still watching her. Frances felt the pleasure of being the center of her daughter's attention and love. She smiled.

"Momma, I almost forgot to thank you. For everything."

Frances looked almost pained as she settled back and closed her eyes again. Her words were hoarse, choked. "You were a lot better to me than I was to you, honey. I should be the one thanking you."

"But you've taught me so much." Sugar tried to explain. This was her last chance. "You've taught me about courage and love and devotion. You are teaching me even now. Thank you."

"You're such a good fixer-rupper, Sugarrr."

The words came slowly and had begun to slur. Sugar couldn't tell if it was the morphine or if Frances was losing control of her speech. She stroked her mother's hair, pushing her bangs back into their usual place on her forehead.

"I love you, Momma."

"Of all the things I know, Sugar, I know that for sure." Frances' eyes were closed and she appeared to be sleeping.

Sugar's tears began to fall freely. Her nose ran and her eyes closed tight as she struggled to control all the emotions that had been grinding up against each other in her stomach for weeks. It didn't seem right that she should feel such joy sitting at her mother's deathbed. Joy and sorrow. Pride and loss. Love and loneliness. Awareness and exhaustion. Excitement and fear.

She'd always thought her life's dream was to raise her children and have a successful career. But she realized that her real life's dream—her original life's dream—was to have her mother like this, open to her, receiving her love. To feel as close as they were, touching. Sugar felt like she still had so much left to give. So much love she had withheld, so much love that Frances had been unwilling or unable to receive. So many words withheld for fear of misunderstanding.

It was a perfect moment. Amidst the putrid smells and the chiseling sounds and the tension of the four green walls, the two of them had found a perfect moment.

Frances leaned into Sugar's touch as she stroked the soft skin of her cheek. She pressed against her daughter and smiled and sighed as a puppy might. Sugar was barely touching her, but it was the greatest comfort Frances had ever allowed herself to receive.

As her mother drifted to sleep, Sugar thought, *Tomorrow I'm going shopping to find a dress fit for a princess.*

24

IT was pretty much a straight shot across the country—New York to Salt Lake City. Randy's gloomy mood changed as soon as he crossed the Pennsylvania state line into Ohio. He didn't like Pennsylvania. If it were up to him, he would never go back. As he drove, Randy considered that he would have to go back to Philly, if only for a day, for his mother's funeral. He expected his mother to hang on for some time, and he'd decided he didn't want to wait in New York. Better to be on the road making something happen.

He popped in a CD and looked at his reflection in the rear-view mirror. As he reached up to adjust the mirror, he bumped the soft spot inside his right elbow on the middle console.

"Damn, that hurt," he said as he rubbed it. Randy always tried not to run into things; he considered himself a careful person. "Get a grip, boy."

His brother was keeping him up to date on all things medical and maternal, so he was aware that she'd finally gotten the guts up to disconnect herself from treatment. While he was glad he wasn't on the death watch, he harbored mixed feelings about being relieved of duty. Later, when he was thinking more clearly, he might conclude that it was his mother's gift to him. But until then, because he didn't realize the extent to which his emotions had overtaken him, he thought of Frances' dismissal as rather abrupt, rude even, the way she pushed him out of the family during its time of crisis.

He blamed his mother for the distance between him and his siblings. She'd always treated him as though he were different than Sugar and William. Or like he needed to be quarantined from them. Yes, that was more accurate. His mother had always kept them apart because she didn't want William and Sugar to catch something undesirable from him.

He hadn't called her in a few days. She always wanted a poem to make her laugh. Randy couldn't seem to come up with anything very creative so he postponed the conversation. He tried for a while as he drove, before he gave up.

"It's really too bad you won't recover
Between this world and the next you hover
I hope you don't become a ghost
And come back to haunt those who lied the most."

No. That wasn't good. It implied she still had some control over him. He wouldn't admit that even though he'd thought of her and little else since he'd left Philadelphia. He was still under the mistaken belief that her power had long since been arrested. Instead he tried a tune, one she would recognize. A lullaby:

"Rock-a-bye momma
In the hospital bed
I don't have to visit
For soon you'll be dead."

He decided to stop the game. He was becoming far too cynical even for his own edgy sense of humor.

The emptiness inside him was as wide as the interstate highway ahead of him. Three lanes were going in his direction, with no sign of life except his flashy car. It was laden with all his memories packed inside brown boxes, taped up tightly where she couldn't get them. On the other side were three lanes all going her way, jammed with stupid rhymes, exaggerated pride and fake smiles.

He had nothing left to say to her.

She'd never known him at all. Randy tried to think of a time when he'd had a good relationship with his mother, a time when he'd felt she really saw him, valued him, as Monica did. Sweet Monica. He had always turned to women to make up for the validation he didn't get from his mother. And he'd found it all with Monica. Randy put thoughts of his ex-girlfriend aside. For now.

His mother had always been so judgmental. That's what made her so different than Monica. Randy imagined his mother as a kind of smoke alarm installed in every room of his life. Whatever he created, whatever expression of himself he tried to cook up, he heard that horrible blast of sound screeching through his initiative, making him stop whatever he'd been doing and think only of her. He found himself looking to her before he even took a step, wondering if she was going to start sounding off before he'd even had a chance to put his foot down.

No matter how many years went by, he still wanted his mother's approval. He wanted her to see him in the same light Monica saw him. Capable, intelligent and strong. That's all he'd ever wanted. He thought back to when he'd been a kid, a teen, then a young man. No, he couldn't think of one good moment. It had always been the same way. To her, he was just a charge. A patient for her to care for. He was never a boy, a man, a person. There was always something she was trying to fix about him. Something she always wanted for him that he couldn't achieve.

She had said she was proud of him at the hospital, he remembered.

"Hah," he said aloud. "I have to wait for her to be on her deathbed to say one nice thing about me." He thought again, trying to remember the exact words she had used.

"And she was talking about my job. She wasn't even talking about me."

Randy drove until late at night and found a chain hotel just outside Toledo. He didn't even bring his suitcases in from the car; he fell fast asleep in his clothes as soon as he hit the pillow. He slept without waking until the sun rose.

On this day, the second day of his new life, Randy Ascher Williams found that something was wrong. Very wrong.

It had been a routine check in the mirror, the same routine check he'd been doing since he was eleven. When he saw the spots on his face this time, the broken capillaries around his eyes, his knees buckled. He sat down on the edge of the bathtub, his skin growing clammy and his heart quickening. *This isn't good. Don't cry, don't sneeze. Don't do anything. Just relax for a minute. Relax.*

Randy took off his blue jeans and they were there, too, on his legs and feet. He opened his shirt; they were there on his ribs and sides, even along the line where the shirt's shoulder seam hit his skin: little purple spots, broken capillaries. *Purpura.*

He caught sight of where he'd hit his elbow on the car console yesterday. There was a deep, purple and black bruise that stretched from his elbow down his forearm. *It's probably still bleeding.* The words echoed in his mind like the clatter of something that had fallen unexpectedly from a forgotten attic shelf.

Mechanically, he put his clothes back on and dialed the front desk.

"Can you give me the location of the nearest hospital?"

"Right across the parking lot."

As chance might have it, the hotel was situated just beyond the rear parking lot of the Greater Toledo Medical Center. Randy put on his shoes and carefully walked outside. He knew he'd be there for at least a few days so he stopped at his car and got a few things out of his suitcase on the way.

As was always the case, the emergency ward was a bustle of activity even at seven-thirty in the morning. There was an ambulance outside with its light still flashing. Flashing red like the memories inside Randy's mind. He didn't wait long before he was called into a little cubbyhole with a triage nurse.

"I am having a relapse of a condition called Idiopathic Thrombocytopenic Purpura. ITP."

"What are your symptoms?"

Randy repeated his symptoms, knowing the only signs of the disease were the little spots. The spots he checked for several times a day in every mirror he'd passed for the last twenty-five years. The spots that on some days, he'd convinced himself would never again appear. The spots that were now growing more abundant and larger inside and outside his body.

The nurse didn't seem to recognize ITP. Randy told her he needed a platelet count as soon as possible, and that he needed an IV with immunoglobulin. She looked at him suspiciously and told him to return to the waiting room.

I could die of a brain hemorrhage while I'm waiting, stupid bitch. He hesitated but returned to the waiting room as instructed, evaluating the other patients, all of whom appeared sicker than him on the outside. He made an effort not to bump his leg on the hard brown chair as he sat. *Without platelets in my blood, it won't clot. I'll just go on bleeding and bleeding inside, like my elbow.* He unconsciously bent his elbow and cradled it against his chest.

I could be dying right now. I could have internal bleeding and they wouldn't even know it. Any one of my arteries or veins or blood vessels could have already burst inside me. Randy began to grow dizzy with the implications of his condition. He shuddered at the thought of hitting the floor unconscious.

He made his way to the check-in window and told them he was going to faint. The young nurse saw he was serious and brought a wheelchair alongside. To his relief, she wheeled him through the double doors into the examination area and made a place for him to lie down in examining room number four. Randy put his head back on the pillow and tried to relax. *I'm safer now,* he thought. *Breathe.*

A young doctor, likely fresh out of medical school, presented himself. "Hello, I'm Dr. Doctor, if you can believe that. That's my real name. And get this: my parents named me Ivan Bartholomew Addison Doctor. That's 'I. B. A. Doctor.'" He was still laughing at his own joke, one he'd surely told a thousand times now. "I wanted to be a lawyer but really, what choice did I have?"

Great, I've got me the class clown. Somebody get me a real doctor.

Dr. Doctor looked at the forms that had been filled out so far. "If you feel better about it, you can call me Dr. Ivan."

It didn't make Randy feel better. Not at all. He began to look around the room for other signs that things were odd here, reasons to get up right now and get in his car and drive away. But he found none. He knew he had to stay.

"So, you think you've got ITP? You've had it before?" The doctor examined Randy's feet and arms then pulled up his shirt to look at his trunk.

"I had it twice. Once when I was eleven, and again when I was twenty."

"Ever had your spleen removed?" The doctor's tone was as if he was asking Randy if he'd ever changed the oil in his car, or even worse, that he needed to. He was fingering Randy's abdomen looking for scars amidst his body hair. Removing the spleen was a last-resort procedure for ITP.

"No."

"Did you take steroids?"

"Yes. I know I had immunoglobulin and steroids when I was twenty. I'm not sure what they did when I was eleven."

"Well, let's get some blood taken and see what we've got. All of our professional blood takers are out today, preparing for Halloween next month. I'll have to send in one of the rookies. Hope they remember what to do. Don't hesitate to give them directions." Dr. Doctor turned to leave.

"Wait a minute, what is this place, anyway? Don't you have any qualified people here? I can't afford to be poked and stabbed. I'll bleed to death."

Randy was beginning to get upset and sat up. Now he was sure he didn't like this place.

"Whoa, hold on," Dr. Ivan took a step toward Randy, opening his hands apologetically. "I was only kidding. Professional blood takers. Vampires. Next month is Halloween. Get it?" He guided Randy back down onto the pillow. "Don't worry. Our technicians are fully qualified to take blood. And we're going to take a lot of it to see what's going on, so don't get your boxers in a bunch."

How could the man still be attempting levity?

"I'm sorry, I don't have much of a sense of humor. My mother is dying in Philadelphia and now I've had a relapse of *this*. I don't find anything about the situation very funny."

"I didn't realize that about your mother. So you're under a lot of stress? On your way to see her?"

"Yeah. On my way," Randy lied. "But not any more."

He put his head back on the pillow and closed his eyes. "I need a blanket, I'm very cold."

The blood test came back indicating that he had a severe case of ITP. The platelet count had come back at about four thousand. Normal is at least two hundred fifty thousand; even upward past four hundred thousand is in the normal range.

"I just wanted to show you all what four thousand platelets look like." Dr. Doctor had gathered the entire staff of nurses and doctors around Randy and was pointing out the purpura all over his skin.

"This guy got here just in time. Really dodged a bullet. He could have died, you know, from internal bleeding." The doctor was filling out Randy's chart for admittance into the hospital's hematology unit.

My mother's dying. I am not dying, Randy told himself over and over until he was safe in his hospital bed by the window on a brilliant fall day with the large bag of clear liquid dripping slowly through the needle inserted into the back of his hand. He could feel the cool liquid passing through his warm skin, he could see the veins plump with their cargo. It would take four hours for the contents of the bag to be assimilated. He slept.

25

SUGAR had agreed to meet with David. Just to talk. One of the hardest things about the divorce was that she no longer had anyone to talk to, and God knows she needed someone now. She'd lost touch with most of her real girlfriends over the years of "having it all," a family and a job. Now she really wasn't that close to the friends she had left. They went out together and complained about their ex-husbands together, but they didn't talk about matters of the heart. When it came to the most important things, Sugar was lonely.

She pulled on her skinny jeans and was surprised to find that they fit. Satisfied with her reflection, she tossed her thick head of golden hair about, fluffing and smoothing. She looked good. Despite all that was happening, she still looked good.

She met David at a nearby restaurant, in a strip mall. It was a small, French-Vietnamese place, one of her favorites. She had never been there with David before, and she hoped that he'd never been there without her.

"Cindy, you look great." David had arrived first and was waiting for her.

While she was annoyed that he commented first on her appearance, she was pleased that he'd noticed. When it came to her face and figure, Sugar knew she could compete with any of his girlfriends.

"Hi, David."

He stood up, reached for her shoulders and kissed her on the cheek. Flustered, she withdrew from his embrace and sat down before he did.

"So I heard from Eric that your mom's in the hospital. He wasn't sure how she was doing. I think he's worried."

Sugar was glad he'd brought it up first. But then again, they never really made small talk so she, too, got right to the point.

"I don't know how to tell the kids my mother's dying."

It had been bothering her for weeks. When she looked at the boys, she still saw children, and she didn't know the words to help them understand her mother's decision when she herself didn't accept it.

David sat back, processing an idea he'd never considered before. His mother-in-law was dying. He tried to think if he'd ever really known anyonc who'd dicd before.

"Wow," he said. How long does she have?"

"Not long. Maybe a week."

"Whoah. And you didn't tell the boys? Don't they need to see her and have some kind of closure? I mean, they don't have any experience with these things. They're kids. You oughta be making it easier for them somehow, you know, help them learn from the experience. This is an important time in their lives."

Sugar felt like she had to defend herself but accepted his criticism because she was already aware she wasn't doing a good job handling it.

"I'm doing the best I can, David. It's my *mother.*"

"Yeah, I know how tough the old broad can be. How 'bout you arrange it so the boys can see her tomorrow? I'll bring them to the hospital. I'd like to say goodbye to Frannie myself."

Sugar was astonished that David had no idea. About anything. More than anyone else, her mother hated David for what he'd done to Sugar and the boys. She'd never been enthusiastic about him from the beginning, all broad shoulders, smiley and handsome. She'd wanted Sugar to marry a regular guy whom she wouldn't have to worry about losing. Frances had always thought of David as a ladies' man and hadn't hesitated to say, "I told you so," when David eventually fulfilled her expectations. Now, she compared him to Satan and tried hard not to see her grandsons as the devil's spawn. Sugar had been fighting for a year to protect David from her mother.

"David, my mother does not want to see the kids. And she'd *never* see you. She won't see anyone but her children. Diane's not here. Mom's even sent Randy away."

"Well, that's kind of selfish, isn't it?" David stirred the lime into his iced tea as he spoke. "I mean, this isn't just about her. It's about the whole family."

"David, if you don't mind my saying, you gave up any say you had in this family when you decided to sleep with Janine." She reached over and patted his hand patronizingly and said sarcastically as she scrunched her face up, "Kind of cancelled out any vote you had."

She tried not to sound annoyed, although she was desperately trying to keep her cool. She needed the evening to go well.

"There you go, bringing that up again. Listen—" David caught himself raising his voice and sitting at the edge of his chair. He sat back and lowered his voice. "Listen, Cindy. What I've been trying to tell you is how bad I've been feeling about all of that. First, I've apologized enough and I'm not apologizing again. Don't expect me to. I'm done apologizing."

Sugar realized she could listen to David apologize a hundred times and she would still find him insincere. "David, I—"

"No, wait, hear me out." He reached for her hand. "I have never been so miserable. I've been in therapy and I think I'm figuring it all out. I thought I was unhappy in our marriage. I thought you had driven me away when the boys were born, so I sort of took the backseat and let you raise them. There was no room for me in the family. So I started fooling around early on. First the secretary in my office. She was just a fling—"

"David, I really don't—"

"Listen to me, Cyn. Please."

Sugar was beginning to cry. She hadn't known about the secretary. She hadn't known anything at all about the "early on." She had thought they were happy. Her head was spinning as she tried to remember back.

"I slept around some. Okay, a lot. But I still loved you. I was just trying to find myself, and I thought my search was over with Janine. She was so full of life, funny, and she was interested in me. She went out of her way to be sexy for me. The sex was great."

"Stop, David. I don't want—"

"I asked you here so I could tell you this. I have to tell you, Cindy. Please, listen to me. It's all gone wrong."

Sugar wondered what David could say that would make any of this better. She also wondered who this man was on the other side of the table holding her hand, and why she was sitting here listening to him. Was he for real? Was he really doing this? Tonight? Now?

"The sex was great," he repeated though she hadn't heard. "I thought Janine and I were so close that I didn't care if you found out about us. It was my way of getting your attention, to pay you back for abandoning me for the boys. I thought that when we split, I would be with her and I'd be happy. But I wasn't. Janine and I have broken up."

Sugar just stared, not moving as a few tears ran down her cheeks.

"You may think you know that woman, Cyn—I know she was your best friend. But just let me tell you, you don't know her *at all.* She is seriously mentally ill. You don't know how she's treated me. I treated her so well, and she—I won't even begin to tell you what she did to me and my reputation. Suffice it to say that she was no friend of yours. Or mine."

Oddly, Sugar was interested in how they'd broken up. And she perversely delighted in the idea that David had somehow been taken advantage of. Any concern she might have had for him had long since expired; he'd used up her reserve of love and caring sometime during the property settlement.

"David." She paused, waiting to see if he would allow her to talk yet. She suddenly felt energized, despite her exhaustion and sleeplessness, to speak up for herself for the first time. To tell David what was really on her mind instead of playing the perfect wife and the perfect ex-wife and the perfect mother of the perfect sons.

"David, you seem to have mistaken me for someone who gives a damn. You must have misunderstood my attempt at civility for the boys' sake as being a genuine concern for you and your well being."

Confused, David dropped her hand and squinted at her. She stood up.

"I am going through a family crisis with my mother dying

right now, and you don't even seem to realize that would be hard on me. Somehow, I thought you'd understand at least that much. My mistake. But the fact is, I can't help you with your problems now. Or ever. I suggest you go back to your shrink to help you deal with your 'feelings,' and I will just go home now and deal with mine."

Sugar turned away from David, from the man in whom she had not once—but again—placed her confidence, only to see him—again, this time more clearly—for the sleezeball he really was. It was not a vision she'd planned on having tonight.

Who was the man she had fantasized about having dinner with? How long ago had David stopped being that man?

David started after her, but she turned.

"Don't follow me, and don't call me. If you know what's good for you, you will communicate directly with the boys to make your plans for this weekend. They're old enough now to handle that."

"I can't believe you're acting like this. Janine was right. You're a bitch." David sat back down, crossed his legs and turned away from her.

Janine was no friend of mine. And you are no longer my husband. I know that for sure now.

But why did you pick tonight to make me say goodbye?

It was still early and Sugar didn't know where else to go but back to the hospital. She justified it by telling herself this might be the last time she could turn to her mother for help. Frances woke up when Sugar came into the room. Visiting hours were over but Sugar knew those were flexible when it came to Frances Baldwin. No nurse was going to tell Sugar to go home.

"What's wrong, Sugar? You look terrible." Frances looked her over then closed her eyes again.

"David told me he wanted to get back together, then he acted like a jerk so I told him to go to hell. I just left him there, sitting at the restaurant after I caused a big scene."

"Good job, honey. David is a jerk. You know that. Leopards don't change their spots."

She was dying, but Frances loved gossip and girl talk as much as any living woman. An "I told you so" wasn't what Sugar wanted to hear, but it would do. At least her mother was agreeing.

"He is a jerk. Now I know it for sure. I don't know how I keep forgetting that." She tucked her hair behind her ears and straightened up in her chair. "I hope it doesn't rub off on the boys."

"Listen, there's something I want to talk about, Sugar." Frances opened her eyes and changed the subject. "I'm trying to make everything right now. Now I can see so clearly where I've gone wrong. I always wanted so much for my sons, and it always seemed to come between us. I guess I projected a lot of my own dreams onto them. I can see why they rejected me." She turned her head on the pillow as if in shame.

For a moment, Sugar wondered if her mother was capable of feeling remorse. Maybe dying made a person able to do things they could never have done during their lives. Maybe when David—.

"Maybe that's why you and I always got along," Frances said. "I never wanted much for you."

"But you did."

"Did I? What?" She didn't remember ever dreaming any

dreams for her daughter. Sugar just always was what she was; there had been no need to turn her into anything else.

"You wanted me to be like you."

Frances laughed. Sugar waited until her mother grew quiet.

"And I am."

"No, you're not, Sugar. You are a much better mother than I ever was. A much better person. You'll never turn out like me. You have patience where I have bitterness. You have compassion where I am judgmental. And you have a really good sense of yourself and what's right for you. Like tonight. You took a stand with your husband and said what was right for you. I never did that, and I should have. Maybe I never had dreams for you because you were already so much more than I was. I didn't want us to get to be too different."

"But you only know of me what I show you, mother. There's a whole other side of me you would be surprised to know! I'm not as perfect as you describe."

Sugar had the sudden urge to stand up and swear, get drunk, and show her mother exactly how bad she could be. Frances reached for her before she could get out of the chair.

"Then I guess it's better that it end this way. I'll always be able to think of you as my little Sugar. Sweet, sweet Sugar."

Sugar was flattered but unsatisfied. She wanted to be seen by her creator. She wanted to be able to remember a real moment of absolute connection with her mother where they'd spoken squarely and honestly, where she was understood as who she really was—different and flawed. Sugar longed to be truly known and forgiven.

Instead, she would go through the rest of her life trying to remember the exact words her mother had used to deliver her compliments, compliments that were years overdue and long imagined. She would end up writing down what she could recall and would read, countless times, from that sheet of paper her mother's assessments about her character and her capabilities. This would take the place of her mother; it would stand in for all the words that would go unspoken when Sugar needed them most.

26

FRANCES had grown accustomed to the pattern of waking and falling to sleep again. She no longer had bad dreams; she no longer watched the clock tick away the remaining seconds of her life. The next time when she awoke, William was at her side.

It must be daytime. "I'm here. Again," she said.

"How are you feeling, Mom?"

"If I were any better, I'd be in heaven, William."

"Do you have pain?" He'd noticed her squirming in her sleep and didn't know if she was in pain or just restless. William had asked the nurses when he came in, so he knew she was receiving morphine every four hours.

"No. I'm just uncomfortable. I want Randy."

"Mom, I'm here with you. I'll take care of you. Remember you sent Randy home."

"I know that. I mean I want to talk to him. He hasn't called me. I need to talk to him."

"I called him this morning but he didn't answer his phone. I left a message on his cell and at his apartment."

Randy hadn't mentioned to anyone that he'd moved out and was on his way across the country.

"I bet he's mad at me."

"For what?"

"For dying."

"He's not mad at you for dying. No one's mad at you for dying."

"Your father is."

"Well, okay, you're right. Dad's mad. But none of your children are mad at you for dying."

"I was going to die sometime. You all knew that."

"Yeah, but I think Dad forgot it."

"Just like him." She paused and returned to her original train of thought. "Then why is Randy mad at me? For sending him away? He wanted to go home, we all knew that. It was too hard for him to be here." She waved her hand dismissively. "Anyway, I couldn't stand to look at his face, so pained, anymore. It made me so sad. He's not like you and Sugar. He can't handle things like the two of you can."

She gestured for him to come closer. He sat in the pink chair and took her hand, inviting intimacy between them.

"You know how much Randy loves me," Frances said solidly, "how close we are. It's always been that way. He's my baby. I've always wanted to protect him. My baby." She was groggy again but her agitation persisted. "Get Randy on the phone. I need him."

William dropped her hand with his lips tight and drawn. Unable to hold it off any longer, Frances fell back to sleep. William took a walk. His footsteps pounded the pavement like the thoughts pounded against the side of his head, thudding with the dull echo of a lifetime's disappointment.

I don't need another reminder that she's always felt closer to Randy. Nothing I do is ever enough. It isn't enough for her that I've dropped my whole life and come here for her, at her bedside every day for weeks. She still wants Randy.

Outside, he tried Randy's cell phone again. It went straight to the recording, as if the phone was turned off.

Why couldn't I just have a normal family?

He got in his car, turned the key and looked to the radio. The sound was turned down completely and he waited for the flicker of the green LED light. These messages from God were the best conversation he'd had since arriving on the East Coast. And there it was, complete understanding:

***Caught In The Middle** By Project 86*

How true, how true. William pounded the steering wheel as he stood on the edge of his loneliness, fighting against the pull that would make him lose his careful footing and plunge into the crevasse of complete solitude.

Sugar and her father were in Frannie's hospital room. They'd opened the shades to let in some light but the walls were still an institutional green, the ceiling was still stained with drips and leaks from some previous mechanical dysfunction, and Frances was still hanging on. Like the ceiling, her blanket carried a laundered-in blotch from some previous misery. No matter how hard Sugar tried to turn it or tuck it in, the stain still managed to come out on top.

The television provided the only distraction. PBS was broadcasting the antiques show again, and someone had just found out that the cameo in her grandmother's jewelry box was worth over five thousand dollars.

Frances opened her eyes. "Randy? Has he called?" As if she'd been thinking about him for hours.

"No, Fran, he didn't call. But I talked to him last night." Bill tried to sound like he wasn't worried.

"Why isn't he calling me? Is he mad at me?"

"He's really busy with work, you know, the new job."

"That's bullcrap. He's not so busy that he can't call his dying mother. Something's wrong. What is it?"

"He'll call you today, Frannie. You just get some rest."

Bill didn't want to discuss it any more. He and Randy had agreed that Frannie didn't need to know that her youngest child was in the hospital in Ohio getting infusions to replace the blood platelets his body had mysteriously destroyed. She didn't need to wonder if he would recover or not; the prognosis was still not in. Her days of worrying about Randy were over. Bill would do the worrying for both of them, and he preferred to believe their son would be just fine.

It was the morning of the second day of Randy's hospitalization. The first infusion had gone well and they had already started him on the steroids. Doctor Mann, with a much better name for a physician, was the hematologist.

"Good morning, Mr. Williams," he said. "Did you have a good night? Any pain?"

Randy looked down at the IV site in the back of his hand. Nurses had come in three or four times to check it during the night. They weren't going to blow anyone's hand up in this hospital, he was sure of that.

"I feel fine, Doctor. I have no other symptoms."

"We'll complete the blood tests today. We're doing a

complete analysis of your blood at the cellular level to determine if there's a cause for this reaction your body's having. You are aware that there are three components to your blood. The red cells, the white cells and the platelets."

"Yes, I'm aware of that."

"And you know that Idiopathic Thrombocytopenic Purpura, or ITP as we call it, is caused by the body's own immune system turning against its platelets and destroying them. For an unknown reason. That's the idiopathic part. That means we don't know what causes it."

"I know."

"Sometimes it's caused by a virus. Have you been sick in any way?"

"No. But I recently spent a few days visiting my mother in the hospital. Maybe I came in contact with something there."

"Unlikely if you had no fever or other symptoms."

"No fever. No symptoms."

"So we will probably never know what caused it. If that's what it is. We're doing a lot of tests to rule out other things."

Randy, who was worried enough, now worried more. Was he going to die, too? Were he and his mother both going to die, hundreds of miles apart in separate hospitals, with the family surrounding her bedside and him, alone? He suddenly had the feeling that he *was* dying now. He closed his eyes. The pain of losing himself now filled his psyche. That was his only other symptom. The doctor's words came back to him like a hockey puck to the head. *To rule out other things.*

"Other things, Doctor? What other things?"

"Any kind of lymph or blood disorders. Leukemia, you know, things like that. We'll check for anything that ends in

–oma. But your platelet count is up, from four thousand to over eighteen thousand already. That's a good sign, one that points to it being a recurrence of your ITP. You're tolerating the steroids just fine. That will help stabilize the platelets, too."

Dr. Mann patted Randy on the foot on his way to the door. "Keep up the progress, Mr. Williams. We need that count to continue climbing. You'll have another infusion today and another tomorrow. If all goes well, we'll let you out of here on Friday. Let's aim for that as the most likely case."

But what hospital patient ever focuses on the most likely case, especially a hospital patient left alone with no one to talk to? As Randy turned on the television for distraction, his cell phone rang. Even though it was against hospital rules, he'd turned it on earlier and left it on his bedside tray. Just in case.

"Hello." His weak voice cracked on the second syllable.

"Hi, Randy, it's your father. Doin' okay?"

"Okay, Dad. Everything all right with Mom? Is she—"

"She's still with us. But she keeps waking up and asking for you. You need to call her."

"I can't. I thought we'd agreed that it's better for her not to know."

"We did, but she knows something's wrong. First she thought you were mad at her. Then when we told her you weren't angry, she said she knew something else was wrong. She's still sharp, Randy. You know you can't fool her."

Lord knows, Randy had tried. But she had a way of seeing whatever he was hiding and it tended to stay in her mind long afterward.

"I'll call now."

Randy dialed her number, which he'd kept on a sheet of

paper next to his phone on his tray. Just in case. Sugar answered, roused her mother and passed the telephone.

"Mom. Hi! It's Randy." He tried to sound upbeat.

"Baby boy. How are you?"

She sounded weak. Randy could hear her labored breathing catch on each word.

He started to reply, but the speaker over his bed spoke first. "Doctor Mann, Code Blue on Five. Doctor Mann."

"Randy?"

"Yes, Mom, I'm here." Now he covered the microphone of his cell with his hand when he wasn't speaking.

"You're in the hospital, aren't you?"

Frances was alert now; Bill and Sugar watched her sit up in bed, something she hadn't done in days. She winced at the pain as she bent in the middle. "Randy? Are you in the hospital?"

Her sixth sense. Randy knew it well. While he violently searched his mind for a way to fool her, he let down his guard just a little and tears began rolling down his cheeks.

"No, Mom. Don't worry, everything's okay."

"Don't lie to me. You're sick again, aren't you? Oh, Jesus. Help him."

"I'm sick, Mom. But don't worry. It's the ITP again but I'm getting better."

"I knew it. I knew it." Frances looked at Sugar and Bill. "You both knew, didn't you? And you didn't tell me."

"Mom, listen to me." Randy was sobbing now. He needed his mother to tell him everything was going to be fine, but it was he who had to do the reassuring. "Mom, the doctor was just here and he said my platelet count is already rising. As long as it keeps up, I'll be released Friday."

Frances ignored his crying and digested the news. She knew all about ITP. "And are they sure it's not something else this time? Not leukemia?"

"They're running all kinds of tests. Jeez, Ma, they've taken like twenty vials of blood." Randy needed her sympathy. Her empathy, maybe.

"Where are you?"

"Toledo."

"Ohio?"

"Yes. I was on my way to Salt Lake City."

"But they're checking for leukemia."

"Yes."

Frances processed all of this. Exhausted, she lay on the pillows again and struggled to hold the phone to her ear. She'd spent all of her energy just talking. "Call me when you know something," she said.

"I will."

"You know I love you, Son. I wish I could be there for you. But I can't. I have to be here now. You're going to have to do this one on your own."

"I know. I'm doing fine. Don't worry about me. I'll call you when I know more."

Frances had already dropped the phone. She had no emotional energy left for her children. It was taking everything she had to separate from them all. But now she couldn't go until she knew that Randy would be okay or whether this time he.... No. She wasn't going to think of that. He had to be okay. She couldn't bear knowing she was losing a son.

Randy hung up the telephone and turned it off. He didn't want to talk to anyone else. All morning he'd been afraid he was dying. Now his fear had subsided and all he felt was hopelessness and resignation. Even his sadness had passed. This was it. The end. *This is where I will die,* he thought. *We're going to die together.*

His gaze and his thought turned to the golden trees swaying in the breeze outside the window. Leaves scattered with every puff. He watched one fall to the ground and felt peaceful. His arms were light and his breathing seemed to make him float above everything around him. *It's my time to fall.*

The light was suddenly dimmer and the sounds of a busy hospital seemed to fade to a gentle hush. He could hear his own heart beat. The breath moved in and out of him like a soft wave in a still lake.

He wanted to ask his mother if this is what dying felt like but as he formed the question, a new energy began to rush through him. With a chill, he felt the fight begin to rise up inside him. No, this wasn't death. It was something else entirely. He sat up in bed and looked around him for what felt like the first time.

Maybe the platelets are making me stronger, he thought. *Yes. This is what life feels like. Maybe dying is resignation, focusing on the way out instead of the way back in. I want to live.*

His heart pumped adrenaline into his fingertips; he felt the oxygen monitor clipped there. He became aware of his toes under the sheet, the backs of his heels burning against the bed's plastic liner. He relaxed back and felt his head against the pillow as he became aware of the conversation in the hallway outside. He was more fully alive in that moment than he could remember ever being.

My mother is indifferent to all of this. When she told us to lower the blinds on her hospital window, she lowered the shade on her life, too. Randy looked out at the tops of the wavering trees and the sunlight burned his eyes. His stomach flip-flopped; he felt himself halfway between knowledge of his impending demise and an unquestionable certainty that death was being pushed out every pore of his body. It was being rejected. But there was nothing yet to take its place except the reality that his mother was leaving him.

His breakfast sat on the tray in front of him like a stack of books, unopened and uninteresting. He couldn't eat. He couldn't take in anything else; he had all he could handle. He needed time to process.

The nurse, an Asian woman named Philomena, came to his bedside to take his temperature as she did every hour. She hooked up a new bag of immunoglobulin and attached it with a tube and a needle into the port in his hand. She saw the food still on his tray.

"You must eat, Randy."

"I can't. My mother is dying."

"Oh, dear, poor thing."

"She's in another hospital right now, in her bed, dying. And now I've upset her by telling her I'm sick. I didn't want to tell her. Now she's upset. We're both trying not to be upset that the other one is sick." He cried and choked back his sobs. "I was thinking we're both gonna die. How sad is that?"

"You cannot cry, Randy, you have to be strong. You can't cry or sneeze or brush your teeth yet. There's danger of bleeding. Please calm down."

Philomena opened a plastic cup of plastic tapioca pudding. She began to feed it to him. "You must eat with this medicine. You need to get well."

Randy let her feed him, spoonful by spoonful, until the cup was empty. She smoothed his hair as the last of his tears fell then held the Styrofoam cup and plastic straw up to his lips for him to drink his fruit punch. Just as his mother had done all those years ago when he'd been sick.

He was a child again, a helpless child with a scary illness with a long name. In a scary hospital where people die and lose pieces of themselves. Where the food was terrible but they expected him to eat it and feel better, where they made noise all night long and expected him to sleep. A solemn place where they told him not to worry but gave him all kinds of things to worry about. And this time he was alone. His mother was not here to soothe him. No one was.

Randy looked over at Philomena and said, "She's dying. My mother is dying."

But what he really wanted to say was, *Who will be my mother now?*

27

THE hospice nurse had been with the family for about half an hour. It was the first time he'd come during the day when they were all there. In fact, until then no one except Frances had even met the man who introduced himself as Nurse Timmy, the man who was supervising her death.

The Baldwins had been politely listening to the nurse's life story. They learned all about his high schooling, his marriage, his son and more than they ever wanted to know about his political persuasion. Frances had politely kept her eyes open because Nurse Timmy was a Democrat. Silently, they all wondered what he could possibly talk about next. There wasn't much more left to be covered.

Perhaps because of Bill's looking out the window, or Sugar's two trips to the ladies' room, or because William finally picked up a magazine, the man decided to get to the point of his visit. Nurse Timmy stood against the wall, affable in all of his six feet three inches and two hundred forty pounds. His big, goofy smile was incongruent with his words.

"So you know the saying, Mrs. Baldwin, 'Piss or get off the pot?' I'm here to evaluate how long it will take you to pass on, and you don't look near ready yet by my measures. There are certain things we look for, certain signs." He pulled up the blanket unceremoniously and looked at her toenails. "If it takes longer than our time limit of fourteen days, I need to know what you and your family plan to do when you can't stay here anymore."

Hospice had started just over a week before Nurse Timmy's sixty-four thousand dollar question. Not even ten days since William heard Kristen Swift say his mother could stay in the hospital and receive hospice care until she died. His impatience quickly turned to anger. He wasn't the only one who couldn't believe what they'd just heard. There was a collective gasp from the family, followed by a resulting lack of oxygen in the room.

The four gathered around the white-faced Frances' bed, listening to her rattling breath as she tried to maintain her stoicism. Without looking at anyone else, William took the nurse by the arm, pulled him away, and said, "Let's take this outside," through his teeth. He motioned to the hallway, but he sorely wanted to take Nurse Timmy out behind the hospital and beat him beyond recognition.

Once outside the door, William pushed the man against the wall. The nurse was clearly confused. He'd tried to be nice.

"Don't you *ever* pull anything like that again. If you have business to talk about, you talk to me. You don't worry a dying woman with financial matters, you fool."

"I was just speaking the truth. Medicare only pays us for fourteen days in the hospital."

"No one told us that. They said she could stay."

"I guess the doctor thought it wouldn't take that long. But I disagree. I do this all the time, and I think she's got a ways to go yet. Her vitals are too strong."

William grabbed the man, this time by the front of his shirt.

They were face-to-face, each feeling the other's heated breath and not liking it.

"Get out of here. And don't come back. Don't you *ever* talk like my mother's living too long. We only have her for a short time more. That's not *enough* time. And you come in here, wasting her precious minutes, and ours, telling us your whole life story. Who cares about *you?* You just spent a half hour taking about yourself while we are trying to appreciate the last hours we have with the woman who means the most to us in the world. You arrogant asshole. Don't come back in my mother's room again. Don't waste her time. Or ours." William dropped Nurse Timmy with a push.

"I have to do my job."

"I'm calling Kristen to tell her to send someone else."

"Don't call her, please. I guess I could do my job just looking at her chart out at the nurse's station." Timmy tried to appear conciliatory so William would stop making a scene in the hallway. People were beginning to watch. "Anyway, most of the time, people like when I visit."

"It only seems that way. Most people are too civil to tell you what a fool you are. When someone's dying, people just accept whatever care the hospital gives them, as if they don't have the right to expect anything better. But my mother deserves more."

"No one could accuse you of being civil, Mr. Baldwin."

Nurse Timmy tucked in his shirt and straightened his collar while William stared him down.

"We never want to see you again. If I see you here, I'll freaking kill you."

William was loud and eloquent. He finally had his opponent by the balls and wasn't content to let him go without humiliating him since he couldn't hurt him any other way. He'd gotten the attention of the nurses at the station, and they were all giving him the thumbs-up sign and smiling.

Timmy tossed his hair back. "Understood. And I guess I should tell you before you call my bosses that exceptions can be made. If it's only a few days' difference, the hospital can file for an extension. I can put in a good word for your mom if you give me a break here."

"I'm not going to bargain. Leave."

Nurse Timmy walked down the hall to the nurse's station to return Frances' chart. He wanted to stop drawing attention his way so he smiled at all of the nurses, took a piece of chocolate from the bowl, and strode as fast as his long legs could carry him to the nearest elevator.

Nurse Pat walked down to William, who was still walking in circles, blowing off steam in the hallway.

"Nice job," she said. "The guy is a nuisance. Your mother hates him."

"The hospice would be appalled if they knew what he did. I'll get another nurse in here tomorrow."

"Good idea," Pat assured him. "Usually people have a good hospice experience. I know the organization. They do good things for people."

"When I met the representative, she made me feel peaceful about all this," William said. "But that guy—"

"Don't worry. When you call them, they'll do everything they can to fix the mistake. You're doing the right thing by speaking up. The idea is to make this easier for you, not harder." Pat looked at the light blinking over one of the rooms in the hallway and touched William's shoulder. "I've got to go. Hang in there."

William reached in his pocket for one of his father's Valium. He hadn't taken one before because he wanted to stay sharp and on top of his game. But he took one now. He still had the rest of the day ahead.

His father, who had remained silent and disinterested during Nurse Timmy's visit, left the room. Sugar and Frances made no mention of the argument they'd overheard. William tried to explain that his mother didn't need to worry about leaving the hospital, but Frances seemed unruffled and happy already. She was glad to see that her son knew how to fight. He was going to need that after she was gone.

William took a walk and waited for the medication to calm him.

Sugar sat at the bottom of her mother's bed on a teal plastic chair. She'd been softly rubbing her mother's feet for the past two hours. She wasn't exactly rubbing them; she'd been just touching her skin in soft, slow movements because her feet and legs were swollen and soft like overripe melons. Sugar was afraid to touch them any harder. They were no longer any good for standing, and the weight of the blanket made them ache.

Sugar delighted in the opportunity to touch her mother; Frances had never let herself be soothed before these precious days when nothing seemed to separate them but the knowledge that it wouldn't last. Frances had always hated to have her hair combed, to have her shoulders rubbed, and to be embraced. But Sugar loved the intimacy that touch created, intimacy she'd never had since she'd learned to walk and her mother had let her go.

William sat next to Sugar, paging through a magazine. He'd calmed down after the hospice nurse had left. The Valium was responsible for that, but he was still so keyed up that he felt sharp and ready to handle whatever came next. From time to time, he glanced up at the antiques show that seemed to be on the public television station incessantly.

Bill came intermittently, taking his place in the pink vinyl chair behind Frances' wheeled tray. The rest of the time he walked the halls by himself. Of the four, though, he seemed to be the only one harboring resentment about the earlier events. The others had put it behind them. Frances awoke and looked around at her husband and two children. They all stared at her as if she were the centerpiece on the table.

"I haven't had this much attention since the day I was born," she said. Then, thoughtfully, "Wait, maybe not even then."

She closed her eyes. Another hour went by. She woke again.

"I can't die with you all sitting around staring at me like this," she said melodramatically. "Lord knows, I've been trying."

Sugar and William started to laugh, amused at what remained of her sense of humor, still so out of context. Bill scowled at his children for laughing at a time like this.

"So here it is, listen to me now. No more death watch. Okay? You can visit, but I don't like this scene where you are all here waiting for me. Each of you pick a time when you want to be here, but get back to your lives, will you?"

"Let the record show I object," William replied.

"I'll smack you all up side of the head if you don't obey a dying woman's wishes. Now say goodnight to me, all of you, and leave me alone." She gestured toward her cheek where they were to kiss her. "I don't need you here. And don't come back too early." She scratched her nose with her bandaged hand and replaced the oxygen line.

Bill took the opportunity to leave. He kissed his wife in the middle of her cheek before he turned, relieved, toward the rest of his life. Sugar gathered her belongings and walked with her father to the parking lot.

Frances looked over at William. He wasn't going home like the others. He lived too far away.

"And you, look at you. You stand out like a sore thumb. Get out of here and take a drive or something. I don't need you now. You've got to let me go."

"I will. I know I've got to give you some room to do what you've got to do now. I've heard you."

Frances changed her tone. "William, this week has been great. Really. I cherish every minute of it. But I've got to go now."

"I know. My work is done. I did what you asked to set everything up and deal with the hospital. You know how much I love you, and that's the most important thing."

"Yes, that's the most important thing. Now take tomorrow off. Get Diane on the phone or enjoy the football game or something. Promise me."

"I'll come up late in the afternoon."

"Just for a visit."

"Yes, just for a visit."

Frances closed her eyes.

28

WILLIAM walked straight to his car and dialed Diane on his cell phone. It seemed like such a long time since they'd spoken. Diane had been away at a conference, one which he'd encouraged her to attend despite his detour to Philadelphia. He thought it was fair. She shouldn't have to put her life on hold just because his was falling apart. It wasn't her family, after all. His mother wouldn't have allowed her to visit anyway, and neither would the hospital. Only first-degree family had been allowed in the CCU. So there was really nothing she could have done to make it better for him even if she'd been there all along. At least that's what he told himself.

It had been hard to talk to her when she was away because she only had a few minutes in between meetings. William didn't like feeling squeezed in, and consoled himself with the idea that Diane didn't really understand what he was going through anyway. But he knew in his heart that wasn't true. When they'd last spoken, she'd known exactly what was going on. She'd said she would be there for him. Yet he hadn't asked her for anything more.

She answered the phone as if she'd been waiting all day for him to call.

"I need you, Di. I need you like I've never needed anyone before. Can you come out here?"

Diane exhaled her waiting and breathed in her new situation. "Sure, Will. I'll be on the first flight out in the morning. I would have come before except I was waiting for *you* to become *we.*"

"I know, sweetheart. You've been waiting a long time for that. It wasn't lost on me."

William's Journal

SEPTEMBER 9, 2005. Driving back to the hotel, I realized I'd been clinging to my mom all week by taking responsibility for her. I've been vital and important. I needed that. I didn't need Diane because I had my role with Mom. But Mom's pushing me away now. Every day she sends me home earlier.

She needs to go. And I have to let her. The events of the last few days have done a lot to pull us together, even though the outcome is to guarantee our separation. But in order to die, she has to feel like she doesn't need to cover me, to be there for me, to make it okay for me. Here I thought that's what I was doing for her, selflessly. But I can see clearly now that she was doing the same for me. Quite a pair we've been.

It's time for me to turn from her and turn back to the adult life I've created. I've been working hard to learn how to be a loving son in these last weeks, although soon that won't matter anymore. My future is in being a loving husband. And father?

I've pushed Diane away from loving me for so long. I only let her love me *this much.* Time for those walls to come down. I need more, and I need to give more. In making my peace with Mom, I've freed up a lot of love, I guess. I never knew I had it in me. In getting closer to her, I've learned I can be close, that I want to be close.

I don't know what I've been doing for the last ten years. I guess I was working hard to stay the same and ended up not being good at anything except computers. But everything's changed now. My life is completely different. In just a few days, I've become someone else. I hope it's not too late.

-whb

29

SHE woke up and realized she'd slept through the night without pain. Sunlight streamed through the window and the leaves danced in the wind. Disoriented, she looked at the clock on the wall. No glasses. What time was it? She sat up in bed, found her bifocals on the rolling bedside table, and saw it was 7:00.

A flood of thoughts.

I'm sitting up. By myself. The sun doesn't hurt my eyes. Nothing is hurting. When is the last time I had pain medication? I was sleeping so soundly. Nothing hurts. She did a quick scan of every incision she had, pushed on her bloated stomach. No pain.

What is going on? I thought I was dying. This doesn't feel like death. This feels like life.

She began to panic. The breaths came harder and her heart raced. *This isn't right. Am I dead?*

She reached for the phone and called her husband.

"I don't know what's happening. I have no pain. I can sit up in bed. My head is clear."

He heard her voice and thought the word, *Miracle*. She encouraged him to stay away from the hospital until she could make sense of it all. Until she could compose herself and find balance and a reasonable explanation. But he, still thinking

Miracle, was already putting on his pants to get to the hospital as soon as he could.

As he drove, Bill thought how he'd never been ready to believe she was dying. He hadn't accepted what the doctors had said and resented the ease with which their children seemed to come around to accepting a fate he so vehemently denied. Now he was witness to a miracle. His wife was being returned to him. He drove a little faster than normal so he could make it all happen quicker.

Frances called William next while Bill was already on the way to the hospital. With her son she couldn't hide her panic.

"Do you all think I'm crazy? What is going on here? What is God doing to me?"

William imagined her, straight up in bed, eyes wide and breathing quickly. He couldn't even hear a wheeze as she spoke.

"I mean, it's not like I can get out of bed and start dancing around or anything. But William, yesterday I couldn't pick my head off the pillow. Now I'm sitting up all on my own! I haven't had pain medication since nine o'clock last night!" Her breath was short and liquid and afraid.

William was afraid for her. Her voice was the tone one would use if a flying saucer had just landed in the back yard and little aliens were coming down the gangway. She had no idea what to make of all this. Should he tell her what he knew?

"I'm thinking that maybe I want some toast? What would you do, would you have toast if you were me? Will I be setting everything back? I mean, what's happening? I don't understand what's happening to me. I don't know what to do. I was ready to die, but now this. Help me." She almost whispered the last two words.

He imagined her heart pounding and became afraid that she'd have another episode of heart failure. He knew that a rally was normal in the last days, so he'd been prepared for this. The patient might want food or a meal where before they had no interest in food. They might even have enough energy to get out of bed.

He didn't know if he should be telling all this to his mother, though. He'd become his mother's sole source for information about dying and he wasn't sure it would be helpful. What if she was deciding to live?

"Mom, I remember when my friend's mother died, something like this happened. She was on comfort care, like you, and she actually got out of bed and had dinner with her family. The next day she went into a coma and died the following day."

Frances was obviously relieved but still confused.

"So it could still happen, then. I could have toast, and I will still be dying." Her mind was rationalizing quickly.

"That could happen, Mom. I've heard of this energy burst happening before." He heard an audible sigh of relief. She was calming down.

"So this could be part of it. Just like the other days were part of it."

He imagined her relaxing back onto her pillow.

"Yes, Mom. You've had good days before. This is another one of them. You keep telling us to go with the flow. Now you've got to go with the flow. Accept what you've been given. You have this day. Be grateful."

"Then I want to spend it with your father. He's been bringing me down so much. I've felt so guilty. He just sits there with that sour puss. I'm not going to feel guilty about feeling good today.

I'm going to watch the football game with your father. And I'm going to have some toast."

"That sounds good, Mom."

"And everything is still on course. This is just another day."

She had calmed down, and her determination was returning.

When Bill arrived, Frances didn't tell him what she'd learned, but she was careful not to let him get his hopes up. She tempered her mood so that it was good enough for him to interact with her but not so good that he could deny she was still ill.

The Eagles won the football game, and Frances let Bill win at cards.

Both, in their own way, were small miracles.

Randy lay in his bed in the Toledo Medical Center, loosened up by his latest positive test results and the anti-anxiety medication they'd given him, wondering why he had ever left New York. He tried to remind himself about the series of events that had led him to agree to the position in Salt Lake City. What was it that he'd been looking for? Why did he feel the need to move from city to city, beginning anew every few years?

He tried to answer these questions but he could only think of one thing. *Monica.* At first, he was under the impression that thinking of her was a distraction from answering the real questions. But then he realized that Monica was the answer to the questions. He had been running to the idea of a woman like Monica while at the same time running away from the real Monica, the woman who loved him. The woman with whom he was deeply and desperately in love, only he'd never before thought to call it that.

Monica represented everything he'd ever hoped he could be, the best of who he already was times ten. He'd been in the habit of moving to a new place every so often with the hope of becoming his best, a quest that usually proved fruitless after the validation of a few years' failures. So he would move again, giving himself a new chance to be this person. This vision of who he could be.

This time, he realized through the clarity of his IV and the humility of his hospital gown, he had really become this man. This time, in the life he'd created in New York, he'd found a partner who saw the man he wanted to be and believed in him. In fact, he had become this man already: strong, capable and loved. His flight to Salt Lake City was a flight back to his helpless and infant self, incapable of loving and being loved. An adolescent, authority-rebelling reaction to the reality that he had really, finally, grown up.

He knew immediately what he had to do.

She answered the telephone on the first ring. She was angry and confused.

"What's going on, Randy? You packed all of your things. What the hell is going on?"

He pictured her in the sweatpants she wore after a day's work, her long chestnut hair in a ponytail. He knew he had some explaining to do, and he did it. He told Monica everything he'd figured out so far: his intentions, his struggle with his mother, his illness. He wove the challenges together with his bad decision and deftly ended the story with a commitment not to leave her again. He spilled out his heart to her, knowing it might be his only chance. He told her everything he knew about her, everything he valued about her. Everything he intended to protect and cherish about her.

"Didn't you think about how I'd feel?" Her voice was slightly muffled, as if she held the phone far away.

"I tried not to. I figured if I didn't think about you, you wouldn't think about me."

"That's like a kid closing his eyes and pretending he's invisible," she said more clearly. She was getting closer.

"Yeah, I know. Dumb. Problem was, I just couldn't stop remembering everything about you."

"I knew you weren't gone for good. You wouldn't do that to me." She was speaking right into the receiver now.

"I tried. I honestly tried."

"But you couldn't. You didn't. I was right."

Randy felt her connect, as if he could touch her now.

"I'm an idiot." Randy smiled and hoped she could see it. "You know how when the light is really bright it's hard to see? And then when you shade the light, things get really clear?"

"Yes." Her voice was uncertain.

"When I got here night was falling and I could see more clearly. I started to figure everything out. Then it got really dark and I couldn't see a thing. I was scared."

"I'm sorry."

"Don't be. It was good for me. Today the headlights came on, and there you were. Right in front of me. Clear as day."

"How do I know you won't leave again?" Her voice took a step back.

He reached for her. "You don't. But I do. I'm tired of running, baby. I can see that now. I'm tired of always trying to be someone else."

"I like you just the way you are."

He had her again. He laughed at the tickle of it. "All red splotchy, nose-running, pathetic hundred-and-eighty pounds of me?"

"Yup." She was crying now. "I love you, too, Randy," she said.

He paused. He hadn't said he loved her. Had he? He tried to think back.

"And I'm really worried about you," she continued. "I can't stay here, with you going through all this alone. I need to be with you. I'm coming to Toledo."

His heart felt heavy, expanding in his chest until it felt as though his ribs would have to move aside to accommodate everything he was experiencing. He was full and weighted in a way he'd never been before. Satisfied. He was warm for the first time in his life.

"I do love you, Monica. Thank you," he said.

Back in Pennsylvania, Sugar called her boys into the living room. She was ready to talk. Summoning up all the courage her mother had given her in the last weeks, she told the boys their grandmother was going to die.

"Granny is dying now. Her body is finished here, and her soul is going to Heaven."

The words were simple. Jason, the youngest, began to cry.

"I knew it."

No one said anything for a minute, then he asked, "How can she just die? I'm not ready for her to die. I love her too much."

Out of the mouths of babes.

"I'm not ready for her to die either, sweetheart. I wish she would live a lot longer. The hospital tried to fix her up, but they can't. It's her time. Everybody has a time to die, Jason, and this is Granny's. She told me to tell you both that she loves you more than anything. She always will." With that, Sugar reached for their hands.

"I'll miss her," Jason said as he wiped his nose. "A lot."

His initial tears had stopped; still his eyes watered at the thought.

"Granny said that missing her is good. She wants us all to miss her. That's how you can tell you love somebody. But she doesn't want us feeling sad for her. Or for ourselves. She will be okay because God is going to take care of her now. He will do a much better job than the doctors can."

"Is she afraid?" Eric asked.

"No, Son, she's not afraid. And she says we shouldn't be, either. Death is a natural thing and she accepts the laws of nature. It's nothing scary, it's just sad. That's all."

"Is she sad?"

"Sometimes, but mostly she's just sick."

"She's been in the hospital a long time," Eric observed. "I had a feeling she was going to die. Is she suffering?"

He was a teenager, he'd obviously been thinking this through.

"Sometimes she hurts, Eric, but they give her medicine for that. Hey, you know it takes nine months for a baby to be born. It takes some time for a person to die, too. It's not always as easy as you see it on TV."

"Yeah, I'm sure," he said. "Nothing on TV is true."

He'd been wanting to ask to see his grandmother, so he did.

Although he wasn't sure he really wanted to, he thought he might be expected to.

"No, Son, you can't. People might gather around someone's bedside when they die on television, but in real life sometimes people just want to be alone. Granny doesn't like visitors. Dying people need to separate from their loved ones, and sometimes having the ones they love best next to them keeps them from leaving. Granny needs to leave now."

Young Jason seemed to accept the news, but he had a complaint.

"But you didn't tell us. That was the scariest part, wondering what was happening. I was too afraid to ask and Eric told me not to because it would upset you. I told Dad I was scared. He said you were being selfish."

Sugar contained a flash of anger, which was intensified by the fuel of her helplessness. She swallowed hard, then patted Jason's hand and tried to smile.

"I know. I didn't do a very good job with that. But I did the best I could. I was so sad, I couldn't really talk very well. I love my mother so much."

Despite her best efforts, Sugar began to sob. It was as if the breath had suddenly been knocked out of her and she couldn't get it back in. She put her head into her hands so they wouldn't see her crying. As if this would protect them somehow.

Both boys put their arms around her. She felt their touch like an electric blanket, warming her and easing the chill that had settled deep in her heart two weeks ago.

"Don't worry, Mom. We'll take care of you now. You can count on us," Eric said, taking his place as the man of the family.

"Yeah, Mom. Granny wouldn't want you to cry. She's going

to Heaven, and you shouldn't feel bad about that. You shouldn't be sad because she's going to be happy. She always talks about God like she knows him really well."

"Yeah," Eric echoed. "She wouldn't want you to be in a sad place once she's moved on."

"I know," Sugar assured them. "I'm just missing her already."

"Missing's good," Jason remembered.

William drove to the airport with a song playing in the background. He didn't hear the words but he knew the title. He knew it very well.

Who I Am Hates Who I've Been By Relient K

He and Diane greeted each other like people do in the movies—running toward each other with arms open wide. They didn't even speak while they waited for her bags; they just held each other closely and smiled a lot.

"I've missed you more than you know," William said as they checked into a hotel near the airport. He picked up her bags and put the room key in his teeth.

"Good," she said.

They stayed in bed together all afternoon. They made love as if for the first time, desperately—William basking in the feeling of being alive and Diane exploring the whole self that William had, finally, undressed before her. Afterward, they lay on pillows next to each other holding hands.

"If we didn't make a baby today, I don't know what it takes." William laughed proudly, making light of a topic that had previously tied him in knots.

"Will, I'm still on the pill," Diane reminded him gently as if he'd really forgotten.

"Oh. Well, in that case, we'll just have to keep on trying." William chuckled playfully as he leaned up on his elbow and kissed the top of her head.

30

THERE was no doubt Frances had taken a turn for the worse, or for the better depending on who you asked. Whether her body had grown too weak to fight the blood infection or whether her organs had just reached the end of their purpose, no one would ever really know. But she wasn't ready to let go yet. Her body might have been ready but her heart and mind had one more job.

She woke occasionally and asked, "Randy? Did Randy call?"

"No, Mom, he didn't."

It was Friday morning, the day Randy was supposed to have learned whether his treatment had worked. William, Sugar and Bill were all in Frances' room waiting to hear. Since Randy had taken ill, Bill was even more despondent, unable to face even the remote chance of losing a child and his wife at the same time. Despite the additional stress, his illness had brought them all closer. They were a family that at least knew how to weather the bad times together, even if they weren't so good at living happily ever after.

Finally, the telephone rang. Bill was the first to jump up and answer it.

"It's me," Randy said. "They're going to let me go."

"Where are you going?" Bill knew his son had been en route to his new job when the illness had hit.

"Home. To New York."

"I thought you—"

"I'm going home. Monica is here, she flew out this morning. We're driving my car back together. We have a lot to talk about. It's all good."

Bill could hear his son smiling.

"I'm really happy for you, kid. Mom's been waiting for you. I don't think she can die unless she knows you're going to live. She's been mostly unconscious since yesterday. The only thing she wakes up for is to see if you're okay."

"Randy? Is it Randy?" Frances opened her eyes and was suddenly alert.

"Yes, Fran. It's Randy. He's going to be okay, the doctors told him. He's getting out of the hospital today."

"Let me talk to him."

Bill placed the telephone on the pillow next to his wife's ear, and she held it in place with her own hand.

"Son," she began, "You're going to be okay."

She said it more as a statement than a question, which surprised Randy. He hoped she knew something he didn't.

"Yes, Mom. My count is up to over one hundred eighty thousand. They said I can go home. I'm on steroids for a few months to stabilize things, but there's no reason why I won't hold steady. Everything will be just fine. I responded really well to the treatment."

"No leukemia." Again, a statement.

"No leukemia. They did loads of tests."

"You're going to live a long time."

A statement, not a wishful thought. Randy hoped the insight of a dying woman was somehow magical.

"Mom?"

"Yes, baby."

"I have a little song for you."

Frances smiled. Randy sang to the tune of "I've Got Sixpence":

"I've got platelets
Lots and lots of platelets
I've got platelets
To last me all my life.
Oh, I've got platelets to spare
So I don't have a care
And my skin
Will always be so fair
So fair.
No worries now to grieve me
No bruises to bleed me
I'm as happy as can be
Believe me,
And I am going to go home."

He heard her laugh. It was getting farther away.

"Now I really know you're going to be okay. I know it." She sighed, finally giving in to the full relaxation her body craved.

"Mom?"

"Yes, Son."

"I love you."

"I love you, too, Baby Boy."

His mother's voice was fading. Randy became sharply aware that this was the last time he would ever speak to her. The last time he would ever hear her voice. He felt his body disappear as his mind raced through the telephone wire to his mother's bed.

"Good bye, Mom. Thank you for everything."

"Good bye, Randy. If I could squeeze out all my platelets and give them to you, I would." Her voice trailed off.

Randy hung up and cried until he couldn't cry any more. Monica sat by his bed, stroking his face and wiping his tears while her own spilled freely.

Frances closed her eyes, relieved but still uncomfortable. She thought she would be able to sleep now, but something was still not quite right. In the muddle of her medicines and pain, she searched her mind for what was left to do. But she couldn't be sure of what it was.

"Bill," she groaned.

Her husband stayed in his seat and looked to his daughter for direction.

"I'm here, Frannie. I'm here."

"Come closer," she begged.

He patted her hand from the pink chair, still not moving. Tears filled his eyes. Still, Frances moaned. She was not comforted.

"Bill." Again, imploring him.

"What does she want?" Bill asked Sugar.

"She wants you to hold her, Daddy. She wants to be close to you."

"I can't."

"You can."

"I don't know what to do."

"Yes, you do."

"No, I don't. I can't do what you two are doing. I'm not like that."

William led his father into the hallway. He squared off with the bigger man and looked at him straight on.

"Dad, we've put up with your distance. We've worked around your lack of cooperation with all of this. But now it's different. Mom's dying now. This is the end. This is it. And in the end, all she wants is for you to be close to her. To comfort her."

"I can't."

"You get in there right now and be her husband. I put up with your abdicating your duty as my father. I could have used your support over the last few weeks, but I've learned to get along without that. You seem to think this is all about you. You can't even see what this has done to your own children.

"One of us almost killed himself with the guilt and pain of losing his mother. Randy's worry and pain put him in the hospital, you can bet on that. And Sugar, poor Sugar, has had to deal with her boys and her ex-bastard all the while taking care of Mom and planning the funeral. And I flew across the country, leaving my own wife behind, to handle this all by myself."

William tried, but he couldn't stop. This was too long in coming.

"And what have you been doing, Dad? Sitting by yourself every day as if you have nothing to do with any of us. Feeling sorry for yourself because you have to go on from here without your wife. Well, boo hoo, Dad. Boo hoo. Poor you. We're all taking this chance to learn what we can from death and you sit in the convenience of denial. Wake up, Dad. Wake up."

William caught his breath after exhaling all of the resentment that had been building up inside him over the last weeks. He wasn't going to let his mother die without her last wish.

"I've grown from a boy to a man during the last few weeks,

Dad. I never knew how far I had to go until I stretched and faced my fears. Now you, goddamnit, better start acting like a man. Get in there and hold your dying wife. Tell her you love her. Be the man I always thought you were, a man I can look up to."

William left quickly, overcoming the urge to hit his father and throw him down under his feet. He couldn't look at his sad face anymore. He couldn't create yet another logical explanation for his father's irrational behavior. His anger had risen past his sorrow, his loss, and he didn't like the feeling.

Sugar met her brother in the hallway. She'd been listening behind the closed door.

"You talked to Dad like he was a child. No one else could get away with talking to him like that."

He had to smile. "I talked to him like I love him. That's how you talk to someone you love when they need a kick in the ass."

Sugar kissed him and gave him a hug. They walked together to the parking lot. William started his car. *Give me a sign, God. Give me a sign.*

***Let Go** By BarlowGirl*

William put the car in reverse and headed to the hotel to have dinner with his wife. He missed Diane more than he could say and needed to make love to her longer than time could allow. Then he needed to hold her for a very, very long time.

Bill washed his face in the men's room and looked at himself in the mirror. He dried his hands and face then straightened his shirt. He walked back down the hall to his wife's room. The door was as heavy as his resistance, but it gave way as soon as he pushed. Sugar had gone and Frances was alone. She opened her eyes and looked at him.

"Bill." She reached out to him with her bandaged hand, smiling.

He went to her bedside and lifted her tiny body over to one side of the bed. He climbed in next to her, on top of the blankets, and put his arms around her. She relaxed onto his chest and fell asleep.

"Frannie."

31

I can hear them talking, but words have no place
In this place…
They talk about me. But not about *me*.
I am more
… Now.
Their tone does not alarm me
Or have meaning…
Nothing pulls me back.
I float away from them, as if it is sleep
… But it is not.
I love this.

… I've done what I must. I did all I could…

This new place,
this ease.
I have no purpose, there is nothing more to do.
The rest is just waiting.
The wait is just resting…

I am not afraid, no, not at all.
This peace, I feel
Relieved.
I hope there's more.
After.
This peace is
Perhaps the God I've waited for.
… I am soothed
for the first time.

My father,
I dreamed of my father. Maybe just my wishful thinking
To see him again. I don't know
What I will see…

But I see nothing more here. Shadows
when I open my eyes
And light when I close them.
The light. I am going to the light, just like they said.

My chest goes
up and down.
Again.
My only sign
That I am still my body, though I want
To let go, I have
Nothing left
here. It is not me.
anymore
… I am …

32

FRANCES died alone.

Sugar and Bill had gone to the cafeteria; William, upon returning from his dinner, had been out in the hall talking to Dr. Al-Biruni. Frances hadn't been by herself for more than five minutes.

"I can't die with you all sitting around staring at me like this..."

William found her when he came in to start his watch. He knew she had passed on as soon as he saw her. She hadn't moved. Everything looked exactly the same, but the air was different: it was lighter, more transparent. It moved freely around her now, passing over and through her as if she wasn't there. Her spirit, quite visibly, had left. There was no radiance, no softness remaining. No pain. The body in the bed was no longer his mother. She was gone.

He walked slowly and sat beside her, holding the hand of the woman he'd known better than he'd ever known anyone. As time went by, he felt her skin grow cool. He noticed how the skin had stopped feeling like skin. Whether the impression was real or imagined, he'd already begun to think of this body as one of the cadavers, unknown and impersonal, that he'd known in medical school. The experiments, the exploration—somebody's father and brother and sister and mother.

That is why he'd had so much trouble. He couldn't concentrate on the science without wondering how someone had died, as if knowing how they'd felt about their death might make it all okay. He'd never known how each person came to be under the sheet in front of the students, and he wondered whether he was violating a person or a soul with his scalpel or whether the body had truly ended up there, right where it was supposed to be, to teach him. As his mother was now—right there with him to teach him.

Now he understood. He understood Frances had wanted him to be a doctor so he could let go of her when the time came. So he could see that a body was just a body and the soul was without death. William was convinced his mother's spirit had gone on, he knew it as surely as he knew her body lay in front of him now. Now he understood.

And he understood why she had waited to take her last breath alone. He understood why it was he who had found her. His mother was no longer in need of a guide; she no longer needed to learn anything here. Her only purpose now, and maybe all along, was to teach him. To teach them all.

Finally, effortlessly, he cried. He cried every tear he'd been saving, reserving, for this moment of what he could only describe as pure happiness. The happiness that comes when the puzzle is solved, when the solution is clear, when the future is unveiled. He thought he'd given Frances everything he'd had to give her. But he had one thing left: his sorrow. He poured it all out until there was nothing left.

At the right time, Sugar and Bill returned from dinner. Somehow they were both surprised, as if Frances' death hadn't been imminent at all, as if it was equally likely that somehow she would regain consciousness yet again and tell them one more thing they needed to know. As if the cycle of hope and sadness would never end.

But it had ended. After the surprise of this revelation, Bill and Sugar felt indescribably relieved and exhausted. William called Uncle Holden; Bill called Randy and passed the telephone to Sugar. Randy and Sugar cried together.

"I'm sorry I'm not there," Randy said, knowing he couldn't have been, wondering if he would have been if his own health had not been at stake.

"You are here, Randy. Just as sure as if you were standing right next to me." Sugar turned to look at him sitting next to her on the bench.

William went to the nurse's station to let them know. One by one, the nurses on duty came by, not to console the family but to pay their respects to Frances. Pat came last.

"They say that people die as they lived. Your wife, your mother," she said, looking at them in turn, "lived and died a courageous woman. And her wisdom was a gift to us all. She will always be in my heart as a leader, someone who took me somewhere I would not otherwise have gone.

"You know, I watch people die all the time. I watch their fear, their struggle—and that's what breaks my heart, when they and their families just can't accept the reality of the situation. Many are desperate to go on living because they're unprepared to die, or they live desperately because they don't know what choices are really open to them. But my heart doesn't break for Frances. How could it? We're all going to die. I just hope when it is my time, I can do it with the grace and kindness Frances showed.

"I will never forget her."

33

William's Journal

OCTOBER 5, 2005. Well, the funeral went just the way she wanted it. She did look like a princess that day, albeit a dead princess; but she didn't look a thing like my mother, so the viewing wasn't as hard as I thought it would be. Randy, Sugar and I sang all of the songs really loud in church, rocking and swaying back and forth the way we used to do, making fun of Mom when we were kids. We thought she always sang too loud and with too much enthusiasm, so we would move down to the other end of the pew so no one would see us with her.

Everyone who could have attended did. It would have made Mom happy to see them all. When the service was over, we whisked her casket away to the crematorium, just like she said. I couldn't help but throw my fist in the air and scream, "Yes," when the hearse rolled away. I think Uncle Holden, among others, misunderstood.

It was a moment I'll always remember—knowing I had come through for my mother, done everything she asked, met all of her expectations. My last try was my best try. I could feel her smiling down on me.

Randy stayed around with his girlfriend for a few days after the funeral. Sugar really bonded with Monica. By the end of the week, they were acting like best friends. Randy never really made peace with Mom and maybe that's okay. Maybe some people only need to make peace inside themselves.

And Dad, well, I think it will be a while before people stop fussing over him, the grieving widower, and he gets a chance to be alone. My dad has never been one to adapt quickly to things. Now that he's out of denial, I think he will figure it out eventually and go on with his life. Maybe at some point he'll even look forward to it.

Diane and I are home now, feeling like we're on our honeymoon. I don't know exactly how, but in learning about and accepting death, I also learned how to live. Before Mom died, I was always looking forward and capitulating as to what would come next, or wallowing in what came before. Now I live each day like it matters. That's what those last weeks with Mom taught me. As hokey as it sounds, each day really is a gift, and life is a succession of everyday miracles, even though they aren't of the sort Dad was looking for. I guess it's always been that way, but I never noticed. I notice now.

Each of those last days with Mom was a miracle. She became accepting of herself and of us, with a clarity that eluded her during life. And day by day, she gave that clarity to us so we could see her and ourselves with forgiveness and accuracy. I guess we can decide to heal ourselves and go on, or choose to die slowly in our own misery. I choose life.

And I choose love, which as it turns out is the greatest miracle of all. In the end, that's all there is. It doesn't matter how much money you had in the bank or whether you had wrinkles on your face or if you were famous or dressed well. All that you have when you lie in that last bed is the love you developed for your friends and family, and the love you earned from them. Love brings peace to the living and the dying; it tears down the walls of status and position, it transcends roles and past transgressions. Mom finally opened her heart to us, loving us as we are instead of how she wanted us to be. And most importantly, she finally learned how to let us love her. For me that was the greatest gift. As Diane is finding out now, I have a lot of love to give.

Ah, what to say about grief?

It's an unpredictable thing for which different cultures have felt the need to create traditions and rules. Interesting similarities, and none of them seems complete. Hindus and Hmong and the Irish have traditions of chanting, a deep rhythmic release of the deepest feeling for the dead. Some Pacific Islanders have a good cry but after that, grieving is not expected. Jews have a custom of Shiva, where a certain amount of time is allocated for deep grieving, but then it's over and everyone goes back to living. Native Americans set aside a year for mourning, and they try to honor the memory of the deceased with their actions and thoughts during that time. Traditional Chinese have long periods set aside for grieving, especially for the first son of the deceased.

Our customs surrounding burial are all about grief, about hanging on to the person, denying that they've departed. We embalm them so they stay whole under the ground. We set up marble monuments so we can know where to find the deceased and visit them. My mother's decision to be cremated and scattered at sea is so consistent with the rest of her plan. She wanted all of us to know that death is a natural rupture in the family's fabric. A force of nature. When we go out on Uncle Holden's boat next month with her ashes, we will say our last goodbye.

That's the way I want you to think of me. Free. That's what she said. Then, things will really be final. She will really, literally, be gone.

I don't know what's considered normal grieving. It catches me by surprise sometimes. Like I have this sudden thought out of nowhere that, *Gotta go to the store and get milk and, oh yeah, Mom's dead,* or *That's a nice car and, oh yeah, Mom's dead.* But sometimes I forget. The phone rings and it crosses my mind, *It's Mom.* Suddenly I need to hear her voice and talk to her so badly that my ears and throat burn. Then the sting washes over me like a hard wave to the face, and my heart stops beating with the shock. Last week was my first birthday without her. No call. No card. Somehow it surprised me, and then it took my breath away.

In those moments when my heart grows hot with sadness, I can be right back at her bedside in a second. But I've learned I have to lift my heavy feet over and over and walk away from that time. I keep mentally returning to her bedside as a way of being with her again. It's where we were last together. But she's not there anymore. I guess I need to find her again somehow—not in the past, but in the everyday miracles.

Oh, and speaking of everyday miracles, there was the rainbow. I'll never forget it.

Diane and I were flying home after Mom's funeral. I was feeling sad to realize that it was all over. All of a sudden, I was overwhelmed with emptiness. We were flying right over our house on approach to the Los Angeles airport.

The pilot came over the speaker and said, "Ladies and gentlemen, if you are on the left side of the plane, take a look out the window. I've never seen anything like the rainbow out there."

When's the last time you heard a pilot talk about a rainbow?

Diane and I were on the right side of the plane. We looked at each other, then leaned and tried to see out across the aisle.

"Whoops," said the pilot. "It's gone. Boy, was that amazing.... Wait, this is unbelievable. Now it's on the right side."

I looked out the window next to me and there it was. A double rainbow. One side coming up from our neighborhood below and the other side ending *right on the wing of our plane. Right on the wing. Right outside my window.*

Diane and I looked at each other, goose bumps on our arms and tears forming. We both knew it was a sign. A sign that the storm was over and everything was going to be okay.

Diane held my hand and pulled herself toward me.

Good, I said to her as the tears ran down my cheeks. *She owed me a rainbow.*

-whb

Author's Note

This story is based on the experiences and decisions that led to my mother's death. She asked me to write down what happened, and after three tries, *Finding Frances* is the result. Although Frances resembles my mother, the other characters are not modeled after my family in particular. They are all of us. I created them to express different attitudes about dying, different roles that people play in a family system, and the many different ways that grief takes form. For those who ask if I am William, Sugar or Randy, I am not just one of them; there is a piece of me and my own experience in all of them.

One of the things that struck me most about the month my mother was dying was the resiliency of the human body and spirit. As she deteriorated, some parts of her tried to heal. As I was losing her, I was finding new aspects of myself and my relationship with her. This was the genesis of the title. In the end, it's about what was found, not what was lost.

Because death has replaced sex as the new taboo, we don't talk about it in friendly company. Instead, we learn about it in sterile hospital corridors from doctors whose training is to help us heal, not to help us die. I believe that fiction can make the topic accessible. I hope that by sharing this story, more people might consider that the death experience can be a normal and beautiful time.

My mother always told people that I was born old, that I was never young. Sometimes I think that's true because I always look contemplative, worried, or responsible in my baby pictures. Sometimes I get to thinking maybe I knew my mother in another life because I understood her so well in this one. But then again, maybe I don't believe in past lives or future lives at all.

There are now many more things that I do know for sure, though. I know that there's more to life than living and more to death than dying.

—J

ACKNOWLEDGMENTS

I could never have written this book without the love and support of my husband Stephen. He held me every time I broke down in tears and gave me the space to grieve and grow in my own way. He is my mentor. I am thankful for the support of all my family, especially Maryellen and Angela, who had confidence that I could tell the story well. Peter and Carolyn were there as I told it for the first time, at the hospital and in those long evenings after visiting hours were over. Their interest and compassion helped me realize that others might want to hear this story, too.

Many people read the manuscript along the way, and I can honestly say that every comment I received made this a better book. Starr Porter, Francine Gianas, Rose Fields, and Deborah Cohn read my first draft and gave me new perspectives to incorporate. Kay Haedicke, M.D., and Paul Phillips, M.D., reviewed the book's medical aspects and corrected my rudimentary understanding of pathology and hospital procedures. Patti Rackstein, RN, shared a valuable nursing point of view. My book club critics Regina Bradley, Valerie Ayers, Cheri DeColibus, Diana Fyfe, Kaye Harig, Barbara Hoskinson and Ruth Ann Volkert enlightened me with their discussion and contributed valuable suggestions for honing the story's characters. And finally, two years after I completed it, Jerry Harris,

Esq., and sociology professor Sarah E. Green, PhD, gave me the encouragement I needed to get this book out of my computer and onto the printing press.

I am grateful to Pablo Rodriguez for the formatting and design. I would also like to thank Mary Rosenblum and Eric M. Witchey for their professional coaching and editing.

I thank all of my readers for sharing this conversation on a critical topic for our life and times. Let's keep the talk going. Tell others about your experiences; share your wisdom. Plan your own future. I will.